OFF THE BENCH

OFF THE BENCH

Bruce Kreisman

SALVO PRESS
Bend, Oregon

Off The Bench

Copyright © 2001 by Bruce Kreisman

Salvo Press
P.O. Box 9095
Bend, OR 97708
www.salvopress.com

Library of Congress Catalog Card Number: 2001086049

ISBN: 1-930486-19-7

Printed in U.S.A.
First Edition

To the women in my life; Beth, Rachel, and the Hound.

Acknowledgments

I've benefited from the help of many wonderful people. I am truly thankful to my parents for their encouragement and the examples they set. The Red Herrings were instrumental to my evolution as a writer, and I am indebted to them all (with special thanks to readers Phoebe Waterman, Steve Mandel and Libby Fischer Hellman, and Judy Duhl of Scotland Yard Books in Winnetka, Illinois). Thanks to Michael Beckman, good friend and fellow writer, for being especially supportive. I greatly appreciate the technical assistance I received from Heather Higgins Alderman, Henry Samuels, the Northbrook, Illinois Police Department and the Chicago Police Department. The Chicago legal community also deserves acknowledgment. I had good days and bad days practicing law, but each one was an inspiration.

Special people deserve special thanks. Beth's love, support, faith and encouragement always keep me going, and for that (and too many other things to mention) I feel eternally lucky. Rachel is a constant joy and amazement. I hope this book will make her proud.

CHAPTER 1

I solemnly swore to tell the truth, the whole truth, etc., etc., a needless formality in my case, since I'm not the lying type. I swear.

I was being questioned by Erin Sitterly, the attorney for our mutual client Bernadette Hume-Goldfarb. Ms. Hume, as she is known professionally, is a partner in a major and very proper Chicago law firm. She suspected that her imminently ex-husband, the Goldfarb part of the moniker, was doing the bump-and-grind with one of his co-workers. While I don't normally take on peek-and-tells, my daughter Gail's bat mitzvah was fast approaching, together with the bills for the hors d'oeuvres and the band and the flowers and...

Erin asked some preliminary questions about my experience as a Chicago police detective and a private investigator. Then we got to the good stuff.

"Where were you the evening of January 24th?"

"I was in a vacant apartment on the eighth floor of 1341 North Dearborn."

"And what were you doing there?"

"I'd set up a telescope, and was looking into an apartment at 1330 North State Parkway, apartment 704 to be precise."

"The lights were on in apartment 704?"

"Yes."

"And the blinds or curtains were not closed?"

"They were not closed. I had an unobstructed view."

"And what did you observe at that time?"

"At approximately 7:35 p.m. I saw Mr. Goldfarb enter the apartment."

"Was anyone else there?"

"Yes, Stacy Cheevers, the woman who lived there."

"And what did you observe?"

"I observed Goldfarb and Stacy kissing, then they undressed."

"Then what?"

"Goldfarb and Stacy put on some outfits."

"What do you mean 'outfits'?"

"They appeared to be leather outfits, with lots of studs. I also saw hand-cuffs and whips and..."

"Objection," screamed Goldfarb's attorney Arnie Hirschberg, a fat guy who exhibited surprising dexterity in getting to his feet so quickly. "This testimony is highly prejudicial and without sufficient foundation."

"Your Honor," began Erin before the Judge cut her off.

"Mr. Hirschberg, your client has elected to contest this divorce. The Court is entitled to hear all the evidence by which the Petitioner believes she is entitled to the requested relief. I have been sitting in this Court a long time, and I can assure you that this Court is not easily prejudiced. Still, if your client fears embarrassment by Mr. Bronk's further testimony, perhaps he would consider stipulating to the petition. I will recess this Court for fifteen minutes. You and Mr. Goldfarb discuss what course you want to take. The objection is overruled."

I've been around enough courtrooms to know that I'd concluded my testimony. People get funny about airing their sexual peccadillos in public. Actually, I felt bad for Erin, knowing how she loved to beat up on wayward husbands.

Sure enough, when Court resumed the judge announced that a settlement was reached and that no further testimony would be required. With that simple pronouncement he adjourned court; no dramatic pounding a gavel like on TV. (I've appeared in dozens of courtrooms without ever seeing a gavel pounded; just another life experience in the waiting.)

"Thanks for your help, Marty," said Erin. "Too bad you didn't get into the really juicy part."

"Yeah, I really wanted to talk about the couple who joined them and what they were wearing."

We were still in the courtroom during this conversation. I felt a tap on my shoulder.

"The judge would like to see you in his chambers," said the deputy.

"Now what did I do?" I asked.

"He probably wants to hear the rest of the story," said Erin.

•

I don't know if Judge William Robert Bobb's parents had no sense of humor or a great sense of humor, but it had to be one or the other. Because to lawyers, courthouse personnel, even fellow judges, he's Billy Bob Bobb. Although I'd bet he was born in Chicago, somehow his face took on an appearance to match his name. His well-lined cheeks and sunken eyes made him look weathered, even while his greasy, combed back hair came with a union card. Sort of the Marlboro man meets the South Works steel plant.

I followed the deputy back to Judge Bobb's chambers. "Chambers" sounds so impressive. In fact Judge Bobb, like the other judges in the Richard J. Daley Center, was situated in a nondescript office which would embarrass most junior associates. It was furnished with a wood veneer desk and three chairs, a larger one for the judge and two well-worn straight back models for visitors. On the wall behind the judge was a single shelf, holding the Illinois statutes and a lawyer's directory. The thin gray carpeting needed replacement years ago, and the faded walls were begging for fresh paint. The view was north, where few of the buildings held any architectural interest.

Judge Bobb had taken off his robe, revealing a short sleeve dress shirt and a coffee stained tie. I could tell we'd get along.

"Mr. Bronk, please have a seat."

"Thanks. I take it I'm not in contempt for my racy testimony?"

"Please, a little S & M isn't going to bother this old boy."

"So is this a social visit?"

"No, it's business. You've testified in my court a number of times, and you seem to be a stand-up guy. I need your services."

"How so?"

"My law clerk is missing."

I turned my head toward the outer office. "In that case I can help you. No charge. She's right there." I pointed to the woman seated behind the front desk.

"No, she's just a temp. My regular has been missing for a week."

"What do you mean missing?"

"She hasn't shown up for work, she hasn't called in, and she doesn't answer the phone at home."

"Have you spoken to the police?"

"Yeah, they've added her to their missing persons list. But I was an assistant state's attorney, and I know that cases involving missing adults don't always get much attention. Especially when there's no family to play the squeaky wheel."

"No family at all?"

"Not that I know of. Her name's Celia Glagovic. She's not married and doesn't have any kids. She lives alone in a two-flat on the southwest side."

"What more can you tell me about her?"

"Not much. I'm sure you've seen her around; she's one of those who seems to have been here forever, although she's really only about 50."

"Anything else I should know?"

"Well, I suppose there's no sense beating around the bush on this. She's not the warmest person you'll ever see."

"Meaning?"

"She tends to be pretty loud and unpleasant. A lot of the lawyers complain that she's rude. Of course you talk about the pot calling the kettle black..."

"Do you have a picture of her?"

"Here's one taken at last year's Christmas party. She's the one on the left." The photo showed two women talking. Celia's head barely reached the other woman's shoulder. Her's wasn't a party look, but that of a nun about to get serious with a miscreant fifth grader.

"And her address?"

Judge Bobb handed me a card from his Rolodex, and I wrote down the information.

I explained that in missing persons cases I charge a flat fee, nonrefundable even if the person walks into work the next day, or is never found. And that I require the fee in advance. He took out his checkbook and paid me on the spot.

"How come you're willing to foot the bill on this, Judge?"

"Something just doesn't seem right. And everyone's entitled to some dignity. Even a pain-in-the-ass."

CHAPTER 2

It was one of those glorious March days, the sun shining and the temperature inching toward that magic fifty degree mark. The type that inspires you to put away the winter coat and snow boots, seducing you to ignore the gnawing sense that the season still has one good snowstorm to go.

I took the Stevenson to Pulaski Avenue, then south on Pulaski till I got to Celia's street, 62nd Street, where I turned west. I get a feel for a neighborhood from the cars parked there. On Celia's block I saw lots of Fords and Chevies, most showing at least some signs of rust.

Celia lived in a two-flat, just as Judge Bobb said. Her apartment was on the first floor. I walked up the steps to the front door, then rang the bell, hoping for an answer, and with it the easiest money I'd ever make.

After ringing three or four times with no response I tried the door. Locked. I then peered into the picture window. The curtains were open just enough for me to see that the living room was in order. No lights were on.

Celia's upstairs neighbor was named Poole, at least if I could believe the name plate by the buzzer. I tried that one next, and within a few minutes a short, thin woman in a faded blue housecoat came to the front door. I'm not sure which was grayer, her hair or her skin.

"Yeah, whadda you want?"

"I'm looking for Celia Glagovic."

"Try ringing her bell, not mine. Dodo."

"I did. She didn't answer."

"Then I guess she ain't home."

"When was the last time you saw her?"

"How the hell should I know. And who are you anyways?"

"My name's Martin Bronk, I'm a private investigator." I held up one of my cards. She still hadn't opened the door. "How about opening the door, Mrs. Poole. No sense shouting through this thick glass."

"Who's shouting." She seemed to consider my request for about a second, then resumed her non-shouting. "Why you want Celia?"

"She's been missing from work. I'm just checking that she's okay."

"Well, she ain't been home for about a week, and her car ain't been here neither."

"You have any idea where she could have gone?"

"No, we ain't exactly friends. She's kinda grouchy."

I bit my lower lip, literally, then continued. "Anybody you know who'd want to harm her?"

"Probably everybody on this block's had a run-in with her at one time or another. But I can't believe anyone would hurt her. Everyone knows her bark's worse than her bite."

"You haven't seen any strangers or unfamiliar cars around here, have you?"

"Only you."

"Mrs. Poole, what you lack in tact you make up for in honesty."

"Huh?"

"Never mind. If you see Celia, or hear anything about where she might be, give me a call." I slid my card between the door and the jamb.

I turned to leave. "Hey mister," in what surely qualified as a shout, "I hope youse find her."

"Thanks for your concern."

"It's not that. I own this building, and she's still got six months left on her lease."

I checked out the alley, but found nothing unusual. I then walked around the block a few times, stopping three passersby. They all knew Celia, hadn't seen her for a few days, didn't like her, and hadn't seen anything suspicious. I was getting the impression that her neighbors looked upon Celia as a wart—you notice it when it's there, but you don't miss it when it's gone.

I might have struck out on 62nd Street, but I still had more at bats to go. Back in the car I dialed up an old buddy of mine from the department, who's always happy to do me a favor.

"What the fuck, Bronko, you go private, and the only time I hear from you is when you want something." The last word was pronounced "sometin."

"It's not like that, Plonski. I'm downtown, you're on the southwest side, it's hard to get together."

"Spare me the soft soap routine. Watcha want?"

"Know anything about a missing person named Celia Glagovic? Lives over on 62nd Street."

"Ain't heard of her, but I'll ask around. Call back in a couplla hours."

"Thanks Plonski. Next time I'm in the neighborhood I'll treat you to a polish sausage."

"Save the shit, Bronko. We both know the next polish you buy will be the first."

Good thing he was one of the guys I got along with.

Next I called my office for messages. Only two. One, a potential new client who claimed that his neighbors had bugged his house. With real bugs, that is, not listening devices. And not just one neighbor, but the two on either side, and the one behind the alley as well. I called him back, told him the case sounded great but I had a full plate right then. That's okay, he said, he thought it over and decided an exterminator would do more good than a private eye.

The other message was from my ex-wife Randee, reminding me that we were getting together that night to make up the final invitation list for our daughter Gail's bat mitzvah. This didn't figure to go smoothly, and I'd succeeded in putting it off as long as I could. I even ran the idea past Erin that maybe she and Randee's attorney could hammer this out, but Erin thought that was the funniest thing she'd heard since the mayor talked about stocking the Chicago River with fish.

Later I called Plonski back. He'd checked around. Celia Glagovic was an open case, going nowhere. Her car had been found at the Jewel parking lot on Cicero near 73rd, two days after she'd been reported missing. No one at the store saw or heard anything out of the ordinary. The cashier thought she remembered Celia checking out about six-thirty. The car was unlocked, the groceries still in the back seat. The car keys were found on the driver's side seat. The cops hadn't turned up any motive or any suspects.

"You know some judge phoned it in," said Plonski. "When the lieutenant over there heard that he went apeshit getting some suits on the case. But the trail's cold as a witch's tit. You can have this one, Bronko."

"Who's in charge?"

"A Detective Crumpton."

Damn. One of the guys I didn't get along with.

•

"Yeah, I remember you Bronk. A pain-in-the-ass college boy."

I remembered Lucius Crumpton too. He was the type who enjoyed getting in the face of anybody he didn't like, whether they were suspects, witnesses or fellow coppers. He also got ribbed by some of the white guys that affirmative action helped him make detective. I wasn't one of those guys, but that didn't seem to make any difference to him.

"I just wanted you to know that Judge William Bobb asked me to look into the Celia Glagovic case. If I turn up anything I'll let you know." Which was the thing to say, even if it wasn't necessarily true.

"If Billy Bob Bobb wants to throw away his money, that's his business. But we're still on the case, Bronk, and I don't want you interfering, ex-cop or no ex-cop."

"I just want to find the lady, Crumpton. I don't consider that interfering."

"Your considerations don't mean shit to me. Just don't fuck things up."

"Got you, Chief Inspector Crumpton."

"And Bronk."

"Yeah."

"Save your humor for the B'nai B'rith."

CHAPTER 3

I made it to Randee's house, formerly our house, only fifteen minutes behind schedule. One of my rules in life is to always arrive fashionably late for parties and get-togethers with ex-wives.

Gail was waiting for me at the front door. "Hi Daddy," she said. I hadn't been "Daddy" since she told me that names ending in "y" were "childish." I don't know where she got that idea, but since that pronouncement I paid particular notice every time Randee called me Marty.

"Hi Pumpkin. Nice sweatshirt." She was wearing something I'd picked out for her at Niketown a couple months earlier. I'd battled the Saturday afternoon throng of tourists, and spent as much as I spend buying two shirts for me, but I still felt good about it.

"Yeah, everyone at school thinks it's really cool."

"So where's your mother?"

"She's coming. She's got to get all her notebooks and stuff together. She's making like such a big deal out of this."

"Sometimes I think it's a bigger day for her than for you."

"Yeah, well I just wish it was over already."

"Hi Marty." Randee made her entrance. She was carrying a three-ring binder, three clipboards, and three pens. In black, blue and red.

"Hey Randee. Tell me, what are we planning here, a bat mitzvah or the Normandy invasion?"

"Nothing wrong with being organized. Different colored pens for me, you and Gail. Let's go into the living room."

I was hoping she'd say that. That was my favorite room, with all our old furniture from when we first got married. Avocado couch, gold chairs. The room may never make House Beautiful, but it reminds me of happier times.

I took a chair, while Randee and Gail sat on the couch.

"Here's my idea," continued Randee. "We'll each make out a list of guests we want to invite. Then when we're done we'll figure out how that matches the budget, and if necessary we can cut down."

"Doesn't it make more sense to just set how many guests each of us gets?" I asked.

"Not really, because it'll probably work out this way, and we'll save the step of fighting over the total number."

Another of my rules in life is that you have to pick your battles. Sensing a bigger one on the way, I left this one alone.

Randee passed out the clipboards, some notebook paper, and the pens. I got the blue one.

Randee and Gail finished in less than ten minutes, which they signified by tapping their clipboards with their pens. "Hey, you guys are quick. You didn't have this planned out already, did you?"

"Maybe we've given this more thought than you, Marty. Don't make that out to be a bad thing."

I finished in another ten minutes. My list had 58 names on it, including some out-of-town relatives I knew wouldn't be coming, and some people I really didn't care about inviting. But I needed them for negotiation purposes.

"All right, let's see what everyone has," announced Randee. She looked over the lists, scrunching her nose a couple of times while reading mine but saying nothing. She quickly scanned Gail's list.

"I think this looks doable," said Randee.

"Cool," said Gail. "Can I go to my room now?"

"Not so fast," I chimed in. "Let me see what we're talking about here."

"Marty, don't cause trouble."

"Trouble! I'm footing the bill for most of this little party, so let's see just how much of my stock portfolio I'm going to have to sell off to finance this."

Randee passed the clipboards to Gail, who passed them to me. Randee had 85 names on her list, Gail 45 on hers.

"Are you guys out of your minds?" I said. "Randee, you know I'm on a budget here. I figured maybe 115 guests, 125 tops."

"Well, that's just not going to work, is it."

"Sure it will. You get 50, I get 50 and Gail gets 25."

"No way," screeched Gail. "I can't leave out half my friends."

I looked again at her list. "Where'd all these friends come from all of a sudden? I've heard of maybe five or six of them, but that's it."

"I've got different groups of friends. From school, Hebrew school, basketball, softball and volleyball. Don't forget, Dad, you wanted me to be a jock. I can't leave out my teammates."

"And I have a bigger family than you, Marty, so it's not fair that you and I have an equal number of guests."

"The fact that you have more second cousins once removed than I do doesn't mean you have a larger family. I'm sorry, but you have to cut down your lists, and that's the way it has to be."

"Who elected you dictator." That was Gail.

"I'm the treasurer, not the dictator, and the budget will allow for 125 guests. I'll cut my share to 45 to help you out, Gail, but that's the best I can do."

"This sucks," said Gail, who threw down her red pen and ran upstairs.

Randee stood up and stretched. "I'll talk to her later, Martin."

"You know I wish we could invite 500 people, but we can't."

"I know. That was nice of you to offer to cut your share to 45. I can probably cut a few people from mine too."

"Randee, you're going to have to do better than a few. Can you get down to 45? With my 45 and Gail's 45 that makes 135. Not everyone who's invited will come, so I can live with that."

"That's not right, Martin. Gail can't run this show, we do."

"But it's her bat mitzvah. And she can't invite some teammates and not others. That will cause all kinds of problems on the teams."

"Martin, she has you so wrapped around her little finger it's scary. But if you want to be mister nice guy, here's my suggestion. You have 40, I'll have 50 and Gail can have her 45. Deal?"

Of course that wasn't fair. So I accepted, in light of yet another of my rules—you never get everything you want when you're married, so you sure as hell don't get it when you're divorced.

We shook on it like businessmen, then narrowed down our lists. Some cuts were easy, but it really pained me to drop cousin Ben from Winnetka, since I'd spent $200 in gifts on his four sons' bar mitzvahs, money I'd hoped to see back.

When we told Gail the good news she said "cool," and that was it. I was amazed at how much emotion she could show when things were going sour, and how little when she got her way.

So everyone left the evening friends. And soon I'd be someone's new best friend. My stockbroker.

CHAPTER 4

By nine the next morning I was back at the Daley Center, which is named after the late mayor, not the current one. The building is steel and glass, and the supports look like they're rusting out. I've heard that the building's designers planned that effect, though I don't get the attraction of dirty brown. A sculpture by Pablo Picasso, which Chicagoans simply call The Picasso, is the focal point of the plaza south of the building. Some people think it depicts a woman, others an animal of some sort, maybe a bird. To me it symbolizes the Chicago Cubs; you can't make sense out of it, but for some reason you can't help enjoying it.

I headed up to eighteen, Judge Bobb's floor. Since no one in Celia's neighborhood could tell me anything useful about her, I hoped her co-workers would fill in some details.

I spoke to Trish, Rita and Derrick, all clerks on Celia's floor. Office workers chat, so I thought they'd know something about Celia's life, from swapping stories around the water cooler. They all agreed on one thing— Celia was a crab, short on small talk, long on complaints. If she was talking to Trish she'd criticize Rita. If she was talking to Rita she'd whine about Derrick. So they pretty much tuned her out. None of them even knew where she lived, or whether she was married. But no one ever heard anyone make any threats against her.

Next I waited to speak to Judge Bobb, who was still on the bench. There are three rows of visitor's benches in the courtroom, and I took a seat in the second row. Judge Bobb was going through his motion call when I felt a tap on my shoulder. I turned and saw Jim Lanter, a classmate of mine at Wilson University Law School.

We shook hands, firmly. "Hey Marty. Let's go outside where we can talk."

I followed Jim out the courtroom to the main corridor. We both played defensive end in college, with one big difference—he actually played, while I sat glued to the bench. Jim was also ten years younger than me, and his muscle mass hadn't yet shifted alignment.

"Shit, Marty, I haven't seen you since Wilson. You still with the police?"

"No, I gave that up awhile ago."

"But you're keeping busy?"

"Can't complain."

"I'll tell you, Billy Bob's courtroom is sure a lot more pleasant without that bazooka of a law clerk."

"So you don't miss her?"

"Hell no. I'll tell you, probably every lawyer in that courtroom is happy she's out. Hopefully she's gone for good."

"Did you know she was missing?"

"Missing?"

"Yeah, no one's heard from her in a week."

"Really? Well, I feel like a shit. I mean, I don't want her dead or anything."

"I know Jim."

"Anyway Marty, I got to run up to twenty-two. Give me a call, we'll have some beers after work sometime."

"Sounds good."

Jim confirmed something I'd already sensed—every lawyer who practiced in Judge Bobb's courtroom was a potential suspect.

I went back inside as Judge Bobb finished his last motion. The deputy announced that court was adjourned. The judge exited the courtroom through a door behind and to the right of the bench. I followed.

Judge Bobb was standing in the doorway to his chambers when I caught up to him. He yawned and rubbed his eyes.

"Rough morning, Judge."

"It's not that. I was up late last night watching the Blackhawks. Overtime game out in Los Angeles. Didn't end till after midnight." I heard they'd lost, but I'm sure the judge didn't need a reminder.

"So, did you find out anything yet?" he asked.

"Only that Celia is universally characterized as a grouch. Other than that, no one knows anything."

"Excuse me Judge." It was his temporary law clerk. "This envelope was on my desk when I got back from the courtroom. It's addressed to you, personal and confidential."

"Let me see that," he said.

It was a plain white envelope, business size, no postage stamp. He tore it open from the top with his finger. His face gave nothing away while he read over the letter.

"Here, Marty. See what you make of this."

Judge Bobb handed me the letter, which looked like it had come off a laser printer. It said:

Pass the word around. I hope everyone is paying attention. This was just a warning. Unless certain people clean up their act the next one won't be so lucky.
ABC

"So what do you think, Marty?"

"Sounds like he might be releasing Celia. But the other stuff, I don't know. Clean up what act? And what people are being warned?"

"What about that 'ABC' at the bottom?"

"I don't know; kidnappers don't usually leave a calling card. Safe to say it's not the television network. Can you think of anyone with those initials?"

After a minute of chin stroking Judge Bobb proclaimed drawing a blank.

"I guess I better give Detective Crumpton a call," I said.

I dialed his direct number, and he answered on the second ring with a phlegmatic "Crumpton."

"Hey Crumpton, it's your old buddy Bronk here."

"Yeah. What do you want?"

"A letter was delivered to Judge Bobb this morning. It may be from Celia's abductor. Not a ransom note, but some sort of warning. I can't make sense out of it."

"You read it? Don't you remember anything about fingerprints and handling evidence."

"It wasn't evidence when the judge got it, Crumpton. It was just a letter. Judge Bobb read it, then he gave it to me. So quit trying to bust my chops. You want the letter, fine, it's in Judge Bobb's chambers. If you don't want it, it's no hair off my chin."

"I want it, hotshot. I'll be there in half an hour."

I looked into the hallway, where some sort of commotion was going on.

"Oh, and one last thing, Crumpton."

"Yeah?"

"I could be mistaken, but it looks like your missing person just showed up."

CHAPTER 5

"Everyone move out of my way," she bellowed. "And you," she said, pointing at me, "get away from my desk."

She couldn't have been more than five feet tall, but she was solid. Squat like a block of granite. Her hair was a nest of black curls, even while her gray eyebrows betrayed its true color.

"Celia," said Judge Bobb. "Are you okay? We were worried."

"Yeah, I'm fine."

Clerks and deputies from other courtrooms began congregating around the chambers, confirming that Celia was really there. Judge Bobb and I shooed them away once their curiosity had been satisfied. None of them said hello to Celia before leaving.

"Celia," continued Judge Bobb, "this is Martin Bronk. He's a private investigator I hired to find you."

"Yeah, I've seen you around," she said. "You really earned your money on this one, huh."

"I'm just glad you're safe," I said. I moved away from her desk so she could sit. Also to escape her odor; her dungeon must not have come equipped with a shower. "So what happened?"

"I was in the Jewel parking lot, and next thing I know someone's sticking a handkerchief over my mouth and nose. It must have had that stuff on it, 'cause when I come to I'm in the basement of a house, my leg chained to the wall."

"Did you see who abducted you?" I asked.

"No. He always wore a mask."

"Do you remember anything about his appearance?"

"He wasn't fat or nothing. He was a white guy, I could tell from his hands. That's about it."

"Did he say why he kidnapped you?"

"He said he was sick and tired of all the 'hostility' that goes around in court. That was his word, 'hostility.' He said I was the meanest, nastiest clerk he's ever seen, so he was gonna teach me a lesson."

"Teach you a lesson?"

"Yeah, like punish me. He pretended he was a judge, and he sentenced me to one week confinement. He had this long chain on my ankle, so I could move around a little. Even had a toilet down there I could reach. Then today he says my sentence is up. He put that stuff to my face again, and when I woke up some wino was making eyes at me."

"What?"

"Yeah, that nut dropped me off on Lower Wacker. Once I chased the bum away I figured, since I'm already downtown I might as well come to work. Way the County works, I was probably docked for unauthorized absences."

"Any idea where the house is?"

"Nah." The guy was smart to knock her out; not only wouldn't she make a fuss, she wouldn't know how long she was in the car.

"All right," I said. "The police will be here soon, and I'm sure they'll ask you some more questions. Anything else you can think of?"

"He said everyone better start acting nicer. He thanked me for being so neat; said it made his clean up easier for the next one. Oh, and he said the next one wouldn't get off so easy."

Soon Crumpton and his cohorts stormed into the office. I took his arrival as my cue to leave, but not before we stared each other down, like two boxers in the ring. Judge Bobb acted the part of referee, leading me to the hallway.

"Thanks for your help, Marty."

"You know, Judge, I feel guilty about my fee. I hardly did any work, and poof, she shows up."

"A deal is a deal, don't worry about it."

"Well, anyway, I'm glad she turned up alive. Catching the guy is a police concern, not mine."

"Right."

"But if you need anything from me let me know."

Sometimes I should just keep my big mouth shut.

CHAPTER 6

A week later Celia called the office. Judge Bobb and Judge Dienstag wanted to see me that morning, in Judge Dienstag's office. She didn't know what it was about, only that I should be there. We set an eleven o'clock meeting time.

"Oh, by the way, give Mrs. Poole my regards," I said.

"That buzzard. As soon as I get back she wants her rent money. Don't care in the least that I been kidnapped. That's the one the guy should have took, he wants someone nasty."

Judge David Dienstag was the chief judge of the Circuit Court of Cook County. The Big Cheese, the most muckety of the mucks. Among other things, he controlled the judicial assignments for the hundreds of Cook County judges. So if you're a judge and you get on his wrong side, you end up in housing court hearing eviction cases all day, or maybe traffic court. Judge Dienstag was so important that he didn't merely have a chambers, he had an office. If he wanted to see me it wasn't for a social visit.

I was greeted by Judge Dienstag's secretary, a matronly woman in her fifties who you just know types two hundred words a minute. She led me to the judge's office. It was at least three times the size of Judge Bobb's chambers, and featured a lake view. Judge Bobb was already there, sitting in a chair which sure looked like real leather.

"Hello, Mr. Bronk. Thank you for coming on such short notice. Please have a seat." Judge Dienstag was little larger than a jockey, he wore over-sized glasses like some science geek, and he combed over his hair to hide his baldness. But no one would dare tease him about his appearance. His sharp tongue could put the meanest bully into therapy. He was the wunderkind of the Cook County judiciary. From assistant attorney general to judge to chief judge within a dozen years. Rumor was he merely had to give the word and he'd be in line for the next opening on the federal court, but he wasn't yet willing to give up his fiefdom.

"No problem, Your Honor. But please call me Marty." I sat. Real leather all right.

"Let me get down to business, Marty. Judge Bobb—hell we're all friends here—Billy Bob was telling me about the work you did when his law clerk was missing. It seems that we have another situation on our hands."

"A situation?"

"We've managed to keep it out of the press, but Judge Miles has been missing for the past two days."

I'd testified before Judge Walter Miles a couple of years earlier. An automobile collision case where'd I'd taken photos of the accident scene. I should have been in and out within thirty minutes tops. But the judge ended up lecturing one of the attorneys for ten minutes, in open court, about the proper etiquette involved in raising an objection. Then he chastised me for referring to an 'accident' rather than a 'collision.' "You're being sloppy in your language, sir. The contact could have been intentional, which would negate this being an 'accident.'" Miles was, in a literal sense, correct, but the defense was based on a third car supposedly cutting the defendant off, and there'd been no indication that the collision was anything but an accident. So the judge was simply being a prick.

"Tell me more about Judge Miles."

"He's been a judge for twelve years. For the past five years he's been a trial judge in the civil division, hearing major personal injury cases. His wife said he left for work as usual two days ago. That's the last anyone's seen of him."

"How does he get downtown?"

"He drives to the Metra station in Northbrook and takes the train."

"I assume the police are involved."

"Yes, both Chicago and Northbrook."

"So what can I do for you?"

"In all candor, Billy Bob was less than impressed with the way the Chicago police handled the investigation into his clerk's disappearance. Seems they didn't even interview any of the other clerks, or her landlord. You were on the job only a short time, but you did all that."

"I'm sure the cops will put their best people on the job if a judge is missing."

"Maybe. Still, this is one of our own we're talking about, and I'd like to go to bed at night knowing that someone's on top of things."

"Well..."

"I should add that money is tight and I can't ask the county to appropriate any funds on your behalf. But Billy Bob was telling me about the rather generous sum he paid you, and the fortuity of his clerk showing up the next day. Plus, I can pledge the gratitude of the Cook County judiciary. While I'm not promising anything, one never knows when that could prove beneficial."

Judge Dienstag had painted me into a corner before I even knew I was in the room. He couldn't, and wouldn't, promise anything so brazen as fixing a case. But there would likely come a time when I'd be picked up for trespassing or assault, and a sympathetic judge could make my life a lot easier.

"Judge," I said, "I'll get on it. But just so there's no misunderstanding, I neither desire nor expect any favors from the Cook County judiciary. The personal gratitude of its individual members is sufficient." See, I know how to play the game too.

"I'm glad we understand each other, Marty. Billy Bob will fill you in on Judge Miles and what we know so far. My secretary will give you my pager number; call me anytime if you need official help. Any questions, you can deal with Billy Bob. Now I have a budget meeting to attend."

We shook hands. In retrospect I was overcompensated for my work in finding Celia. But while judicial gratitude is fine, it doesn't pay the caterer.

•

"Bronk, I figured I was through with you when the Glagovic woman showed up."

"No such luck, Crumpton."

"Where you calling from, a fucking tunnel?"

"Must have a bad cell. I'm on my way up to Northbrook."

"Northbrook? Don't tell me you're butting your nose into Judge Miles' disappearance."

"Now I can see why you made detective, Crumpton."

"Unfortunately, Bronk, as much as I'd like to—and you know there's nothing I'd rather do—I can't help you with this one. Northbrook's taking the lead, since that's where he was last seen."

"Maybe you can tell me what's going on with the Glagovic case. Have you found her kidnapper?"

"We're still working on it."

"What about that letter Judge Bobb received. Have you figured out who or what ABC is?"

"Like I said, we're still working on it."

"Do you see a connection between Glagovic and Judge Miles' disappearance?"

"I don't have to answer your questions, Bronk. If you want to make a pest of yourself in Northbrook that's between you and them. But I don't want to hear from you again. Got it?"

"I don't know what your problem is, Crumpton. We made such a good team on the Glagovic case. You sat on your ass at the station, I asked a few people some questions, and next thing you know she showed up safe. Seems like a pretty good setup for you."

"You've been warned." With that the connection broke. It could have been a cellular phone problem, or it could have been a hang up. Not that it really mattered.

Although Crumpton had it in for me personally, his territorial attitude was pretty typical of how cops feel when outsiders get involved in an investigation. Even though everyone should be on the same page in trying to catch the bad guy, the locals feel disrespected if they're not running the show. I know from experience, because I was that way too. Locals don't like the state, they don't like the feds, but they especially don't like private investigators nosing around.

Some p.i.'s don't confront this issue; they do their work, and deal with the cops only after the shit hits the fan. But I figure the cops will find out about me sooner or later, so I try to be professional about it from the beginning. I make a point of introducing myself and explaining what I'm doing there. Usually I get reactions like Crumpton's. But not always.

I walked in to the Northbrook police station and asked to speak to the detective in charge of the Miles case. The officer at the desk phoned someone, then directed me down the hall to the third door on the left.

The office was open. The nameplate on the door said "Criminal Investigations." I knocked, then walked in before getting a response. The room was no larger than Judge Dienstag's office, but was set up to accommodate a lot more activity. Four desks, two facing one wall, two the opposite wall, formed the perimeter. A long table surrounded by six chairs was in the middle of the room. Papers and files were spread out on the long table, and the other desks displayed the standard police-issue clutter. Only one of the desks was occupied. The detective was talking on the phone, but signalled me over.

"Hello, I'm Detective Moyer. How can I help you?" she said to me after hanging up. She then stood and extended her hand. She was tall, at least six feet, and wore her strawberry blonde hair in a single braid which reached just below the shoulders. She had a long face, cheeks a bit sunken, and green eyes which were slightly crossed. Her eyebrows were a shade darker than her hair. My description may not be terribly flattering, but I found her appearance more unusual than unattractive.

"Hello, Detective, my name is Martin Bronk. I'm a private investigator." I gave her one of my cards.

"Can I see your identification too?"

"Sure." I dug out a laminated I.D. card.

"Okay," she said after maybe five seconds, "what can I do for you? Or what can you do for me?"

"Are you in charge of the investigation into Judge Miles' disappearance?"

"Yes I am."

"I wanted to touch base with you. The chief judge of the Cook County Circuit Court asked me to look into Judge Miles' disappearance. A week ago I helped locate a court employee who was missing, so now it seems I'm their resident expert on missing persons."

"The Celia Glagovic case" she said without hesitation.

"That's right. You do your homework."

"Does that surprise you?"

"A little. I used to be a detective in Chicago, and frankly not all my colleagues were that efficient." I was surprised to hear that come out of my mouth. I don't normally bad rap my old co-workers, especially to a stranger.

"I saw your name in Detective Crumpton's report, so I was kind of expecting you," she said without emotion.

"I don't want to step on any toes here, but when the chief judge asks you to do something..."

"Can't very well turn down the chief judge, can you. Don't worry, we'll extend you every professional cooperation, and in return I expect you'll do the same."

"That's fair."

"We all want to find Judge Miles, and catch the bastard who took him. I'm sure you know your way around an investigation, so if you can help, we won't take offense." How refreshing to find someone with a sensible attitude.

"Thank you for your understanding. Now, Detective Moyer..."

"Amanda."

"Okay, Amanda, what have you turned up so far?"

"Not much. Judge Miles left his home at his usual time to catch the 7:34 into downtown. Every morning he buys coffee at the stand in the station and kibitzes with the guy who runs it, but the guy doesn't remember seeing the judge that day. Also, Miles always sits in the same train car, but the conductor didn't see him."

"Did anyone see him in the parking lot?"

"No. Oh, his car is missing too."

"How do you know he didn't just run off with some cute young thing?"

"I suppose we can't know for sure, except that he has no history of cheating or unexplained absences. So we're assuming that wherever he is, it's not by choice, and work from there, hoping we're wrong."

"Anything in Judge Miles' past to suggest who might have done this?"

"We're still checking."

"Of course any judge can be expected to have some enemies."

"Right. I can tell you that we haven't gotten any ransom notes."

"Do you think it's connected to the Glagovic case?"

"Can't tell yet. That ABC note suggests the possibility, but other than that we don't have a connection."

"Except they're both Cook County court personnel." I paused briefly. "The one thing I kept hearing about Celia was that she was unpleasant to deal with. From my limited experience with Judge Miles, he too would have flunked charm school."

"Yes, we've heard he can be loud and short-tempered."

"Is it okay if I speak with Mrs. Miles?"

"Sure, go ahead. Not that she knows much. We have an officer there keeping an eye on things. Give him this note when you get there." She scribbled something on a memo pad, folded it, stuck it in a Northbrook police envelope and sealed the envelope.

The phone rang at one of the other desks, and Amanda walked over to pick it up. Her long, fluid strides earmarked her as an athlete. I've always been turned on by athletic women, which is ironic since Randee's most strenuous activity was pulling out her credit card.

While holding the phone Amanda turned to face the wall. I took her body language as a sign that I should leave, so I did.

It was nice meeting someone who realized that people working the same side of the law for the same end aren't enemies. Professionalism is so rare.

I wondered what she thought of me.

•

I made the short drive to the Miles house. As Amanda said, a Northbrook patrol car was parked in front. I handed Amanda's note to the officer. He opened the envelope, read what was inside, and smiled. I asked him what the note said, but he wouldn't say.

Mrs. Miles looked a week past tired, even though her husband had only been missing two days. She invited me to join her in the living room, which was tastefully furnished in traditional style. She served me tea and butter cookies, as if this was an afternoon social.

Between puffs of cigarettes Mrs. Miles recounted that her husband had seemed fine, they hadn't received any threatening phone calls or letters, and she didn't know of any enemies. The only time he'd ever been missing was twenty years earlier, when he got drunk at a colleague's going away party, passed out on the train, and missed his stop. Their marriage was good, and while she knew from watching TV that such things could happen, she couldn't imagine her husband running away with another woman. She had a feeling something bad happened, but she didn't have any idea what, or why.

After rambling about how wonderful her husband was I cut the interview short, since I wasn't getting anything out of Mrs. Miles other than a serious helping of secondhand smoke. In the fifteen minutes we'd talked she'd already finished three Winston lights. Sensing the imminent arrival of number four, I hastily thanked her for her time before it emerged.

"Nice lady," I said to the cop as I walked back to my car. "Hope things turn out okay."

"I'll bet he offed himself."

"Why do you say that?"

"She give you tea and cookies?"

"Yeah."

"She comes out here every hour on the nose with that stuff. I know she means well, but it drives you nuts after awhile. Imagine living with someone like that."

"She does seem a bit compulsive. So tell me, what was in that note from Detective Moyer?"

"Why does that bother you so much?"

"Just curious. It's nothing that will embarrass me, right?"

"Nothing like that. I'll tell you, but don't let on to Moyer."

"I won't."

"Okay. The note says nothing."

"Come on, stop crapping me."

"Here, look for yourself." He handed me the note. "If he asks for the note, tell him it says nothing," it said.

"I don't get it," I said.

"If you knew Moyer you would."

•

I used the drive back to the city to plot strategy. I could have stayed around Northbrook to interview Miles' neighbors, people at the train station and so on, but Amanda seemed to know what she was doing, and I doubted that retracing her steps would turn up anything. Instead, I decided to concentrate on two other areas. One, was there a connection between Judge Miles and Celia? And two, who was ABC?

It was around three o'clock when I got back to the Daley Center, and the courthouse's morning frenzy had given way to afternoon lethargy. Sort of like the difference between Division Street on New Year's Eve versus Christmas Eve. Courtroom use diminishes as the day winds down, which doesn't mean the judges aren't doing their jobs. Cases get resolved, often when it's too late in the day for the judge to start a new trial. And when that happens there's not much need for the judge to stick around. So I wasn't surprised that Judge Bobb had left for home.

But Celia was still in. She was working a crossword, and didn't look up until my third ahem.

"Oh, it's you," she said.

"Hello Celia. How does it feel to be back on the job?"

"Chained to a wall, chained to a desk, no big difference."

"Come on, aren't you glad to be back dealing with Chicago's many friendly attorneys?"

She gave me a "you're an idiot" stare, then waited for me to continue.

"Did you ever work for Judge Miles?"

"Yeah, I worked for him about ten years ago. Lasted three weeks. Why?"

"Just curious. You haven't clerked for him since then?"

"No, not even for one day. We didn't exactly see eye to eye."

"What was the problem?"

"He's a screamer. Probably don't mean anything by it, but I don't take well to that. Someone yells at me, I yell back, louder. Miles didn't like that too much."

"Who does he scream at?"

"Just about everyone, but especially anyone who challenges him, or people he thinks are stupid or have a bad attitude. He's a loud guy."

"You ever hear lawyers complain about him?"

"Lawyers complain about everyone. That's what they do best, you know. Complain."

"What do they say?"

"Depends on who you listen to. Most say he's too unpredictable. That he flies off the handle and tries to embarrass them. But they say that about half the judges here. The other half, they say they're too soft. You just can't win. Lawyers. They ought to lock the bunch of them in a room for 48 hours and see what happens. I'll bet they'd come out with a whole new attitude."

"I'll suggest that to Judge Dienstag next time I see him. But in the meantime, when you see Judge Bobb in the morning ask him to clear about fifteen minutes for me. Maybe around eleven."

"Yeah, okay."

"You know, Judge Bobb really was concerned for you."

"Yeah, he's okay."

"Was that a compliment?"

Celia went back to her crossword. "What's a five letter word for 'get lost'?"

"Scram?"

"You figured it out. Now figure out how to do it."

•

The Cook County Law Library is located on the 29th floor of the Daley Center. Nothing fancy here. Computers are virtually unknown, chairs are mismatched (some seats are so worn through you sink), and the desks are so chipped and scratched that you need a backing, like a clipboard or a thick legal pad, in order to write. But it does offer an unobstructed view of Lake Michigan to the east, and it's a great source for legal information, provided you're not spoiled by CD-ROMs and online services, which I'm not.

I found a number of stories about Judge Miles in the Chicago Daily Law Bulletin, going back twelve years. Walter Miles grew up on the northwest side of Chicago, the son of a butcher. He attended Gordon Tech High School, then Loyola University and John Marshall Law School, which he completed at night while working days as a paralegal. He followed a path common to Cook County judges, starting out as an Assistant State's Attorney before being appointed an associate judge and then being elected a full judge. Before the last election he was rated "qualified" by the Chicago Bar Association. Not its highest rating, but not its lowest either.

An article written four years earlier caught my attention. Practicing lawyers had been surveyed concerning judicial temperament. All the circuit judges were rated from one to ten, ten being the best temperament. Judge Miles got a three. Only five judges had lower scores. The article also noted that Judge Miles was one of a handful of judges targeted for removal by a group of attorneys I'd never heard of—the Society for Civility in the Courts.

And I found another noteworthy article, from this past January. The Judicial Inquiry Board, or JIB, was reportedly investigating Miles for sexual harassment. According to the article Miles vehemently denied any impropriety, and proclaimed that he'd be vindicated if a complaint was filed. He said the allegations were nothing more than an attempt by certain unnamed individuals to get him off the bench. Which, to my mind, was more an accurate observation than a refutation. The story was not specific as to the alleged harassment, other than to say it was verbal, and not physical, in nature. It went on to describe the judicial inquiry process, and how the JIB must complete its investigation before deciding whether or not to file a complaint.

Now that I'd read up on Miles I needed to find out more. If there's one person who really knows what a judge is all about, it's his law clerk. So on the way down from the library I stopped at Judge Miles chambers. Locked. A clerk walked by, trying to look casual, but she was moving so slowly that she must have been checking me out. I asked her where I could find Miles' clerk. I guess I didn't look too disreputable because she answered. He must have been reassigned, she said, but she didn't know where. Call Angie on eight, and ask where Eldrick is working.

The eighth floor is the Clerk of the Court's office, but instead of calling I stopped over. The room is set up with a long L-shaped counter, where different stations allow you to do such things as request a court file or file a document. Behind the counters are dozens of people working at small desks. Doing what I'm not exactly sure, but either they've learned the fine art of paper shuffling, or they were truly busy.

I asked the woman at the information area where I could find Angie. She pointed to a desk in the first row behind the short side of the L, to the right of the cashiers. That's where I went, but when I was still thirty feet away the woman seated there got up and walked out of view. I continued on and stopped at the counter in front of the desk. But not only had Angie left, the nearest worker was four rows back, and she was on the phone.

I waited a few minutes, and I'm big enough that someone must have noticed me, but no one offered any assistance. Maybe the desk sitters don't deal with the public. Or maybe it's easier to be rude than helpful. I suppose I could have shouted to the woman on the phone for some attention, or maybe jumped up and down waving my arms until someone noticed. But I learned early that the best private eyes are usually the most discreet, and I aim high.

The counter itself was a good four feet tall, but a shorter pass-through gate connected it to the wall. The gate was locked, but because it didn't quite reach my hip I figured I'd have just enough clearance to get my legs over. I brought my right leg up and swung it over, then repeated with the left. My hamstrings weren't happy, but I made it.

If anyone saw me they were keeping it to themselves. I was working my way back to the lady on the phone when a short, bald man with an unlit (but not unchewed) cigar intercepted me.

"You, instead of standing around doing nothin', go make yourself useful," he rasped. "Rush these things up to Dienstag. And be back in five minutes, or else I'm writin' you up." He held out a couple of file folders, crammed with enough papers to gladden a bureaucrat's heart.

In response I crossed my arms over my chest.

"What are you waitin' for?"

"A 'please' would be nice."

"You crappin' me? When was the last time you heard a 'please' around here. Now get to it."

"No."

"No? Whaddya mean no."

"I'm working."

"I know you're working. That's why I'm givin' you work."

"But I don't work for you."

"If you work in this office you do." He gave a head-to-toe look. "Hey, where's your ID card?"

"In my wallet."

"Cripes, don't you know nothin'? It's supposed to be showing at all times."

"It is?"

"C'mon, moron, take it out."

I showed him my ID. "What's this? Private detective?"

"Yeah, that's me. Like I said, I'm working. Now, tell me where I can find Angie. Or, better yet, Eldrick, Judge Miles' clerk."

"Why'd you let me go on like that?"

"Because you were rude, and rude people don't bring out the essence of my sweet nature."

"I thought you worked here."

"So that excuses your bad manners?" I unclipped the ID card fastened to his shirt pocket. "I'll tell you what, Sid, I'll be sure to mention you to Judge Dienstag. He's the one I'm working for."

"So tell him. He ain't my boss." Which was true; the Clerk of the Court is a separate office from the Chief Judge's. Still, Sid's voice lost some of its snap.

"I'm waiting, Sid. Angie. Eldrick."

"Angie ain't here. Eldrick is over there." He pointed to a desk set up near the back wall.

"Thank you." I re-clipped his ID card.

He pivoted to walk away. "Aren't you forgetting something, Sid?"

He turned back to face me. "What?"

"A 'you're welcome' would be appropriate."

His upper teeth met his bottom lip, but he kept enough control that the "F" never came. Instead he mumbled something which sounded enough like "welcome" that I let it pass.

Sid had pointed out a black man, mid-forties, bald, mustache. And wearing a jacket and tie, a classy departure from the ragged sport shirts most clerks wear. I walked over, introduced myself and explained why I wanted to talk. Eldrick said he'd be happy to help in any way he could. He had a gentle voice, and even without knowing him I pictured him as a soothing influence on Miles.

I suggested we talk over coffee at the Starbucks in the Daley Center basement, but Eldrick thought it better to stay in the Clerk's office. "I already had my break," he said, "and I don't want to give the supervisors any excuse not to assign me to another judge."

"So you're here temporarily?"

"Right. And the more temporary the better. Paperwork's not my thing. People are."

"Even lawyers?"

"Even lawyers. Treat them right, they'll treat you right. At least most of them."

"How long have you worked for Judge Miles?"

"Almost four years."

"Tell me about him."

"I know people think he must be terrible to work for, and God knows he can be loud and insensitive. But really, he's usually a regular guy. I guess I even like him. I sure don't want anything bad to happen to him."

"But I take it he can rub people the wrong way."

"Yes, that's true."

"He have any enemies?"

"Enemies? Not really. He's had shouting matches with some lawyers. And even with other judges. But, you know, that happens where big egos are involved."

"Can you give me some names of who these shouting matches were with?"

"Gee, there've been a lot, and I don't know the names of everyone. Can you let me think on it? I'll put a list together tonight, and fax it to you in the morning."

"That'd be great. Aside from the shouting, he ever get any threats?"

"You know, I've been thinking about that myself. Once, a couple months ago, I walked past his office while he was on the phone, and it looked like he was trembling. When he hung up I asked him if everything was okay. 'Just a pissed off asshole who wants a piece of me' he said."

"You have any idea who he was talking to?"

"No. That's all he said."

"Did you answer the phones?"

"Yeah. Oh, I see what you're getting at. I didn't answer that call, so the judge must have phoned out." Or Eldrick wasn't being totally candid. But he seemed honest. Besides, if he was going to cover up who Miles was talking to, he wouldn't have told me about the call in the first place.

"Maybe Miles was returning a call. Do you have a message book with a record of incoming calls?"

"I did, but it's with the police." If Crumpton had it maybe he'd share the information. And maybe the Cubs will meet the White Sox in the World Series. Hopefully Detective Moyer in Northbrook could help.

"Can you be any more specific about when this took place?"

"Just a second." Pause. "It must have been a Thursday because I remember the judge asking me to buy him a bunch of tomatoes at the farmers' market downstairs."

"And the farmers' market is only on Thursdays."

"Right. And it's only every other Thursday too."

I saw Sid out of the corner of my eye, and gave him a wave. He stuck the cigar back in his mouth, then grimaced. Must have bit off a little too much.

"What can you tell me about the complaint against Miles with the Judicial Inquiry Board?"

"You have to understand something about the judge. He's an old school guy, where women are girls or gals. But he doesn't mean anything by it."

"That's what the sexual harassment complaint is about?"

"Yeah, as far as I know. I never saw him say or do anything worse than that."

"But you weren't with him at all times?"

"That's true. Like I told you before, he can be insensitive, but I don't think he means to be nasty. Take me. Sometimes he calls me Eric, because Eldrick is a 'colored' name. If I told my friends and family about that they'd want me to go to the NAACP or the newspapers, or sue for harassment. But in his mind my name identifies me in a way which can be a disadvantage, and he was making what he thought was a helpful suggestion. So I don't take it personally." This Eldrick was all right.

"How about outside of work? Did Miles have any interests that could get him in trouble with the wrong people?"

"I don't think so. He wasn't into gambling or anything like that."

"Any doubts about his integrity?"

"You mean like taking a bribe or something?"

"Right. Maybe he took money from someone and then double-crossed them." Within the past decade a number of Cook County judges were convicted of accepting bribes. In one particularly notorious case the judge conducting a bench trial of an alleged mob hitman found the defendant innocent of murder despite what most impartial observers thought was overwhelming evidence of guilt. Once the bribe came to light the appellate court held that the hitman could be tried for murder a second time, despite the double jeopardy clause of the Constitution. Because he was never in jeopardy of being convicted in the first trial.

"No, he doesn't seem the type who'd take a payoff." As far as I know, the judges caught taking bribes were hearing criminal cases, not civil cases like Miles. So I wasn't surprised by Eldrick's answer. Then again, many judges start off in traffic court, so even if lately he's been clean, it's possible Miles has a history. Something to think about, at least.

"He ever talk about his home life?"

"As far as I know it was okay. Occasionally he'd be arguing with his wife on the phone, but that's been true with every judge I've worked for."

"And probably anybody else you'd work for too." Spoken like the divorced man I am.

"I've been down that road too, Mr. Bronk."

I didn't have any more questions, so I thanked Eldrick. He seemed sincere in saying he hoped I'd find the judge, and he was certainly a pleasure compared to the Celias and Sids I'd been dealing with.

•

That night I had dinner plans with my girlfriend. I'd met Colleen Tobolski a couple of months earlier, and we were still taking things kind of slow. I'd worked closely with her on a matter I handled for the Wilson University School of Law, where she was Assistant Dean. We almost made love one evening, but there were too many ethical issues for me to go through with it. Among them being that she was both a client and a potential suspect. After a rather stormy period we came to grips with the situation, and decided to remain friendly but otherwise cool it until I finished my job. Now that the case was wrapped up I was seeing her about once a week. We were dating, in the sense that I would ask her out and pick up the tab. And we'd kiss and hold hands and share secrets. But we still hadn't made love, and I didn't have a feel for where the relationship was going. Still, she was the only woman I was seeing, and for that matter the only woman I wanted to see. I just couldn't tell if she felt the same.

We met at an Italian restaurant near the Wilson campus, a red and white checked tablecloth sort of place which would have been a pizzeria ten years ago but is now called a trattoria. Colleen was waiting when I arrived fifteen minutes late. She gave me a teacher's tsk tsk, followed by a delicate kiss on the lips.

"I'm usually the late one, Marty. Did you get stuck in traffic?"

"Sorry. Research project for my new case took longer than expected."

"Research, eh? Sounds scholarly."

"I needed a break from beating information out of people."

Our waiter was a college student who was as Italian as me and Colleen. Colleen requested a Pinot Grigio, me a Valpolicella, and I ordered a calamari appetizer. In true Chicago fashion the "cal" came out like "California," and the "mari" like "marry."

"So what's new at good ole Wilson these days?" I asked.

"The University is putting together a search committee for a permanent dean." Colleen's former boss had recently resigned, and she was the acting dean.

"Are you going to apply?"

"Yeah, but I'm going to try the old squeeze play."

"Squeeze play?"

"Yeah, I know they want someone experienced, probably a snooty old guy who'll fit the traditional image. The type who looks like he was born in a tuxedo. And I really don't want the job anyway. But if I throw my hat in the ring they'll have to make some kind of accommodation, or else I'll scream sex discrimination. So that should put me in line for one of the teaching positions that's opened up."

"Colleen, I had no idea you were so calculating."

"Unfortunately you have to be. Higher education isn't the genteel world people think it is."

"You think your plan will work?"

"It will work. If not, I may need you to find me a good lawyer."

"First I have to find me a not so good judge." I explained about Judge Miles and my involvement in the case. I stressed the part about the chief judge asking for my assistance, and even threw in that he'd given me his pager number. Colleen made a big deal about that, but I suspect she saw through my ploy to impress her and was doing it for show.

"So do you have any leads, Marty?"

"Nothing concrete. Just the letters ABC."

"The first three letters of the alphabet? What is it, some kind of code?" I hadn't told her about Celia because that case wrapped up so quickly, so I described the note, and the possible connection between the two abductions.

"Why would someone identify themselves on a note like that?" she asked.

"They wouldn't, unless some weird psychological stuff is going on and they want to be discovered. Or they're so cocky that they have no fear of getting caught. But I'm not satisfied by either of those possibilities."

We finished up the edible rubber, as Gail calls calamari (a little too much garlic, but good). For dinner Colleen ordered a Tuscan breast of chicken, while I got the four cheese ravioli, because I liked the sound of quattro formaggi.

"Colleen, in your academic circles have you ever heard of a group called the Society for Civility in the Courts?"

"No. But you know who you should ask about that? Fred Nickles. He teaches ethics." Fred's a professor at Wilson who I met during my investigation there. Seeing as I'd saved his life he owed me a free consultation.

"Okay, I'll call him in the morning."

"I know where he is tonight. Why don't we stop back at the school when we're done with dinner."

"Colleen, I thought we were on a date, not a fact finding mission."

"Marty, don't be like that. Maybe it's important to your case, and you can be the hero again." She took hold of my left hand and batted her eyes. "I do love a hero, you know."

Her obvious clowning aside, after dinner she led me to a room on the second floor of the Wilson student union. Fred Nickles was one of about a dozen people hunched over chessboards.

"Fred loves the game," Colleen whispered. "He's always talking up the chess club, trying to recruit new members."

Fred was concentrating on the problem at hand, and didn't notice us hovering over his table until after he made his move.

"Well, if it isn't my guardian angel," he said. "What brings you back to Wilson?"

Colleen and I looked at each other in a way which made words meaningless. "Yes, of course," observed Nickles. "Then perhaps I should rephrase my question: What brings you to the chess club?"

"I know how to show my dates a good time."

"Actually I think intellectual stimulation is a good time. But I suspect there's another purpose for your visit."

"Just a few questions about something that's come up in one of my cases."

"Okay, as soon as I'm finished here. Which shouldn't be long seeing how I have my young opponent here on the ropes." He shot his opponent an I-know-something-you-don't smile.

"Oh, I resign," said Fred's foe, a student still trying to lick an acne problem. "You better watch him, mister," he said to me, "Fred's on his game tonight."

The kid got up from his seat. I took his place, and Fred arranged the pieces.

"Shouldn't we go in the hallway to talk?" I asked.

"Not necessary. That image of chessplayers requiring absolute silence is nonsense. This isn't a tournament—we're just a bunch of guys exercising our minds."

"Okay. Have you ever heard of a group called the Society for Civility in the Courts?"

"Sure. The S.C.C. But it broke up a couple of years ago."

"What can you tell me about it?"

"As far as I know there were five chapters, in New York, L.A., Chicago, Philly and D.C. Some rather prominent attorneys and professors in these cities would get together on an ad hoc basis with the goal of improving the climate in which law is practiced."

"What does that mean?"

"They tried to make attorneys more cognizant of being considerate toward each other. They sponsored seminars stressing cooperation over antagonism. They also identified judges who were not respectful of attorneys, and publicized who those judges were."

"You said it disbanded a couple of years ago?"

"Right. It didn't get results. Also, many of the targeted judges took offense, and made life difficult for the S.C.C. attorneys who practiced before them."

"That's a pity. The system could do with some more civility."

"But the fight hasn't been abandoned, it's just gone underground. The S.C.C. spawned some other groups with the same aim, only the attorneys now stay anonymous so as not to antagonize the judges. The people involved in these groups generally aren't as prominent as the S.C.C. attorneys, but they're just as dedicated."

"Any of these groups in Chicago?"

"There's three that I know of. Lawyers for Decency, Bring Back Manners, and Attorneys for the Betterment of the Courts."

"What was that last one again?"

"Attorneys for the Betterment of the Courts."

"ABC."

"That's right. They refer to themselves as the ABCers. It's the group I know the least about. I've never been able to find out any information about them, other than the fact of its existence."

"So you've never spoken to anyone in the group?"

"No. I haven't even been able to find anyone who knows any members."

"Would they resort to violence?"

"Violence? I doubt it; these groups use the pen, not the sword. But like I said, I really don't know much about them. Can I ask what this is all about?"

"I can't say, except that I hope I can put my guardian angel role back into action."

"Do you play chess, Marty?"

"A little."

"How about a quick game?".

"Sure." Far be it for me to dispel the image of the dumb jock, but this former football player plays a tough game of chess. Fred opened up with some aggressive but unsound moves, the kind you play against an inexperienced opponent so you can quickly mow them down. So when I moved out my king knight to protect everything he went into a deep think. He continued to attack, and I easily parried his obvious threats. Soon he overextended himself and I forced him into retreat. Then he overlooked a knight maneuver which won material for me. After that my attack couldn't be defended.

"You play a good game Marty," he acknowledged as he tipped over his king in defeat. To his credit Fred remained graceful, even though I must have done some damage to his academic ego. "Want to play again?"

"Another time. I think I need to get Colleen home before she collapses from excitement." Colleen had been roaming around while Fred and I played. Heads which were otherwise steady turned expectantly, if furtively, as she passed by. Attractive females have that effect on chess players.

On football players too, for that matter.

"Congratulations on beating Fred," Colleen said as we left. "So for all his talk about chess, he's a lousy player?"

"Hey, give me some credit. I do possess certain mental abilities, you know."

"Maybe for chess. But you'll never beat me in Scrabble."

"Oh yeah? Are you familiar with the word 'rotl'?"

"Of course."

"What's the plural."

"'Artal,' a-r-t-a-l."

"Wrong. Try a-r-t-e-l."

"Close, Marty, but that's a different word. Not that it matters in Scrabble, since you don't need to know what they mean."

"Don't try to rattle my confidence."

"Would I do that?"

Earlier Colleen had mentioned a seven a.m. meeting the next morning, so we called it an early evening. We walked to her car, which was parked at the law school. Normally I'd have continued on the Scrabble theme, but I was preoccupied. As we neared her car I got the same feeling I had before asking Kerrie Monoghan to the prom. Kerrie said yes, and I knew Colleen would say yes to what I was going to ask her. Even so it seems that the human psyche needs a certain dose of anxiety, maybe to keep us in line from our more foolish thoughts.

"Thanks for dinner, Marty. Sorry I have to cut the evening short."

"Colleen, I have to ask you something."

"Oh." Probably sensing my anxiety, her face got all serious.

"No, it's nothing like that. I just wanted to ask you to be my date for Gail's bat mitzvah."

"Of course." She answered quickly, obviously relieved that was all I was asking.

"You might want to think about it a little. My family will be there, Randee will be there. And lots of yentas."

"Lots of what?"

"Busybodies. They'll talk about you, the shiksa. Most of the talk will be behind your back, but there's always a few whose voices tend to carry."

"I think I can handle the yentas."

"Well, Miss Colleen Tobolski, when someone asks you about your name you're not going to repeat that cock and bull story you told me, are you?"

"You doubt me?"

"Come on. Your mother doesn't speak much English, and after you're born the nurse asks her what she's naming you, and she says "co-lean" because she thought the nurse asked her what she did for a living."

"It's the truth."

"Tell me the real story. I can handle the truth." Doing my bad Jack Nicholson impression.

"I'd rather handle you." She drew me close and worked her lips into mine. The lip lock that seemed never to end.

Finally we released. "Colleen, you keep that up and you'll have no problem handling me any way you like."

She gave me another kiss. "That's what I'm counting on."

"Do you really have a seven o'clock meeting tomorrow?"

"Yeah, and it's with some major benefactors. I'm sorry, sweetie, but I'm going to have to call it a night."

"I see. Trying to make an impression on the guys with the big bucks. Good thing I'm not the jealous sort."

"You got something big that's much more important to me than their dollars."

"Oh."

"Your heart. What'd you think I was talking about."

"Well, you know...." We laughed, then wished each other sweet dreams.

I was feeling pretty good about things until I got home and checked the dictionary. How could I have mixed up a Moslem unit of weight with a group of people working collectively?

CHAPTER 7

Next morning I got to the office five minutes late for Judge Bobb's call. His message said not to call back, but to get over to his chambers ASAP, something important had come up.

Ten minutes later I was directed to Celia's desk.

"This was here when I came in this morning," said Judge Bobb, pointing to an envelope on the desk. "Celia said she got here at eight-thirty, unlocked the door, then went to the ladies' room. I came in a few minutes later, and saw the envelope. Celia said it wasn't there when she got in. After the way that detective carried on the last time, I thought I better not touch it."

"The hell with that. The last note didn't have any fingerprints, and neither will this. Besides, we give it to the cops and we'll never learn what it says." I picked up the envelope and slit the top with Celia's letter opener.

Again it was a single sheet, computer generated. I read it aloud:

You didn't listen, and you didn't pass the word. Because our earlier warning has not been heeded we have taken matters into our own hands. Disrespect will not be tolerated, and future transgressions will not go unpunished. If lessons must be learned the hard way, so be it.
ABC

"That ties it up. This ABC who kidnapped Celia must have taken Walter too," said the judge.

"Sure seems that way," I said.

"So that's why you were asking me about Miles yesterday." The note stirred something in Celia; her words came out so fast I had trouble understanding.

"I'm going to make a call," I said to Judge Bobb. "While I do that, you call Judge Dienstag, tell him about the note, and that we need to see him right away."

"Do you need me at the meeting too?" he asked. "My motion call starts at nine-thirty."

"Yeah. I have an idea to run by Judge Dienstag, and if he goes for it I'll need your help too."

Judge Bobb went into chambers to make his call. I used Celia's phone. I didn't ask, and she didn't protest. Maybe the note scared her.

I got through to Amanda Moyer and filled her in. Naturally she wanted to see the note, but she didn't raise the stink about handling evidence that Crumpton had. I told her I'd save her a trip downtown and drive the note up by early afternoon. The sooner the better, she said.

But I didn't tell her about my discussion with Fred Nickles and my lead on ABC. While Fred's information seemed solid, I wanted to dig around before spreading the word. And by leaving the cops out of it I was free to follow up any way I wanted. I was following the advice of one of my old partners: "If they don't know, they won't no."

Judge Bobb emerged from his chambers, with the word that Judge Dienstag would be down in three minutes. He made it in two.

"Men, what's this about another note?" he asked.

I showed it to him. He read it, then slammed his right fist into his left palm.

"Damn. Does this mean what I think it does?"

"I'm afraid so, Judge," I said.

"Then we must find this ABC and stop him. Now!" Another fist, this time his left to his right palm. I kind of hoped for another outburst; I was curious what he'd hit next.

"Have either of you ever heard of a group called Attorneys for the Betterment of the Courts?" I asked.

"I haven't," said Judge Bobb.

"Me neither," said Judge Dienstag. "Why?" But he continued before I could answer. "Oh wait, I see. Attorneys for the Betterment of the Courts, ABC. You think that's what we're dealing with, some wacko terrorist group?"

"It's possible. I have an idea how to track them down." I laid out the plan. Both judges said they'd go along. Judge Dienstag made a call, then passed along the information to me and Billy Bob. He wished us luck.

•

Judge Bobb took the bench about fifteen minutes late, which may have been unusual for him but certainly isn't unheard of in the Circuit Court of Cook County. He was conducting his morning motion call, where the attorneys seek (or oppose) various court orders. In the first motion an ex-husband moved to reduce alimony payments because he'd lost his job. The second motion concerned a request that one of the parties turn over financial records which were needed to determine a fair distribution of the marital estate. In the third motion an ex-wife wanted to terminate the ex-husband's visitation rights to their three children because he was ten minutes late picking them up and five minutes early returning them. That's how it goes, some motions are serious, some laughably petty.

As the third motion was being argued I walked up to Celia, who was seated to Judge Bobb's right. I did this even though there was a sign taped in front of her work area stating, in big block letters: "Do Not Disturb Clerk While Court Is In Session."

"Make it good, Celia" I said once I reached her.

The motion finished, and Judge Bobb was waiting for Celia to announce the next case. Instead she said, in a voice which would make a drill sergeant proud, "Can't you read the sign, counselor? Now take a seat and wait your turn."

"But I just have a simple question," I replied, loud enough that the lawyers in the front of the courtroom would hear.

"Next time get here before court starts and I'll answer your question. Now sit down."

"It's a very basic question. I just need to know..."

Before I could finish she announced the next case, but I stood my ground.

"Can't you answer a simple question?" My voice must have carried, because I heard gasps from the back of the room.

"Counselor," said Judge Bobb, "please stop harassing my clerk and take a seat."

"I'm not harassing anybody, Judge, I just need a little courtesy here, which obviously this woman," I pointed at Celia, "sorely lacks."

"Approach the bench, counselor," barked the judge.

Usually there's background noise in a courtroom, lawyers whispering or papers being shuffled. Now there was total silence.

"Counselor, what is your name?"

"Martin Bronk." Loudly so everyone would hear.

"Mr. Bronk, you seem to think that the rules of this courtroom don't apply to you."

"No, Judge, I seem to think that your clerk is in serious need of an attitude adjustment."

"Sir, I will not have you insulting my staff." He paused, looking for a reaction from me, but I gave none. "I'm waiting for an apology, counselor."

"Then you'll be waiting a long time."

"Counselor, I'll give you one more chance. Apologize to my clerk and the Court for the disrespect you've shown."

I stood my ground for a good ten seconds. Then, recalling Gail at her most insolent, "Fine. I apologize."

"Thank you. Despite your apology, which for the record I'll assume was sincere, although personally I have my doubts, I find your conduct disruptive to the Court and highly disrespectful." He waved over the deputy who was standing to Celia's right. "Sheriff, take this man into custody. Mr. Bronk, I find you in contempt of court, and sentence you to detention until eight o'clock this evening. Additionally, I am fining you in the amount of five hundred dollars."

"Contempt? Is this a joke?" But before I could continue the sheriff's deputy pulled my hands behind my back and cuffed them. Then he grabbed my left arm and pulled me away from the bench. "You'll be hearing more from me, I promise," I shouted as the deputy led me out.

The deputy and I didn't say anything until we were in the service elevator, heading to the detention room in the Daley Center basement.

"How'd we do?" I asked.

"Shit, all that yelling made me nervous," he said as he unlocked the cuffs.

"So you think everyone bought it?"

"Hell yes. I never seen such a bunch of scared looking lawyers in my life. Kind of good to see, actually."

"If all goes according to plan I'll make today's Law Bulletin." The Chicago Daily Law Bulletin comes out in the afternoon with news of the day's goings on. An attorney found in contempt for disrupting court is highly unusual, so the story figured to make page one.

"You better lay low for the rest of the day," he said.

"Yeah, I'm going straight to pick up my car and drive out to the burbs. Guess I better stay there till eight. I don't know what Judge Bobb was thinking. He could have ended the sentence at five or six."

"More realistic this way. Louses up the guy's dinner. And from the looks of you, that'd hit you where it hurts."

"You better watch it. Insult the wrong guy and Celia's abductor may get on your case next."

"Hey, you gotta have a sense of humor on this job. I lose that, I might as well work for streets and san."

We got off the elevator and filled out some paperwork in the detention area, just in case some nosy reporter called for verification. From there I took the pedway to the State Street subway and caught a train south to Harrison. Then I got my car from the garage, picked up the expressway at Congress, and headed for Northbrook. The first person to serve a contempt sentence battling expressway traffic.

•

Amanda read the ABC note three times before saying anything. "I don't like the sound of this, at all. We better catch up to this guy soon."

"You don't have any leads?"

"Nothing. Judge Miles simply vanished. You have any ideas on this ABC?"

"Not yet, but I'm working on it."

"What kind of moron leaves his initials on a note like this?"

"Someone who wants the attention, I guess. I talked to Miles' clerk, and he said you guys have his message book. Anything interesting in there?"

"Not really. No messages from any known criminals, if that's what you mean."

"Can you copy part of the message book, Thursdays, starting one month ago and going back two months before that?"

"I guess. Do you have something?"

"Miles' clerk thinks the judge may have gotten a phone threat."

"That's funny. Detective Crumpton talked to the clerk, but he didn't mention anything like that to me."

"With Crumpton it's 50-50 whether he forgot the question or the answer."

"Even so, I guess I better call him and let him know that ABC is back."

"That may be the protocol, but I know Crumpton. He's not going to do much. His case was an abduction where the victim turned up safe. He might like to find the guy, but at this point he'll figure it's your play."

"So you don't think I should clue him in, even though he was first on the case?"

"If it was somebody else I might. But Crumpton will just sit on his ass, until you find the guy. Then he'll get up just long enough to take the credit."

"I guess we can keep this our secret for now. But once my boss gets word of this I'll have to bring Crumpton up to speed."

It was about one o'clock and I hadn't eaten lunch, so I asked Amanda if she wanted to grab a quick bite.

"Sorry, I can't. Too much paperwork."

"Aren't you going to eat anything?"

"Usually one of the officers brings in sandwiches and coffee."

"I can do that. Besides, I'm starving."

"Sure, why not. There's a deli about a mile east on Dundee. I'll take a turkey on a kaiser roll with lettuce and mayo. And a large coffee. The stuff around here's graded 10 W 30."

I never seem to have a problem locating the nearest deli, and this was no exception. I got Amanda's order, and a hard salami on rye and a Coke for me. And a bag of chips. And a brownie large enough to split.

Amanda was on the phone when I got back. She gave me a simple palm up, which I took as a thank you. Thinking there must be a lunch room and that we'd eat there, I didn't start on my sandwich until she finished her call. But Amanda said she just couldn't get away from her desk, though I could eat at the long table in the middle of the room.

Amanda was a real dynamo. She'd go from a phone call to paperwork to reviewing reports without missing a beat. She wasn't cold toward me, but she was wrapped up in her work, so I skipped my normal instinct toward small talk and let her work in peace. I ate in silence wondering if she was this intense about everything.

After finishing our lunches, Amanda worked the phones some more, while I pulled a *Sports Illustrated* out of my briefcase. "Shouldn't you be doing something to earn that big fee of yours?" she asked after her third call, when it must have registered that I was hanging around for no apparent purpose.

"Actually I need to keep a low profile for awhile. You see, I'm supposed to be in jail."

"Really? Are you confessing?"

I explained my little masquerade in Judge Bobb's courtroom, and my possible lead on ABC. She sat stony faced while I talked. Only when I finished did I realize that I hadn't planned to tell her any of this.

"You could have told me about this ABC connection sooner," she said.

"But there's really nothing to tell. One, it's a secretive group, so we don't know anything about its membership. And two, we don't even know that the ABC from the note is the group I'm looking into. I mean, I doubt they're a terrorist outfit looking for publicity."

"Even so, I'll have someone get whatever information they can on them."

"Go ahead, but I talked to an expert, a law professor who teaches ethics, and even he knew nothing about them."

"With due respect to your professor, I'm going to try to scare something up on them. Would you excuse me for a minute while I make a call."

I went out to the front desk and shot the breeze with the officer there. I wasn't offended by Amanda's kicking me out. She probably had a secret source, maybe FBI. And it was a good reminder that I wasn't yet in the inner circle, and maybe never would be.

After about five minutes Amanda came out. "Let's go for a walk," she said. She tossed me my jacket, which I'd left in the Criminal Investigations office.

"Marty," she said once we were outside. "I realize you were a cop and that you know your way around an investigation. But I don't like what you're doing."

"Why not?"

"I have to wonder about your agenda. We just want to solve a crime. But you're private. You need to generate business. So you might have ulterior motives, like gaining publicity, or selling your story."

"That's bullshit, Amanda. What's your real beef?"

"That is my real beef. I don't want some hot shot messing up things, that's all."

"Hot shot! Who'd you call back there, Crumpton?" She didn't say anything. "Let me tell you, to him a hot shot is anyone who wants more out of the job than putting in his twenty years. I'm as far from a hot shot as you can get, unless doing a competent job fits your definition. And frankly, I don't think what I do in Chicago for my client is your concern."

"Take it easy. I'm not ordering you to stop, I'm just voicing a concern.

As long as we understand each other, I don't see why we can't work together on this. Here, I even have the copies from Miles' message book you wanted." She handed me a large manila envelope.

I got the impression that Amanda was playing me, winding me up before settling me down. And I wasn't sure why. Of course another explanation is that I overreacted.

"Okay, well I got the ball rolling on this, and seeing that I'm a licensed attorney I'm the logical one to try and infiltrate the ABC group. And I promise to keep my P.R. people in check."

"Good. Just don't be a hero. You find anything, let me know. Agreed?"

"Agreed."

"Now, I'm afraid I'm going to have to kick you out. You can't stick around the station all day. Unless you want to serve out your sentence in a nice cozy cell."

"That's a tempting offer, but I'm going to head back to my apartment. I assume the press won't be camping outside my door. And if they are I'll say the judge let me out early for good behavior."

Amanda had managed to steer our walk to the parking lot. If she really thought I was a hot shot, my four-year-old Taurus should have dissuaded her.

During the drive home I called Erin Sitterly, who confirmed that I'd made the afternoon Law Bulletin, page one no less, but below the fold. Though Erin was confused why I was calling from jail to see if I was in the paper. I told her I'd made a bet with my cellmate, who now owed me a pack of Marlboro's.

Talking to Erin reminded me how my testifying in her case led to my work on Celia's disappearance. Which brought something else to mind.

I got Plonski on the phone. "Any unsolved murders of court types you know about?" I asked.

"Court types?"

"Judges, law clerks, bailiffs, lawyers, people like that."

"Like I need more work?"

"I know you're the hardest working man in law enforcement, Plonski, the James Brown of the CPD. But humor me and check, will you? You might as well look at other types of mysterious deaths too. Suicides, accidents. Just go back a couple years for now. And check the whole area, not just the city."

"Is that all, Sherlock?"

"That should do it."

"What's this about?"

"Remember Celia Glagovic, the law clerk who was kidnapped? She said the kidnapper told her that he'd killed before. Maybe it was just talk, but maybe not. And there could be a link with Judge Miles' disappearance."

"Oh, the missing judge. In that case give me a call tomorrow around this time. And don't forget..."

"I know, when the case is solved I'll be sure to mention your invaluable insight and assistance."

"Fuck that. Don't forget you owe me a polish sausage lunch. Only now it's two."

At that point I had little to do but wait for the phone calls to pour in. Fortunately, I was listed as an attorney in the Sullivan's law directory, and had a phone listing with directory assistance as an attorney. Other than wrong numbers, I hadn't had an incoming call on that line since I set it up for one of my early cases.

I checked with my answering service when I was on Irving Park a mile from my apartment. No calls. Five minutes later I was in my apartment, but there weren't any messages on my home machine either. Not that I really expected the ABC bunch to call so soon. Still, a guy can hope.

Miles' message book didn't produce the epiphany I was hoping for. On average Miles got about twelve messages a day, so for the eight Thursdays I was interested I was looking at nearly a hundred calls. The farmer's market Eldrick had mentioned is only held every other Thursday, so I could cut the list by about half. But even fifty people are about 45 more than this one man agency can check out. There were a few repeats, so I suppose I could have started with them. But playing phone tag, or even being a pest, hardly qualifies someone as a kidnapper.

As for the callers, I recognized a few prominent lawyers, as well as some judges, including Judge Dienstag, but most of the names didn't mean anything to me. Also, about a dozen of the callers were female. If one of them turned out to be a complainant in the sexual harassment inquiry, then I'd have something. Maybe. Eldrick said Miles referred to the caller who upset him as an "asshole," a word men don't use in describing women. That's assuming Eldrick's memory was correct, not necessarily a good assumption where events took place at least a month earlier.

My head was spinning with possibilities. To unwind I began a new David Lodge novel. I was turning a page when the phone rang, and I dropped the book.

"Hello."

"Hey, Dad, were you really in the slammer?"

"Gail? Since when do you read the Law Bulletin?"

"I don't. But Katie's dad is a lawyer, and he told Katie and she just called me. Why'd you yell at a judge?"

"I didn't really. I mean, I yelled, but it was planned. It's part of a case I'm working on." This came out quickly, probably an instinct against Gail thinking badly of me. But as soon as I said it, I realized that it was information I probably shouldn't have given a chatty seventh grader.

"I don't get it."

"I'll explain it to you another time. But no, I didn't get in trouble and I wasn't in jail."

"Oh."

"You sound disappointed."

"Well, it's not like I want you to be locked up or anything. But it would have made a cool story."

"Yeah, real cool, being the only kid in school with a Dad doing hard time. And no matter what Katie or the other kids at school say, don't tell anyone that the argument was staged. If word gets out it might mess up my case."

"I won't tell anyone. Besides, the jail thing might help my rep."

"Gail, I'm not kidding."

"Chill, Dad, I'll be good."

"So how's the bat mitzvah practice going?"

"Okay."

"Can you elaborate?"

"I'm working on it. But it's still a couple months away, you know."

"Gail, do yourself a favor. Do the work now so you won't be under so much pressure as it gets closer."

"Yeah, sure Dad."

"Oh, you'll be happy to know that Colleen's coming."

"That's like so cool. I can't wait for Mom to meet her."

"Yeah, that'll be good. Anyway the screws are about to take away my bread and water, so I better get going."

"Okay. Let me know if you want me to smuggle you some cigarettes."

"And where are you going to get cigarettes?"

"From my purse."

"What are you talking about?"

"Oh, Dad, be cool. All the kids smoke."

"Mine doesn't!"

"Dad."

"Give me your mother!"

"Dad."

"What!"

"Joke."

I always thought having a sense of humor was a good thing. But seeing it in my daughter, I'm not so sure.

CHAPTER 8

The phone didn't ring again that night. And by ten the next morning my only call was from Amanda, asking how I was dealing with all the calls. I replied that I couldn't talk because I had two people on hold.

As promised Eldrick faxed over a list of who he'd seen Miles shouting with. Eight names were on the list, and Eldrick added a note that there were others whose names he didn't know. Three of the shouters were judges. Including Judge Dienstag.

Combining the phone message with the shouting, I could at least consider Dienstag a suspect. But I certainly didn't have enough to accuse him, and frankly I'd expect conflict between the demanding chief judge and one of his ill-tempered charges. Besides, it was Dienstag who hired me, and while that could have been a ruse to deflect attention from him, I considered that unlikely.

Calling the Judicial Inquiry Board was next on my to-be-done list. Unfortunately I didn't have any sources there, so I had to do like John Q. Public and ask to speak to anyone who could help. I was connected to an Investigator Redding. To me she sounded college-aged, but now that I'm forty anyone under thirty sounds young.

"Can you confirm whether your office is investigating Judge Walter Miles?" Cutting to the chase.

"Why do you want to know?"

"He's a public official, and I'm a concerned citizen."

"Investigations aren't made public. Only prosecutions are public."

"Is your office prosecuting Judge Miles?"

"No."

"But it won't be long before you do, right?"

"Nice try. As I said, investigations are confidential."

"I suppose that if the fact of an investigation isn't public, then the names of the complainants aren't public either."

"That's correct."

"Would the facts of the investigation be passed on to Chief Judge Dienstag?"

"No, that's not our policy. Actually, the judge being investigated might not even know that a complaint had been made."

"How can that be?"

"We might do an initial investigation and find no merit to the complaint. It's only when the Board finds there's some possible merit that a judge will be asked to respond."

"So you'll write the judge if you require a response?"

"That's correct."

"And the letter will identify the complainant?"

"Usually. But on occasion we mask the identity, depending on the nature of the complaint." So even if I found the Board's letter to Miles, it might not tell me who filed the complaints. These protections sure make a private detective earn his pay. Figuratively speaking in my case, seeing how I was doing this pro bono.

I thanked Investigator Redding for her help, such as it was. Getting nothing from the JIB, I re-focused on ABC.

I could have stuck around the office and willed ABC to call. But I made myself feel productive by hanging out at the Daley Center, hoping that witnesses to my performance before Judge Bobb would point me out to others, eventually leading to recognition and contact by an ABCer. I loitered in the corridors, sat in at various courtrooms, even ate lunch in the restaurant in the Daley Center basement. But if any of the hundreds of lawyers I encountered recognized me, they didn't let on.

I also stopped to see Eldrick. He recalled seeing an envelope from the Judicial Inquiry Board, but it was marked Personal and Confidential, so he left it for the judge to open. "Son of a bitch" was the judge's response, and that's the last Eldrick heard about it.

"Can you look around the office, see if it's still around?" I asked.

"Sure. But you might want to speak to the judge's lawyer. They've been talking a lot lately. His name's Hicks Pepper III."

"You're kidding."

"I couldn't make up a name like that."

"Wait. Wasn't he on your shouting match list?"

"Yeah, they really went at it. Something about broken promises, owing each other, stuff like that."

"How'd it end?"

"Mr. Pepper stormed out. But they've talked since then, and as far as I know Mr. Pepper is still the judge's attorney."

After finishing with Eldrick I resumed my man-about-courthouse routine, but by four o'clock nothing was happening, and I decided to visit Mr. Hicks Pepper III. Pepper worked for Markus & Stevens, a large firm known for defending major litigation on behalf of insurance companies. The Markus & Stevens office was located on the 45th floor of a building on North LaSalle. Exiting the elevator, I was greeted by a perky young receptionist with short dark hair and even darker fingernails. Behind her were floor to ceiling windows, the lake in the background.

"I don't know how much they're paying you here, but you have a million dollar view."

"Not really. I get to look at the elevators."

"But you must sneak a peek back there every now and then?"

"I suppose. But it's only water."

"True, and you know what W.C. Fields said about water."

"Who?"

"Never mind. Sorry, I didn't get your name."

"Valerie."

"Valerie, pretty name. I'm here to see Hicks Pepper III."

"Do you have an appointment?"

"No. I'm here about a new case. A big one." Protocol dictates that I should have first called for an appointment. But protocol can be damned when big money is involved.

"I'll need to clear it with his secretary. What's your name?" I told her.

While Valerie made her call I scoped out the area. There were no security doors, only open hallways. If Pepper wouldn't see me I'd have no problem gaining access to the offices. My only decision was whether to head left or right.

"Mr. Pepper's in a meeting right now. He suggested that an associate could help you." Valerie must have passed the word that I didn't look the big money type, and Pepper made the call that I didn't dignify a meeting with a partner.

I made my move. Guessing that Pepper belonged to the WASPy,

Stevens side, I went right wing. "Hey, you can't go back there," Valerie said.

I kept walking. I held my head up and locked my eyes forward, trying to give the impression I belonged there. A couple of secretaries and a young associate nodded at me as I passed, so maybe it worked.

I read the office nameplates as I walked, and found "Hicks Pepper III" at the end of the hall. "Rebecca, I need that research by ten tomorrow," he bellowed, and a harried looking associate scurried out of his office. I poked my head in, not sure whether to address him as Mr. Pepper or Mr. The Third.

"Who the hell are you?" he asked.

I entered, then quickly shut the door behind me. Hicks Pepper III wasn't at all what I would have expected. About fifty, roly poly, with a mop of gray/black curls much longer and more unkempt than you normally see in upper management. The top button of his shirt was undone, and probably the bottom two as well.

"My name's Bronk. I'm a private investigator hired by Judge Dienstag to look into Judge Miles' disappearance."

"Dienstag is full of shit."

"What's that supposed to mean?"

"Seems self explanatory to me."

"What about Judge Miles? What can you tell me about him?"

"I could tell you quite a bit, Bronk. But I'm not going to tell you anything. And you're leaving."

"What's your problem, Pepper?"

"A little thing called attorney-client privilege."

"Ah, so you are his attorney. See, I knew I'd get information out of you."

If Pepper was ticked off by losing this point he didn't show it. "The fact of an attorney-client relationship isn't necessarily privileged," he said without hesitation. "Another fact is that I don't have to tell a p.i. anything. Especially one I don't like."

"Come on, Pepper. I'm just trying to figure out what's going on. I've seen Miles' phone records, and I know you two talk a lot. Give me something."

"I'll give you ten seconds to find the door."

I used those ten seconds to check out Pepper's office. Again it didn't fit the man's name. Instead of fox-and-hounds, it was a virtual shrine to the

University of Michigan, with newspaper clippings of football and basketball national championships prominently centered along the side walls.

Finally I spoke. "Look at it this way, Pepper. The sooner I find Miles, the sooner you get a paying client back."

Pepper snorted. "That's a joke. Now out."

"You mean he's not paying?"

Pepper's response was to snap his fingers and point to the door.

"We'll talk again when you're in a better mood," I said on my way out. "And then you can tell me about the disagreement you and Miles had in his chambers."

I exited stage right, hoping for a "Get back here," but it didn't come.

In my experience, two types of people are best at keeping quiet when provoked. Three hundred dollar an hour attorneys are one. People with something to hide are the other.

•

Later I was back in the office, disappointed and frustrated. I had two messages. Amanda wanted to know if anything was new. The message from Crumpton was: "What the hell are you doing?" Which was indeed a perceptive question. Not that I blamed myself for trying that contempt of court stunt, but I may have been shallow to think a secretive group would recruit me based on one run-in with a judge.

I didn't return either of the calls. The only cop I wanted to talk to was Plonski, and I caught him on his way out, or so he said. "No unsolved murders of court types, as you call them," he said. "But three lawyers croaked themselves in the past two years. One was on vacation in Mexico at the time. Left a note in his room, then dove off a cliff."

"Lots of people cliff dive in Mexico."

"But this cliff didn't have no water at the bottom. The other two are local." He gave me their names. One was seventy years old and apparently depressed by the death of his wife of 45 years. A gunshot to the head did it. The other was strychnine poisoning, a 50-year-old who'd suffered a recent setback in his career. I took down the information and got off the phone before Plonski could hit me up for another lunch.

It was Friday, and I had no plans for the weekend. Gail was staying at Randee's, and Colleen was out of town in search of untapped benefactors for Wilson Law. With nothing to hurry home to, I stopped by the Bar Bar for a couple of beers.

Chicago's a no nonsense town, and that's reflected in the names given some of its bars. My favorite bar name had been the Stop and Drink until a club one-upped that by simply calling itself Drink. Most people think the Bar Bar was so named to attract the attorney crowd. In fact the owner of the place has a daughter named Barbara, and Bar Bar is named after her. Even so, its proximity to both the Daley Center and the Dirksen Federal Building makes it a natural watering hole for attorneys looking to calm their nerves or swap war stories.

Friday afternoons see lots of office groups getting together for an after work drink, so the place was SRO. It's in these situations that my size comes in handy. I can bull my way to the bar without meeting much resistance. I suppose small folk also do okay by squeezing between people. It's the average sized person who has problems, and I've often found myself unwittingly leading a virtual conga line through a bar, me a head taller than everyone following.

I made it to the bar and ordered a Bass Ale. The six o'clock news was on the overhead TV, though the noise from the bar drowned out the volume. I wonder why bars bother to have the TV on in those situations. Must offer comfort, along the same principle as background noise.

I'd just ordered my second Bass when I felt a tap on my shoulder. I looked down, which is my normal reaction, and saw a chest, but no head.

"Up here, shorty."

It was Jim Lanter. I stand a good six-four, but Jim has a couple of inches on me. And, truth be told, he could whip me in arm wrestling without breaking a sweat. No wonder he was a starting defensive end at Michigan, while I was third-string at Illinois.

"You should be honored, Jim. I don't look up to too many people."

"Ah, save the bullshit. I hear you ran into some trouble with Billy Bob Bobb on account of his charming assistant. Bet you wished she never turned up."

"I guess it's just too much to expect any common courtesy these days."

"I hear you. So what was it like in the hoosegow?"

"They just kept me downstairs at the Daley Center detention area. No big deal. The worst part was the bologna sandwich for lunch. Two measly slices. And no mustard."

"That is rough. Good thing you didn't have to go to County. Any of those scumbags found out you used to be a cop, you might have ended up as their dinner."

"I could have handled them. After all, I used to play football." I knew Jim would find that funny, seeing how my most strenuous action was cheering on my teammates, but he laughed more enthusiastically than was polite.

"You know," said Jim, "we ought to get together. I got some Bo Schembechler stories that will kill you."

"Sounds good. Funny, I just came from a guy's office, big Michigan fan. If he wasn't such an asshole I'd introduce you."

"Probably know him already. What's his name."

"Hicks Pepper III."

"Yeah, big booster. A little overbearing, but not a bad guy once he's got a couple drinks in him."

"If you say so."

"Anyway, I've got a buddy coming to my office five o'clock Monday. Played college basketball. How about stopping by? We'll go out and have a few drinks, tell a few lies, make fun of the English majors. You know, like old times."

"I was an English major."

"Better yet, we'll make fun of you."

"I'll be there. But if you're gonna dish it out be sure you can take it too."

"I'm up to that challenge, Bronkman. Anyway I got to run. I'm supposed to be meeting some chick. Candace Sweet. Must be a joke, right? But my buddy, who fixed us up, swears it's on the level, and that she's a real knockout. Of course my buddy is single, so it makes me wonder. But shit, it's only a drink, right?"

"Good luck. Hope she lives up to her name. And I'll see you on Monday."

After Jim left I hung around for an uneventful forty-five minutes. Someone asked me to pass the pretzels, otherwise I was left alone. The highlight was when Wheel of Fortune replaced the news on TV, and I guessed each of the puzzles faster than the contestants. I realize the object of the show is to amass money, not solve the puzzle as soon as you can. Still, I take my excitement where I find it.

No messages awaited me at home. By Monday the events of the previous Thursday would be old news, forgotten in the wake of the NCAA basketball tournament or Tiger Woods' latest victory. While crops don't sprout the day after the seeds are planted, my growing season was short, and I sensed a drought.

•

I called Amanda the next morning, figuring she wouldn't be in on a Saturday, I'd leave a message, we'd stay on good terms, but I wouldn't have to detail my lack of results. But she was there, and the first thing she asked was whether I got any nibbles from my "little plan." I think she knew what I'd say, and when I answered truthfully her much too pregnant pause made me feel like a schoolkid who draws a blank when asked the easiest question.

"There's nothing new here either," she offered. "The car still hasn't shown up. I'm starting to think it's keeping company with the fishes."

"Anything come of the note?"

"No. All the fingerprints were accounted for. The only thing we can tell is that they both came from a high quality laserjet printer. But we're not sure yet if it's the same printer."

"So what's the next move?"

"We keep looking for the car and hope the guy makes a mistake." Again she paused. "Or maybe you'll get lucky."

"You don't believe in my plan?"

"No, because I don't think this 'betterment society' or whatever it's called is behind this. I think ABC is somebody's initials, in code. Like add a letter to ABC, so the guy's real initials are BCD."

"Well, humor me, because I'm not giving up yet. Besides, there's always Plan B."

"I don't even want to know what that is."

Good, I thought, since I'm not very convincing at making up plans off the top of my head.

She surprised me with her next question.

"Where do you work out?"

"YMCA. How'd you know I worked out?"

"You seem to be in pretty good shape. Maybe you could lose a few pounds, but you're not all flab."

"Thanks for the kind words."

"I didn't mean anything bad. It must be tough to keep the weight down after a certain age."

"Keep talking, Amanda, you're digging yourself into a deeper hole."

"Marty, all I meant was I could use a workout partner. We get privileges at a health club in town, and if you're not doing anything this afternoon how about joining me? Maybe around three?"

"Sure," I said without thinking. She gave me directions to the club, and said she'd see me later.

I'm pretty good at analyzing possibilities and probabilities. But I admit I didn't see this coming at all. Amanda had been strictly, and I mean strictly, business. Till then the closest thing we'd had to a personal conversation was her thanking me for getting lunch.

Once the shock subsided I thought about Colleen. Was I doing wrong by her? No. Amanda asked me to a workout, not her sister's wedding. If a guy invited me to the gym there'd be no problem. This was a new century, and a woman and a man can exercise together without any ulterior motives. Besides, maybe Colleen worked out with guys. I'd never asked, and she'd never volunteered.

After a light lunch and a trip to Sportmart for a new t-shirt and shorts, I met Amanda in the health club's lobby. I paid the guest fee and we went to our respective locker rooms.

I get a great workout at my Y, even if some amenities are lacking. Half the lockers are broken, and I always bring my own towel, because I'm never quite sure about the ones they provide. But here I was in a sparkling locker room that smelled of disinfectant, not sweat. Shaving cream, razors and after shave lotion were available, and plush, blizzard white towels were strategically placed throughout the room. They even had private showers. If only my basketball buddies could have seen me.

I met Amanda by the Nautilus machines, which were in their own, glass encased room. Her hair was pulled back in a pony tail. She was wearing a navy blue Chicago Bears t-shirt and gray shorts. I had on a gray Nike swoosh t-shirt and black shorts.

"You don't need new clothes for this place," she said.

"What makes you think they're new?"

She put her hands in back of my neck, I heard a snap, and she handed me the price tag. "I'm a detective, you know."

I assume my face reddened, which I expected would happen during the workout, not before. "And quite a good detective, I see." When stuck for something to say, throw out a compliment. "So, you're a Bears fan." Smooth change of subjects, Bronk.

"Yeah. One of the guys on the team gave this to me."

"Amanda, fixing a ticket for a t-shirt? I'm surprised at you."

"I hear that's a Chicago trick."

"Touche."

"Actually I dated the guy for awhile."

"Really. Who?"

She told me the name of a former defensive tackle, a three-time Pro Bowler. First Jim Lanter, now this. Maybe I needed a few more reminders of my feeble football career.

"So where should we start?" I asked.

"How about the upper body and we'll work our way down."

We started with curls, three series of ten repetitions. Amanda performed her three with effort but successfully. I, on the other hand, had to play the bigshot, so I put more weight on than usual. Inevitably I struggled through, barely making my ten reps during the first two series, and quitting after four on the third.

Amanda didn't say anything on our way to the next machine. There I used thirty less pounds than usual, which insured that I'd make it through the three series, but made me feel like a wimp. By contrast Amanda used an impressive amount of weight for a woman (which I know sounds sexist, but it's what I felt), and completed all her lifts.

That's the way it went. Until I was totally humiliated at the incline board. I managed thirty sit-ups, total; Amanda did sixty, and with the board at a steeper angle. And I'll bet she could have done more. No doubt about it, Amanda was more fit than me. Of course I could always challenge her to arm wrestling.

The workout must have lasted an hour, but we said very little during that time. Amanda was purposeful in her exercise, while I tried hard to keep up. I didn't compliment her on her performance, and she didn't hassle me on mine.

"Woooo, that felt good," Amanda said when we were done. When I didn't say anything in response, she asked if I was all right.

"Yeah, just a little winded. The Italian beef sandwich I had for lunch weighted me down." I really had a chicken pita.

"You seem tense too."

"No, I'm okay, really."

"Maybe this will help." She walked behind me and rubbed my neck and shoulders. She used just the right pressure, firm enough that I felt its effects into my back, but not so hard as to cause any discomfort.

"Amanda, that feels great. We should have skipped the workout and started with this."

"It's not the same unless your muscles ache." She kept it up for a couple more minutes. By the time she was done I felt so good that I was ready to do further battle with the incline board.

"Okay, my turn," she said, and we each rotated 180 degrees.

I pressed my fingers into the base of her neck, where it meets the shoulder. I was afraid to apply too much pressure, but she told me to work the fingers harder. From the neck area I spread out, first across the top part of the shoulder, then to her back.

"You have the touch, Marty," she said between periodic "mmmms."

I continued rubbing, she continued mmmming, and next thing I knew I was kissing her neck. She turned to face me, eyes wide, and I pulled her in to me. I pressed my lips onto hers, and after a slight hesitation I felt hers pressing into mine. When our lips finally parted she stepped back, then began jogging. "Come on, catch me," she said.

We ended up on the running track, an eighth-of-a-mile oval overlooking the tennis courts. She had a head start and was going at a pretty good pace. I gamely followed, but jogging isn't my thing these days. I'm used to short bursts while playing basketball or softball, not sustained distance running. I went into a sprint, but she also turned on the speed, and I lost ground. I could see I wasn't going to catch her, so I did the next best thing. I stopped, and flagged her down as she lapped me. But she kept going.

"Come on, don't give up yet," she said.

"I can't," I said between huffs.

She stopped and jogged back toward me. She put her arm around me, presumably for emotional comfort. I put my arm around her, for physical support.

I caught my breath as we got off the track. I took my arm off her shoulder and stroked her hair. Then I leaned over and gave her another kiss. Her response lacked the passion of the first time.

"Marty," she said, "I need to tell you something."

"Oh no, you're still dating that Bear."

"No, it's not that. I like you, Marty. I like you a lot. It's just that there're some things going on in my life right now and, well..."

"What kinds of things?"

"Let's just leave it at that. But, I hope you didn't get the wrong idea when I asked you here today."

"No, Amanda, I might have gotten a little carried away." Actually, if given the chance I'd have gotten a lot carried away. Which wasn't a comforting thought, given my feelings for Colleen.

"Why don't we shower down?"

It would be clichéd to say I took a cold shower, but I did, because the hot water in the fancy locker room with the individual stalls didn't work right. Just a coincidence I'm sure; God wouldn't be concerned with my testosterone.

I met Amanda outside the women's locker room. She smiled at me, but, like strangers in an elevator, we avoided each other's space.

We reached the parking lot. Her car was parked at the opposite end from mine. Since this obviously wasn't a date, and she was a cop, I dispensed with the chivalry of walking her to her car. We promised to give the other a call if anything broke on the case.

"We should do this again," she said. "You're a good workout partner. We'll just skip the rubdown."

"Sure, anytime."

I spent the rest of the day moping about my unprofessional behavior and my betrayal of Colleen. I'm seeing someone I really care for, and who I find incredibly attractive, yet I'm all over the next woman who comes my way. Maybe my interest in Amanda was normal; I'd had some lean years since the break-up with Randee, so I could have been playing catch-up.

Or maybe I was a jerk.

I didn't sleep well that night. My mind danced from Amanda to Colleen to the case. So I was pretty groggy when Amanda called at eight-thirty the next morning. At first I thought she said she wanted to break my face. My "huh" prompted her to repeat herself, and this time she made sense—there'd been a break in the case.

CHAPTER 9

They found Judge Miles' car in the Lincoln Park neighborhood, in the parking lot next to the Diversey Avenue miniature golf course.

Yellow police tape cordoned off the area around the car, but I caught Amanda's attention, and she got the beat cop guarding the scene to let me in. Evidence technicians worked over the car. Amanda stood back, watching the goings on. Crumpton directed a tech taking samples from the car's interior.

"Lucky you that the car was found in Chicago," I said to Amanda. "Now you get to deal with Crumpton."

"He seems to be on top of things," said Amanda.

"The only thing he's on top of is the number of days to retirement."

Crumpton's back was toward me when I arrived, but now he jerked his body my way and headed over.

"Crumpton, I'm so glad you're on the case. Now we can all rest easy."

"You don't wanna be busting my chops, Bronk. I'll whip your ass three ways to Sunday."

"This is Sunday, Crumpton. And you don't whip asses, you wipe them."

"What're you doing here anyway, Bronk? This is official police business, not showtime for civilians." Crumpton made "civilians" sound like a Class X felony.

"Haven't you heard, I'm an official consultant. So go back to telling your men how to do their job. They'll probably forget unless you remind them."

"Is he your idea, Detective?" Crumpton said to Amanda.

"Mr. Bronk is assisting us, yes," she said. "And I don't see the harm in having him here, seeing how he used to be a detective."

"Not anymore he ain't, Detective, and since this is my jurisdiction I'm kicking him the hell out."

"Lighten up, Crumpton," I said. "Can't I stay and observe? Maybe I can pick up some pointers on the fine art of looking busy."

"Am I gonna have to get some patrol officers to toss you out, smart mouth?"

"Look, I'll leave in two minutes. Promise. But I need to talk to Detective Moyer before I go."

"Two minutes, and the clock's running."

Crumpton went back to the car, where he made a production of gathering the techs around for a talk. Probably brainstorming suggestions for lunch spots in the area.

"Why'd you call me down here, Amanda? You must have known Crumpton would have a shit fit."

"How would I know that? I thought you exaggerated your low opinion of him."

"That I could not exaggerate."

"Anyway, we found a note in the front seat."

"What did it say?"

"It was a poem. It said: 'A nearby place, Where they ply his trade, Is where you will find him, If you make the grade.' Followed by the letters ABC."

"Was it typed like the other notes?"

"Yeah. Obviously we'll see if it matches up to the other two."

"How'd the car look?"

"Clean. No blood, no signs of struggle. A few dark hair strands, men's length, that don't look to be the judge's. But give me a call later and I'll fill you in."

"So now ABC's speaking in riddles. Any thoughts what the note means?"

"Just that he's toying with us. Chicago police are searching the Daley Center top to bottom. Personally, I think the riddle hints of someplace else, but don't ask me where. One thing I do know; we better figure out what this ABC is all about. And quick."

"How'd the car come to be found?"

"Anonymous tip phoned into the Chicago cops this morning."

"Probably the kidnapper. Which means he wanted the car found. And with the note, he obviously wants Miles found too."

"Two minutes," shouted Crumpton. I told Amanda I'd call her later, then loitered for another couple minutes till Crumpton took a step away from the car. I waved, he froze, then I waved again. How could he think I didn't like him?

•

Judge Miles plied his trade in the courthouse. But nearby to what? If nearest to where the car was found, then the kidnapper would be referring to the Daley Center. Maybe he meant the one closest to Judge Miles' home, which would be the courthouse in Skokie. But where would the "making the grade" come into play?

I took Diversey west to the Kennedy expressway north. I stayed to the right at the junction of I-90 and I-94, picking up the Edens expressway. As I passed Touhy a thought hit me. The kidnapper may have been referring to a court, not a courthouse. Northbrook Court is an upscale shopping mall. Miles lived in Northbrook. And one of those obscure factoids imbedded in my head is that the northeast parking lot—where Randee and I always parked—is lot A. And if you "make the grade" you earn the letter A.

I got Amanda on her cell phone and told her my theory. She sounded dubious but agreed to have a patrol officer meet me.

I drove to the northeast parking lot, only now the signboards attached to the lightpoles depicted a drawing of a shoe instead of the letter "A". Seemed like a silly change to me, but I'm sure some consultant's out there with a study showing that shoppers are more likely to remember images than letters. That the image might also suggest an item for the arriving customer to purchase is surely incidental.

It was just after eleven, still kind of early to be shopping, and no more than thirty cars were parked there. The black and white patrol car was parked six spaces away from the nearest car, and I pulled up next to it.

I introduced myself to Officer Kim Breeden. If she was male her hair length would still conform to army regulations. But she also had a squeaky voice that was higher pitched than my daughter's. The amateur psychologist in me concluded that her tough appearance was compensation for her adolescent voice. Then again, maybe she just liked short hair.

Amanda had filled her in on what I'd need. I rode in the front seat as we went up and down the aisles. She'd punch the license plate numbers into her computer, and the name and address of the registered owner would appear. The computer would also indicate if the car was stolen, or if the owner had any outstanding warrants or unpaid tickets. I was interested in each car's status; a stolen auto can make a mobile coffin.

Nothing unusual was turning up, and I was losing focus by the time we reached the last aisle. I missed the '89 Skylark which came up stolen. But Kim caught it.

The car was registered to a Tony Disellendro from Melrose Park, and had been reported missing five days earlier. Northbrook, a well-to-do northern suburb, doesn't normally mix with Melrose Park, a blue-collar western suburb. Something smelled rotten.

But something smelled even worse as we approached the vehicle. Not an overpowering smell, and we might not have noticed it if we weren't sensitive to the possibility. But it was there, that unmistakable scent of decay. We looked inside the vehicle, and except for some McDonald's wrappers on the passenger side floor nothing seemed out of order. The trunk was the source of the odor.

Kim and I looked at each other. "I better call this in," she said. "The boss will want a technician out here to open this. And maybe a search warrant."

She went to the patrol car, but I stayed put. I didn't want to wait around for some tech to get over, or take the chance that some super-cautious captain wouldn't act without a warrant. I could handle this on my own.

When Kim wasn't looking I took the pick set out of my inside coat pocket, testing a few before finding the one that worked.

"Look, it's not locked," I called to Kim before lifting the top. She hurried over.

"That wasn't open before."

"In our excitement we must have missed it."

"Don't give me that. Personally, I don't care if you picked it, but what if we need a warrant?"

"We don't. But even if you did, I'm a private citizen, and the constitutional right to be protected against illegal search and seizure only applies to the government, like the police. You didn't direct me to open the trunk. So no right's been violated."

Kim thought about that, shook her head, but said nothing further. I didn't say anything either as I put my hands under the trunk. We prepared ourselves for what we might see, then I lifted the trunk, the hinges squeaking until the top came to rest.

There was blood in the trunk. Also necks, livers, kidneys and other things I don't know the names of, all inside an unsealed garbage bag. But they weren't Judge Miles. They weren't even human. They were chicken parts, and maybe some cattle innards thrown in as well.

"Can you believe this?" Kim asked.

"This is nothing. Once I pulled a guy over for speeding and found a back seat full of mice. The mice were being bred, then sold to labs for scientific experiments. The lock broke on the cage, and there must have been fifty of them running around back there. The guy didn't even know they got out because they never went to the front seat. It was like they knew not to tip him off, and they'd make their break when he opened the back door."

"What happened next?"

"The guy freaks out that the mice got loose. He runs out of the car, and the mice follow, never to be found again. Turns out the driver wasn't the breeder, but the breeder's cousin, and he's afraid of the damn things. Kind of a heart-warming story, don't you think?"

"I'm afraid these chickens weren't so lucky."

I kind of hoped that these parts were going to be put to a weird use—maybe a religious rite. Something to top my mice story. But it turned out that Tony Disellendro was a butcher, and the parts were leftovers from the shop, which his wife used for soup stock. He'd stopped at a 7-11 for milk, left the car running, and it was boosted. The story sounded plausible, and I really was glad that it wasn't Judge Miles. I was equally happy that the Disellandros didn't invite me for soup.

That was the highlight of Northbrook Court. Not one of my better hunches.

So it was back to my original destination, the Skokie courthouse. I picked up the Edens going south, exited at Old Orchard Road, and headed west a half mile. I parked on the courthouse driveway, the parking structure being barricaded shut on Sunday. I walked up to the east entrance, and after banging on the door for a good five minutes got someone's attention.

A deputy sheriff finally responded. Gianakis, according to his name tag. A wiry guy with a dark complexion and slicked back black hair. He inched open the door just enough to yell "We're closed," but I seized that chance to give him my pitch. I laid out that I was on official business for the police and the court, and needed to investigate the premises. I hoped my blustering, official-sounding talk would get me in. Gianakis wasn't buying it, but he didn't shut the door either.

"You can come with me, see that I'm on the level," I offered.

"I can't let nobody in."

"But this is an emergency. We're talking about a missing judge."

"He ain't one of our judges." Like if it was a Skokie judge that'd make a difference.

I could have pursued the argument, and if it was a debating contest I would have won. But I needed results, and there was one sure way to get it.

I pulled out my cell phone and called Judge Dienstag's pager number. A minute later the judge returned the call. I explained the situation, then gave the phone to Gianakis. His end of the conversation consisted of "Yes," "I understand," "I can't," and "How do I know who this really is." Gianakis then handed the phone back to me, and Dienstag barked to stay put.

I hung around outside after Gianakis kicked me out. Within fifteen minutes a Lincoln Continental drove up and screeched to a stop. A round man, fiftyish, bounded out of the car, slamming the door behind. He waved me over without losing stride.

He had a key card for the courthouse door, and once we were in he yelled for Gianakis, who came running out of the men's room.

"Captain," Gianakis said, "what's going on." Gianakis looked my way; I waved.

"Didn't Judge Dienstag tell you to escort this man wherever he wants to go?"

"How could I know that was really him on the phone."

"Shit. Who's gonna pretend they're the top judge?"

"He's right," I said.

"What?" said the Captain.

"Deputy Gianakis didn't know for sure that it was Judge Dienstag. He shouldn't have let me in."

"Then why's the chief judge of the entire goddam Cook County court calling me at home on a Sunday yelling about an insubordinate deputy?"

"I wasn't insubordinate," said Gianakis, "just doing my job."

"Look," I said, "I need to check out the building. This other business can wait. Okay if I look around?"

"I'll go with you," Gianakis volunteered. A way to escape the boss.

"Fine," said the Captain. "I'm waiting here." Bad manners— he never did introduce himself.

The courthouse is two stories high. Long and narrow, it reminds me of the terminals at O'Hare. The courtrooms were lined up on the right, administrative offices on the left. The first courtroom we came to was Courtroom A. Making the grade!

The door was locked, but after fumbling to find the right key Gianakis opened it, then got the lights. The first thing to strike me was the room's green carpeting, bringing to mind a miniature golf course. The second thing was the judge sitting at the bench, a gavel in one hand, a piece of paper in the other.

Judge Miles was quite dead, but he looked good. He was wearing his judicial robe, his tie was straight, even his hair was combed. Undoubtedly looking more judicial than he ever did alive.

"What the hell!" Gianakis threw up his hands, then ran out of the room, mumbling something about calling the police. I walked over to examine Miles more closely. He was rigid to the touch; if it was full rigor mortis he'd been dead somewhere between twelve and twenty-four hours. No noticeable blood stains, bruises, scratches or wounds. His death may have been unnatural, but it wasn't violent.

Using a handkerchief, I removed the piece of paper from the judge's hand. It was in the form of a legal order, and was captioned People vs. the Honorable Walter Miles. In practice most orders are handwritten by the attorney in court after the judge makes his ruling, but this one was typed. It said:

Judge Walter Miles having been found guilty of unconscionable conduct with respect to his duties as a judge of the Circuit Court of Cook County, and having failed to offer any mitigating circumstances for such conduct, IT IS HEREBY ORDERED that the sentence of death be imposed forthwith, without opportunity for appeal.

At the bottom of the order, in the space provided for the judge's signature, the following was typed in: "The grateful lawyers of Cook County, Illinois, by and through ABC." It was dated the previous day.

I put the order back in Judge Miles hand, then waited for the excitement. First came Gianakis and the captain, both breathless from running, soon followed by uniformed cops, detectives, evidence techs, and, last but not least, news crews from every Chicago TV station.

I'd been kicked out of the courtroom by the first cops on the scene, but thanks to Judge Dienstag's connections the police let me hang around in a cordoned off area. Because I was in the restricted zone the TV crews figured I knew something, and they kept trying to get my attention. It was downright unnatural ignoring entreaties from so many young, attractive women, but my name and face on TV would blow my cover, and any remaining chance with ABC.

But Judge Dienstag didn't have my problem. He'd arrived with the first wave, and spoke to anyone with a mike or notepad. Not that I heard him say anything of substance; just the standard line about being shocked and how Miles' death will be felt throughout the Cook County judiciary.

I'd counted six television interviews when Dienstag waved me over, then led me outside Courtroom C where we were alone. "I want you to keep working on this," he said. "I won't have a murderer terrorizing the judicial system."

"I don't know. Cops don't take well to outsiders poking around murder investigations. They take these pretty seriously."

"Don't worry, I'll talk to the Chicago Superintendent of Police and the Skokie and Northbrook Chiefs. I know them, and I'm sure they'll go along." I didn't even want to know what pull Dienstag had with them.

"The cops have a lot more resources than I do. Why do you want me on board?"

"I'll be honest, Marty. I want to know that someone is looking out for the interest of the Circuit Court and its employees. And that someone will be responsive to the urgency I feel. With the police, I feel they work for themselves, not for me." Spoken like a person accustomed to power. Someone who wants to call the shots.

"I'd like to find the killer too, Judge. So I'll keep on it. As long as we understand that I'm a professional, and that I'll do things my way."

"Of course," Dienstag said, although I had little doubt he was placating me. Nor did I doubt that he knew that I knew what was going on.

The cops were well into their work before Amanda arrived. She checked in with the Skokie detective in charge of the scene, then came over to me.

"You must have had a nose for the football when you played," she said.

"More like a knack for getting in the way."

"Whatever, it looks like you're in the middle of things again. But I thought you said we'd find him in Northbrook Court."

"Slight miscalculation. So how did Judge Miles meet his demise?"

"The smart money's on poisoning."

"Funny that the killer drove into Chicago after killing Miles in Skokie, only to park the car in a public lot. Why not just leave the car in Old Orchard?" Old Orchard is a major shopping center about a mile from the courthouse.

"Probably toying with us, like with the riddle."

"I suppose. You get anything more from Miles' car?"

"Nothing that jumps out. But it'll be awhile before the testing is done."

"Well, I think I've overstayed my usefulness here. I'll give you a call later."

"Okay. Oh, and good work."

A cop praising a private investigator? This day was full of surprises.

CHAPTER 10

I spent Monday in the office, calling my lawyer friends and clients to see if they knew anything about ABC. I got smart-ass comments like "Comes before DEF," "Monday Night Football," and "It's a type of gum, Already Been Chewed," but nothing useful. I also spoke to Amanda. The medical examiner found that Judge Miles died of arsenic poisoning, with time of death between ten a.m. and six p.m. Saturday. The m.e. couldn't say with certainty whether Miles had died at the courthouse, or earlier and had his body brought there, although the lack of any unusual marks on the body suggested no undue physical force.

And the cops had no new leads on the killer.

Poisoning is an unusual cause of death. And now this was the second one I knew of. Plonski had mentioned Keith Forrester, the lawyer who died from strychnine. That death was declared a suicide, and the poison was different than the one used on Miles, but even so I made some calls, got the m.e.'s report and checked the newspaper records. Because you never know.

Forrester had been the managing partner of a large, prestigious (and therefore well-paying), law firm. A big shot, including a stint as president of the Chicago Bar Association. But three months prior to his death he moved to a different firm, one that was considerably smaller and, undoubtedly, less remunerative. The buzz in the legal community was that he was forced out of his old firm after losing a power struggle.

People who knew Forrester described him as a tough, experienced commercial litigator, and a son-of-a-bitch in his dealings with people. A go-for-the-guts guy who played hardball with the best of them, and suffered no fools. He was variously described as abrasive, egotistical, bombastic, tyrannical and cold-hearted. Or, as some would say, a typical lawyer.

He'd been divorced for fifteen years, and had no children or significant others. He hadn't taken a vacation in ten years, worked twelve hour days six days a week, and had no known hobbies.

Forrester's body was found in his office by the cleaning crew on a Friday night. A suicide note on his desk said he'd been depressed "now that my career is nowhere." He acknowledged "that my death doesn't come too soon for some people." The note had been generated on the office computer, and was unsigned.

Forrester fit the profile of the other ABC victims— unpleasant, loud, unpopular. And the poisoning and computer note aspects of his death were ABC-like. Besides, I'm always suspicious of suicide notes; they're much less common than most people think. But there were also differences, the main one being that ABC hadn't been shy about taking credit for Celia and Miles, and made no attempt to conceal that Miles was murdered. There was nothing like that with Forrester.

So here's what I had. A southwest side clerk and a north suburban judge. Someone released unharmed and someone killed. Letters from the elusive ABC. A poisoned lawyer whose death may or may not be related.

The pieces weren't fitting together, and I needed a release. A workout would be good, a couple of beers better.

Which is when I remembered my invitation from Jim Lanter. Throwing down some cold ones and talking sports does wonders for my outlook.

Weiss & Lanter was located on LaSalle Street, the sixth floor of a forty floor building. Not a prestige height, but Jim was a young guy, and just the fact that he'd done well enough to get his name on the door was a sign that his career was shaping up.

I got there a little after five. The door to the waiting area was unlocked, but the receptionist had left for the day. I gave a yell into the office.

Jim came out a minute later, laughing.

"Hey, Marty, I thought you forgot about me."

"Not at all, I got caught up talking to an important client."

"No problem. The guys are back in the conference room. Come on."

I followed him past the reception desk into the main corridor. On the right were offices, on the left were three secretary work stations.

"Nice set up you have here, Jim."

"Yeah, we have some room to grow too. Right now we have three attorneys, but we may be adding another."

"So business must be good."

"Not bad. But don't talk to Bryant about that." We were passing by a large office, where he introduced me to Bryant Weiss, who was pacing behind his desk. "Weiss" means white in German, and while his hair was approaching that color the rest of him hadn't conceded to the aging process. His handshake stung, he had no belly, and I was certain that he could go five sets and still have enough left for 18 holes.

"Don't talk to me about what?" he said.

"I was just telling Jim that business must be good, judging from the office," I said.

"Business should be a lot better," said Weiss, before Jim hustled me out of the room.

"What was that about?" I asked.

"He's still got his ass in a sling over a personal injury case he lost a few weeks ago. Big injuries, so could have been big bucks. But the judge granted the defendant's motion for summary judgment. That got Bryant in his soft spot—the pocketbook. I think he'd already figured out how he was going to spend the fee."

"Hopefully thinking is all he did."

"He's not irresponsible or anything. Just greedy. Which, I should add, isn't all that bad a trait in a partner."

The next office we came to was half the size of Weiss's. "Here's the guy who does the real work around here, Josh Pindler."

Pindler looked to be only a couple of years out of law school. He had a full head of wavy black hair, neatly trimmed and all perfectly in place. Black wire-rimmed glasses with fashionably small lenses accented a slightly elongated face. He'd rolled his shirt sleeves to the elbows, as you might do when you're entrenched in a major project. His suit jacket hung from a coat rack in the corner of the office. Like Bryant, Josh had that fitness glow. With Jim also in good shape, I wondered if workouts were a job requirement.

"What're you working on?" asked Jim.

"What else? Bryant has me researching appeals of summary judgments."

"Figures."

"I've told Bryant it doesn't look good, but you know how he is. Wants me to keep digging. Well, I better get back to this if I'm going to get out before eight."

"He's a good kid," Jim said once out of the office. "A little too into himself, but what Generation X'er isn't?"

We kept walking and took a left into a conference room, which doubled as the firm's library. A distressed oak table surrounded by eight highbacked chairs anchored the room. Four of the chairs were occupied.

Jim introduced Dennis Abbott, Scott Anders, Jerry Grieg and Will Rockland. All were litigation attorneys in their thirties. They each greeted me and shook my hand. Then Scott continued with a story he was telling.

"So Judge Ferris says 'you two keep interrupting me and interrupting each other. So how about if I just pass your case and we'll decide it at the end of the call.' Remember, this is the afternoon motion call, and Ferris never finishes before four-thirty. One of the lawyers says, 'Judge, my daughter has a dance recital after school today. I won't be able to wait to the end of the call.' And Ferris says 'you should have thought of that sooner.' Then the other lawyer has to add his two cents. 'This is what I have to deal with, excuse after excuse.' That really sets Ferris off. He says 'That's enough. I've reconsidered; I have three daughters, and I know how important recitals are. We'll continue the motion tomorrow at four-thirty. But you' and he points to the other attorney, 'that last comment was totally uncalled for. So I'm ordering that you must also attend the dance recital. You'll have to come back tomorrow with a note from the principal, attesting to when you arrived and left.' The lawyer starts to protest, but Ferris will hear none of it. Well, I have to be there next day at four-thirty to see what happened. Sure enough, the guy comes with a note, they argue the motion, and it's wrapped up in three minutes, with no bickering."

"Who needs contempt when you can sentence someone to a dance recital?" said the tallest one, who I think was Dennis.

"Marty, I'll bet you wish Judge Bobb had been creative like that," said Jim.

"Billy Bob Bobb's usually a pretty good guy," said Jerry, before I could respond. "What happened?"

I related my contempt story, sugar-coating my conduct but embellishing the detention part. I claimed I was put in a cell with a drunk who kept exposing himself.

"That's unbelievable," said Scott Anders, a small-framed man with large framed glasses. "Are you going to do anything about Billy Bob?"

"I'd like to, but I don't want to make waves."

"Fuck that," said Jerry. "Haul his ass before the Judicial Inquiry Board."

"I don't know about that," said Dennis. "You don't want a reputation as a crybaby."

"Don't be such a wimp, Abbott," replied Jerry. "There's nothing wrong with standing up for yourself. But there are more anonymous ways to make a point. A dark alley, for one." He laughed, and the others followed.

"So how 'bout we all go down to the Bar Bar," said Jim. "Second the motion" someone said, and we followed Jim's lead out of the conference room. He wished Josh good night and waved to Bryant as he passed his office. Both waved without looking up from their computer screens.

The Bar Bar wasn't nearly as crowded as on Friday. We put together two tables for four, giving us plenty of room to spread out. This was an imported beer bunch, and since the Bar Bar carried Heineken's, Beck's, Guiness and Bass on tap we had a go round with each. Talk shifted between sports, women and law. Dennis played basketball at Northern Illinois, so he, Jim and I swapped stories about our old coaches and some of our nuttier teammates. I admit Jim won this round when he told us about a teammate who'd stuff himself into a locker for a half hour before each game, the better to focus.

The woman talk was predictable. How they were illogical and contra-dictory, impossible to figure out. My contribution was the bat mitzvah invitation scene, and the guys all ribbed me about what a sucker I was and how Randee would end up running the whole show while I get stuck for the tab. Like I didn't know that already.

The law talk focused on personalities. Judges they liked, judges they didn't like, lawyers they liked, and so on. Naturally discussion turned to Judge Miles. His death was the lead story in the morning papers, and undoubtedly the talk of the courthouse.

"I know a lot of lawyers wanted him off the bench," said Will. "But murder does seem kinda drastic."

"You think a pissed off lawyer could have killed him?" asked Jim.

"Sure, why not," said Dennis.

"I don't know," said Jim. "I mean, we all have our rough times in court, but we just figure it goes with the territory."

"I think it's entirely plausible for a hacked off lawyer to kill a judge," said Scott. "Just think about the system. You got one guy passing judgment. He might not be particularly competent; maybe got his job by knowing the right people. And you got these lawyers, who are ego-driven and fairly bright, pleading with this guy to rule in their favor. The judge may be lazy and didn't read the motion papers, or he may not be interested in the subject, or he may not understand it. Still he's empowered to make these major decisions. And on top of that the judge is human and might lose his temper or embarrass the lawyer in front of his peers. And lawyers have to put up with this every day. No, I don't think it's at all unexpected that a lawyer would say 'enough.'"

"But putting the body in the courtroom? That's awfully strange shit. Even for a lawyer," said Jim.

"There are ways short of murder to challenge a bad judge," I said.

"But obviously not as effective," said Dennis. "I see Scott's point. Still, I'd think it would take more than a bad day in court to lead someone to kill."

"I don't know," said Will. "Day after day, week after week of this shit can wear anyone down."

"Admit it," said Scott. "Everybody here has thought of doing something to a judge who's screwed you."

"What're you talking about?" asked Jerry.

"You never hoped that a judge who screwed you over got his comeuppance?"

"Sure. But that's not the same as murder."

"Torture, yes. Murder, no," said Will, which brought approval around the table.

"Enough of this," said Jim. "How about a change of scenery. Anyone up for some pool? We can go to the Eight Ball on Halsted."

Scott and Jerry had to catch trains to the suburbs, but Will and Dennis said they'd play, and so did I, since I didn't have anything going that night. I offered to drive, but Jim said they all had cars, so we should just meet at the Eight Ball.

I drove up Halsted, taking it slow looking for parking once I got within two blocks of the Eight Ball. As I drove up level to the club I saw Jim, Dennis and Will getting out of a taxi. Why pay a cabbie when I'd offered a free lift? No good answer came to me, but I did find a parking space a block up Halsted.

Near Halsted and Diversey, the Eight Ball was in the center of Yuppieville. Sometimes I go to a pool hall on Montrose Avenue, a couple of miles from my apartment, a beat up place where guys in soiled t-shirts named Victor or Nick take their games seriously, and where all strangers are sized up as potential hustlers. But the Eight Ball wasn't a pool hall. It was a billiards emporium. Neon lights and perfectly smooth tables, with the players just as likely to be Peggy or Becky as Jason or Alan. Where Montrose was Old Style and White Owls, the Eight Ball was Martell and Ashtons.

Jim and the others were set up on a table in the center of the room, but a waitress intercepted me just before I got there. I ordered a Beck's, then grabbed a cue and chalked up like I knew what I was doing.

"Looks like we have a pool shark here," said Will.

"More like a beached whale," joked Jim.

"You're not exactly welcome at all-you-can-eat buffets either," I retorted.

"You guys can keep up your battle of wits, such as it is, but I'm breaking," said Dennis. Which he promptly did, producing a satisfying crack and scattering the balls everywhere except in the pocket.

Our game evolved into team nine ball, Jim and me versus Dennis and Will. Nine ball takes more skill than straight pool because you have to make the balls in order; for example, you can't shoot the two until the one is made. Skill being something we all lacked, it took half an hour just to finish the first game.

We were into our second game. Jim made the three in the corner, then pulled back from the table. "Marty, the guys and I talked this over before coming here. How'd you like to be a regular member of our group?"

"What do you mean?"

"We get together once a week, usually on a Monday or Tuesday, to drink beers and let off some steam."

"Sure. Just you three?"

"No, the guys from earlier too."

"We're kind of a closed group, though," said Dennis, "so don't tell anyone about it."

"No problem."

"Not that we're snobby," continued Dennis. "It's just that we like things the way they are. A small group of guys with common interests, who like to go out, have a few belts, tell bad jokes, shoot shitty pool."

"Yeah," said Jim. "Bryant wants in, but we scare him off by saying we're part of a civic group. He's into money, not social change. And the married guys tell their wives they have meetings for this civic group. That way they're not hassled."

"I won't mention the group to anyone," I said.

"Good," said Jim, who went back to the table and made a beautiful bank shot on the six. Too bad he was shooting for the four.

We shot four games, tied two-to-two, and called it quits. Will got a little hot when he missed some easy shots, but for the most part the pool never got very intense, which is amazing with a bunch of lawyers involved. The guys were much more interested in having fun and flirting with the girls at a nearby table. Jim was especially attentive to a curvy blond in a tight red dress. At one point she had a difficult shot requiring her to lean over the table. Jim rushed over, supposedly to give her a pointer, but really to get a bird's eye view of her stretch.

As we were leaving Jim said the next get-together was the following Tuesday, five-thirty at his office. I'd be there, I said.

"By the way," I said, "what kind of civic group are you supposed to be a part of?"

"Something to improve the court system. Attorneys for the Betterment of the Courts." I nearly coughed out my Certs. "But it's really a joke," he continued once I regained control of my throat.

"A joke?"

"Yeah. The letters ABC, they really signify the Attorney Bullshitters Club."

"I don't get it."

"We use the official name when we need to, like with the wives or guys like Bryant. But it's our little secret what ABC really stands for."

"So your group has no real interest in improving the court system?"

"No more than any other lawyers. If screwing around somehow improves the court system, great. If not, fuck it."

CHAPTER 11

I called Amanda the next morning with the latest development. Her response surprised me.

"Now that you know who's in the group we can bring them in for questioning."

"Hold on. What will that do? It's not like anyone will confess."

"We'll shake them up a little, see what happens."

"I don't like that idea."

"Then how about giving me their names and we'll check them out."

"I can do the background work on them."

"I thought the idea was for you to infiltrate the group. You've done that."

"I've only met these guys once. I don't know anything about them, what they're about. Who knows, the killer could have a connection to the cops. If he gets word that we're on to him we could blow the investigation. And some of your colleagues, especially in Chicago, can be a little heavy handed." I didn't necessarily believe all that, but getting more people involved would complicate things. I was also playing to the suburban bias, their belief that Chicago cops can be thuggish. I could easily handle the background checks, and I knew I could keep things under wraps.

"You'd rather just play along for awhile?"

"Exactly, so I can get a better idea of what they're up to. Because for now, I've got to say, I think they're a lot more interested in having a good time than wreaking havoc on the judicial system."

"All right, but keep an eye on these guys. We don't want any more dead judges."

"I've got something else for you to check out."

"What's that?"

"A lawyer named Forrester died about seven months ago. A big-mouthed, unpopular guy, like Miles. Poisoned. Computer generated note near the body. Chicago cops concluded it was a suicide, but there seem to be a lot of similarities to our case."

"An ABC note?"

"No; just a suicide note. So far I haven't found any ABC connection."

"I'll look into it."

"Anything new at your end?"

"Nothing. Stone cold."

"Any ideas how Miles ended up in a locked courthouse?"

"Good question. Our best guess is that the killer used Miles' keycard from his days as a judge there."

"Why would Miles be carrying that on him? He'd been sitting in Chicago a long time."

"I don't know."

"Isn't there a record of what keycards are used?"

"No. The cards aren't coded by user. Judges, sheriff's deputies, the night cleaning crew, they all use the same cards."

"Any security cameras?"

"No."

"Pretty nervy for the killer to put the judge on the bench like that."

"Very. If he gets away with this I'm sure we'll hear from him again."

With a week until the next meeting I had plenty of time to gather information on the ABCers. What I didn't have was a lot of sources. One was the Attorney Registration and Disciplinary Commission, the licensing authority for Illinois attorneys. I phoned over and told the young woman who answered that I wanted to know if the lawyers I was considering hiring had any record with them. I gave her the names of the five ABCers, and Hicks Pepper III. Why Pepper? Not necessarily because he was a suspect, but hopefully to get some leverage on him.

"You're sure looking at a lot of attorneys," she said pleasantly. I detected a touch of southern twang in her voice.

"One of the curses of being cautious. Every time I talk to one attorney, I figure it won't hurt to check another one out."

"You can't be too careful. We've censured and suspended a bunch of lawyers in the past few weeks."

"You sound proud."

"I don't know about that. But I wish lawyers were better about weeding out the bad apples." At least one seems to be, I thought. "Anyway," she continued, "give me about an hour and I'll have the information for you."

Exactly fifty-eight minutes later she called. Only Will, Jim and Pepper had had complaints filed against them by the commission. In Will's case he'd threatened to punch out an attorney after losing a motion. He was found guilty of unprofessional conduct, but the least serious level of punishment—censure—was imposed, based on the finding that his conduct was out of character and unlikely to be repeated. Jim allegedly made a sexist remark toward a female attorney, but after a hearing the complaint was dismissed, upon a finding that the attorney provoked Jim and therefore shared the blame.

Pepper's charge was the most serious. He was accused of theft of client funds by false billing. His defense was that any overbilling was unintentional, the result of sloppy recordkeeping. He further represented that he'd instituted a new system to prevent future problems, and that he'd refund any overcharges. I can see how a disorganized attorney can duplicate charges without intent, but, unfortunately for Pepper, any irregularity involving client funds is certain trouble, and he was suspended from practice for 90 days. This was eight years ago. He hadn't been in trouble since, and undoubtedly his firm had now instituted safeguards and checks to insure the accuracy of Pepper's billings. So my hoped for leverage was about as useful as a week old newspaper.

After finishing with the ARDC, I got Plonski to check if any of the ABCers had criminal histories. None did, except for Scott Anders, who had a misdemeanor charge for cannabis possession when he was nineteen.

Then I tracked down the ABCers home addresses and phone numbers. My theory was that the killer/abductor lived alone in a house. If Celia was held in a basement, she must have been in a house rather than an apartment. And I suspect the wife or kids would discover a stranger chained to the wall, and not welcome this addition to the household.

Scott Anders and Jerry Grieg had houses in the suburbs, but they were married. All three of the single ABCers lived in apartments or condos in the City.

As a double check I called Anders's house, and a woman answered. "Mrs. Anders," I asked. "Yes," she replied. That was enough for me, and

I hung up. I got an answering machine when I called Jerry Grieg, with a female voice delivering the "we're not available, leave your name and number..." message. That too was enough.

I was staring out the window, contemplating my next move (deli versus fried chicken for lunch) when Judge Dienstag called.

"How're things going?" he asked.

"Not great. But it's not unusual for investigations to start slowly."

"Remember when you asked if I'd ever heard of that Attorneys for the Betterment of the Courts group?"

"Sure."

"I had my secretary do some checking. We did get a letter from them, almost a year ago."

"Really?" This surprised me; from what I'd seen, I'd have bet ABC was strictly a social group.

"I'll fax it to you."

"You've only received the one letter?"

"I'm having my secretary double check, but so far that's it."

The letter came through a few minutes later. The letterhead identified the group's name and gave an address in Glenview for an address. No phone number.

The letter said:

We are a group of attorneys concerned about the lack of civility pervading the judiciary. Because we fear repercussions if our identities become known we have designated ourselves Attorneys for the Betterment of the Courts. We are all litigators who regularly appear in court, and we call upon you to investigate this situation before things get out of control.

It's become all too commonplace and accepted for judges to lose their tempers with attorneys, deny reasonable requests for continuances or extensions of time, and to needlessly make things difficult. Too many judges seem to have forgotten what the real world practice of law is like, such as that the lawyer doesn't always have the time or opportunity to thoroughly familiarize himself with a file, that attorneys have other commitments or other matters in court besides the one before that judge at that time, and that the attorney standing before them is not necessarily the attorney responsible for any problems with the case. Instead of being considered fellow professionals we're treated as enemies, as necessary evils,

entitled to little or no courtesy or consideration. Not all judges are disre-
spectful, but we would say that more than half are. While this letter will
not name names, future ones may.

Please accept this plea to monitor your judges, and to counsel those
who are not exhibiting the proper respect and understanding to improve
their acts. Only bad things can happen if judicial attitudes don't change.

Someone signed the letter with the group name.

I faxed a copy to Amanda, and she called a minute later.

"Still think they're just a bunch of good time Charlies?" she asked.

"Yeah, I do. The letter's pretty general."

"'Bad things can happen if judicial attitudes don't change.' That sounds threatening to me."

"Not necessarily. It could mean that lawyers becoming disenchanted leave the profession, or public perception of our judicial system erodes."

"Or that an attorney goes off the deep end and kills a judge."

"I suppose that's a possible interpretation, but it doesn't refer to an ABC attorney. They could be warning that any lawyer is capable of something bad if provoked."

"I think you better face up that these aren't overaged frat boys looking for cheap beer and cheaper women."

I'll admit the letter made me anxious for the next meeting. I knew Jim pretty well, and he seemed the type who left his mean streak on the football field. But the others? Maybe one of them had run amok. Or maybe ABC really did have an agenda underneath the partying.

I tracked the address on the ABC letterhead to one of those private mailbox centers and drove out there. I played it straight and told the manager I needed some information as part of a murder investigation. No, I'm not the police, I admitted, I'm private. After that the manager did his job much too well for my liking; he wouldn't say who rented the box, if they received much mail, or even if the box was regularly emptied.

On the drive back to the City I called Hicks Pepper III from the car, hoping Miles' death had loosened his resolve concerning the attorney-client privilege. Instead I got his secretary. After screening my identity she put me on hold, then came back with word that Mr. Pepper was in a meeting, would I care to leave a message. No thanks, I'll try later, I said. In person, I kept to myself.

Maybe there was another source I could tap at Markus & Stevens.

When I visited Pepper an associate was leaving his office. Associates are often assigned to particular partners, so maybe she'd worked on Miles' case too.

I redialed Markus & Stevens and asked to speak to an attorney named Rebecca. One moment please, I was told, then a few seconds later I was greeted by a new voice. "Rebecca Ellsworth."

"Ms. Ellsworth, my name's Martin Bronk. I'm a private investigator, and I'm calling regarding Judge Miles."

"I was wondering when someone would want to talk to me. But did you say you were a private investigator?"

"Yes, I am."

"I thought I'd hear from someone official. But I guess this is how it works."

"Yes, at least in this case. When would be a good time for us to get together?"

"I'm free this afternoon."

"Good. There's a coffee place on Clark near Monroe. How about if we meet there around 2:30?"

"Okay. But why there?"

"My office isn't real convenient to you. And I presume you'd rather not have certain people in your office know we're meeting."

"I appreciate that."

I gave her my description, and she gave me hers, which really wasn't necessary, because even my brief glimpse of her in Pepper's office stuck with me.

Two-thirty rolled around, I'd been at my cafe window seat for ten minutes, and in came Rebecca. I waved, and she shot me a smile that could quiver knees. "I'll be right there," she said, and she ordered something which must have been loaded with caffeine, seeing how she only got coins in change from her five.

Most people might describe Rebecca as the girl next door type..I can't do that because the girl who lived next to me would make a Russian shot-putter seem like Kate Moss. So let's just say that Rebecca was so pleasant, articulate and downright cute that after two minutes of small talk I was in love, like the crush I had on Marsha Brady when I was fourteen. But being a professional, I'm not easily distracted, even by the brightest smile in the universe.

"I'd like to talk to you about Judge Miles," I said. "Since you're here I presume you don't have any objections."

"Objections? No, not at all."

"Great. You did know Judge Miles, right?"

"Yeah, that's one way to say it. But I didn't kill him."

I burst out laughing. A sense of humor on top of everything else; she was amazing. Except she wasn't laughing. Or even smiling.

"Why do you find that amusing?" she asked.

"The idea of you killing anyone, it's just so absurd."

"Sorry if I don't get the joke. You know some people might think I had motive."

"What motive could you possibly have?" I don't have a problem playing straight man.

"What motive? Why did you ask for this meeting?" Okay, she wasn't perfect. She needed work on her comedic timing. Unless what I took for deadpan was totally serious.

"I assume, since you work with Hicks Pepper, that you represented Miles."

"Mr. Bronk, this is either a very bad joke, or you are one lousy investigator." It's a terrible feeling souring Marsha Brady's mood.

"Hold on a minute. Hicks Pepper is, er was, Judge Miles attorney, correct?"

"Not as far as I know."

"I have it on reliable authority that he was."

"Well, that doesn't really seem possible, does it?"

"We're talking in circles here. Why couldn't he be?"

"Because of the conflict." I didn't need a mirror to know how lost I must have looked. Maybe Rebecca took pity on me, because she didn't wait for my next meaningless question. "You do know that I filed a complaint against Miles with the JIB, right?" The Judicial Inquiry Board. The rumored sexual harassment complaint.

I have no idea how long I took to shift gears, except that I eventually said, "Unofficially I've heard something about a JIB investigation, but they're confidential until the Board actually prosecutes."

"But Miles must have known it was me who made the complaint, right?"

"Maybe he could have guessed, but at this stage the JIB wouldn't necessarily reveal who made the charges."

Now it was Rebecca's turn to crack up, and I followed her lead, more as a tension release than anything else. "You wanted to talk to me because you thought I was one of Miles' attorneys, seeing that I work for Hicks?"

"Yeah, that's it."

Another burst of laughter. "That is just sooo funny." I don't remember who followed whose lead, but we ended up clinking coffee mugs.

"So tell me about your complaint."

"About six months ago I was before Judge Miles on a pretrial conference. You know what that is, right?"

"Yeah, where the judge and the attorneys meet in chambers trying to settle a case."

"Exactly. The plaintiff's attorney was a guy I went to law school with, Mike Gelman. He makes a settlement demand of $50,000. I had authority from the insurance company I represented to settle up to $35,000. So I offered $20,000, to give me some negotiating room. We talk a little more, kind of general, he can come down if I can come up, yadda yadda. Then Miles sends me out of the room, to talk to Mike in private."

"That's standard, right?"

"Oh absolutely. That's how the judge gets a feel for what's really needed to settle the case. So after they're done Miles sends Mike out and asks me in. He starts by saying he thought Mike's figures were off. But that my figure is just right."

"Which you took how?"

"Flirty, sexist."

"Could he have just been making a bad, insensitive joke?"

"Sure. I even sort of laughed that one off and changed the subject to the case. But then Miles says, 'If you want this case to settle, lose the long skirt, show Gelman some leg when he comes back in. He'll take $10,000 off the case, like that. Hell, give me a look and I'll get him down to 30k, right now.' Now that was too much, especially after what he said before. I mean, no one should act like that, but especially a judge. So I pretended that I had to cover another matter and left. And that's what the complaint's about."

"That must have been terribly offensive."

"It was. And I'm not really the type to cause trouble. I know some young lawyers, especially women, feel the need to prove themselves, so they act real tough, like that will get them respect. Me, I always just try to be myself."

"You're saying you didn't file the complaint just to make a name for yourself."

"Right. I've hardly even told anyone about it. Only my husband, and a few friends. No one at the firm."

"So Hicks doesn't know about this?"

"I don't see how he could, unless, like you said, Miles put it together and told him. But Hicks has never said anything about it to me. Now that I think about it, I'm not even sure Miles knew my name."

"Secrets have a way of coming out after someone dies. So if Hicks says anything to you about Miles, would you call me?"

"Sure. Do you think I should talk to the police about this?"

"I don't think you have to. But if you feel the need, this is who you should call." I wrote Amanda's name and number on the back of my card.

Rebecca studied the card, back and front, before putting it in her purse. "Thanks. Oh, and I'm sorry for calling you a lousy investigator."

"That's okay, I was sounding pretty stupid there for awhile."

"I'm not usually insulting like that. It's just..."

"You don't have to explain yourself. I know the pressures young lawyers are under."

"It's not just that, it's...Well anyway, I may give you a call."

"Good."

We stood and shook hands. My thoughts as she left? I knew Miles wasn't the sharpest pencil in the box, but to harass Rebecca and chase her away, he was an absolute fool.

•

Rebecca was totally credible, so besides being ill-tempered, Miles was also sexist. But that part of him wouldn't much impact the ABCers. Actually I suspected that some of the members, like Jim, worshipped at that same altar. So if ABC was involved in Miles' murder, the link would lie elsewhere.

With Judge Dienstag's help I got a computer printout of the cases Judge Miles had presided over within the past five years, and the attorneys in those cases. From this I learned that all of the ABCers, except Scott Anders, had tried cases before Miles. As did at least a hundred other lawyers.

Judge Dienstag also told me that Miles was a substitute motion judge. In Cook County certain judges preside over trials, and other judges hear those motions filed prior to trial. Judge Miles was a trial judge, but he also heard motions when one of the regular motion judges was absent. In that role he'd hear about fifty cases a day. Meaning the ABCers, and every other litigation attorney in the City, could have appeared before him dozens of times. Meaning an endless number of potentially aggrieved attorneys.

The next ABC meeting wasn't until next week. I'd have liked to talk to them now, not so much to interrogate, but to get a better sense of the guys. But other than Jim, I didn't know them well enough to just call and chat, and it was important to stay in character if I was going to get anything out of my ABC connection. Patience may be a virtue, but it's also a pain-in-the-ass.

That left me with trying Pepper again. He'd already ducked a phone call, but I have foolproof ways of getting in to see people without creating a scene.

Like the workman routine. I changed into my blue workshirt, "Ed," (the most unremarkable name I could think of) stitched over the left pocket. Valerie was again the receptionist, and from her double-take I could tell she recognized me but something wasn't clicking within her. "I've seen you at church, right?" I said.

"Maybe that's it," she said. "You look familiar, but different."

"It's the clothes. They make the man, you know."

"I guess."

"I need to check something with the electric." And that got me to Pepper's office.

His door was open but he wasn't in. I walked in, shut the door, then took Pepper's chair.

I was tossing up a University of Michigan paperweight when he came in. "What the fuck?" Which caused me to miss the catch, and the paperweight thudded onto his desk.

"Hello Hicks. Have a seat."

"Are you out of your mind? I can have you arrested for trespass."

"Relax. Just tell me who you think killed Judge Miles, and why, and I'll leave you alone."

"How the hell would I know?"

"As his lawyer he must have expressed some confidences to you."

"As I told you before..."

"Hicks, it's just me and you talking. I'm not going to broadcast this to the world. I won't even tell the cops. And your attorney-client privilege is a lot weaker with a dead client."

Pepper hesitated before responding. "Here's the deal, Bronk. I'll tell you the one person he said hated him more than anybody. Someone Walter said was out to get him. Only you didn't hear it from me."

"Fine. Who?"

"David the Almighty Dienstag."

•

David Dienstag was, by acclamation, the smartest guy around. Leaving aside questions of motive, could he kill, then hire me to find the killer, figuring he'd be too smart for me to catch?

A murderer hiring an investigator; it seems like such a shallow ploy that I'd never believed it plausible. But maybe Dienstag had covered his tracks so well that he could pull it off.

A few things were clear. He'd known about ABC even before Celia's abduction, in light of the letter he'd given me. He could easily adopt the ABC persona to his purposes. He'd made Eldrick's list of people who Miles had blown up at. And as chief judge he had ready access to the Skokie courthouse, where Miles was found.

One more thing. By hiring me he could keep tabs on my investigation, for which, incidentally, he wasn't even paying me. Now that would truly be genius.

So now I had a new problem; Do I investigate the person who hired me?

And if so, how?

CHAPTER 12

Gail stayed with me that weekend. Saturday we visited the Art Institute. I don't think either of us was all that enthused about it, but we go once a year, and our year was just about up. Judging by the number of kids with single parents I saw, it's a regular stop on the weekend custody circuit.

Sunday was much more to her liking. Colleen joined us, and we drove north about fifty miles to Gurnee, site of Gurnee Mills, home to over 200 factory outlet and off-price stores. The mall is over two miles long, and I'd have been happy to pack it in within the first 800 yards. But by then Gail was just warming up, and Colleen wasn't far behind. They shopped with a purpose, buzzing around like bees in a flower garden. If a store didn't have what they wanted they were out within a minute. Before they were done they each came away with a bunch of sweaters, tops and pants. Not that I went away empty handed; for me it was a package of Jockey shorts, irregulars.

After the shopping we grabbed an early dinner at a place which called itself a Texas-style saloon, but the closest thing I saw to a cowboy was a photo of Troy Aikman. Our waitress was Gabrielle. Probably Gabrielle Bird Johnson. Over barbecued beef sandwiches and thick-wedged french fries talk turned to the bat mitzvah.

"You getting excited yet?" asked Colleen.

"Not really."

"What is it, five or six weeks to go?"

"Whatever."

"Have you been practicing your haftorah?"

"How do you know about that, Colleen?" I asked.

"I picked it up from some of the Jewish faculty members. I even know the difference between Rosh Hashanah and Yom Kippur."

"I'm impressed."

"Did you know Mom calls Colleen the shiksa?"

"Gail," I said, "You know better than to say that."

"It's not me, it's Mom."

"It's okay," said Colleen. "Besides, Marty, you say some not so nice things about her boyfriend."

"You mean Thad the Bad? I don't bring religion into it. I just call him things like weasly and stupid. Non-denominational insults."

"Can we change the subject?" said Gail.

"Actually, clever daughter of mine, you managed to sidestep the question, which is whether you've been practicing."

"Yeah, I've been practicing." Her eyes were directed at the steer head on the wall. Non-Verbal Communication 101 said she wasn't telling the whole truth. But Parenting 201 said now wasn't the time to call her on it.

After dinner we drove Gail to Randee's house. Colleen waited in the car when I walked Gail to the door. Normally I'd have suggested to Colleen that she come with and meet Randee. Hopefully Randee would be in her unwashed hair/sweat clothes/stay-at-home mode, all set up for maximum embarrassment. But this didn't seem the time to create an awkward situation simply to indulge my vengefulness. Patience rearing its ugly head again.

"Gail's a great kid," Colleen said on our drive to my place, "but I think she's a little overwhelmed by this bat mitzvah."

"It can be a lot of pressure. You have to learn your reading, in Hebrew. Then you have to give a speech, which is usually on some lesson-of-life topic that no thirteen year old would ever voluntarily think about. And you have to do this in front of your friends, who just want to goof around, and your relatives, who'll be fussing all over you. And in Gail's case you have the divorced parents element. So yeah, that's a lot of stuff going on."

"She'll do fine."

"Maybe. I get the impression that she's not being too diligent about practicing."

"That could be her coping mechanism. Some people get more nervous the more they work at something."

"And some people flunk out the less they work at something."

"Marty, it's a ceremony, not school."

I pulled into my building's garage and parked in my reserved spot.

After turning off the engine I took Colleen's hand. "Leave it to a shiksa to put things in perspective."

She withdrew her hand and started beating me around my upper arms with soft punches. I drew my hands over my face, and she switched to punches in the stomach.

"Have you had enough, mister," she said.

"Stop. Stop."

"If you call me shiksa again I'll, I'll..."

I pulled her close before she could finish. I forced my lips onto hers, she kissed back, and those hands which had been balled up were now working their way under my jacket. I ran my hands through her hair, my lips not letting go of hers. A car came screeching through the garage. We dropped down below windshield level, but didn't stop the action. I'd never made love in a car before, not even as a teenager. Definitely something I missed out on, I realized that night.

Afterward I got to thinking about the crazy things I did do when I was young. Like the time a bunch of us smoked pot in Dena Goldman's basement, and how my parents flipped out when they heard about it. Luckily they didn't find out we were doing it in our underwear or I'd still be grounded. Which got me to thinking that in a few weeks Gail would be a teenager, and some day soon I'd be the flipper (or is it the flippee). Damn reality check.

Colleen and I made it up to my apartment for another round. Reality could wait.

•

Judge Dienstag called Monday morning asking for an update. I suggested that I stop by his office, and he agreed.

I'd thought about how to handle him, and decided on the Bronk the Subtle approach. Dienstag would never suspect that his update was my interrogation.

The judge stiffly greeted me when I got to his office later that morning. "Any progress?" he asked before I could even sit.

"I'm afraid the investigation's going to take time. The more I look, the more enemies I find."

"What about this Attorneys for the Betterment of the Courts?"

"That's my focus, but anybody with a word processor and knowledge of the group could have made up the notes."

"True." First point to Bronk. Dienstag didn't ask "What notes," and I'd never mentioned them before; I'd simply asked if he knew of ABC. And the cops keep details like that to themselves, so I doubt they'd have said anything about them. Although I suppose Celia or Billy Bob could have told Dienstag about the notes they received. So maybe only a half-point.

"I'm finding a lot of lawyers didn't like him. Why, I'll bet some of his fellow judges didn't care for him either."

"I don't doubt that. You don't suspect a judge, do you?"

"Not at all. Just making a point."

"Yes, Mr. Bronk, many people disliked Walter Miles. But dislike is not a motive for murder."

"You're right, something deeper is needed. But, out of curiosity, what was the judicial consensus on him?"

"That he was an average jurist in terms of competence. His major failing was his boorishness."

"Is that your opinion as well?"

"Essentially. Although I'm trying to improve the quality of the judiciary, so average isn't good enough for me. Unfortunately some judges are so accustomed to mediocrity that it'd take an infusion of new people to elevate judicial standards to the level I'd find satisfactory."

"You ever talk to him about his performance?"

"Sure. We even raised voices, which I rather regret because it's not very professional. But Walter had a manner which sometimes made it difficult for one to maintain composure."

"You ever consider transferring him somewhere out of harm's way, so to speak?"

"That would have made things worse in various respects. I'm sure Miles' performance would have gotten that much worse. And if I demote—and that's what we're really talking about—an experienced judge like Miles without specific cause, the other judges get anxious, figuring I could do it to them too. I don't want nervous judges always looking over their shoulders. Besides, the best way to keep tabs on people is to keep them close at hand."

"You ever try to force his resignation?"

"I don't really have that power. But even if I did, trying something like that would really cause some nervous judges."

So you killed him to get him off the bench, I was tempted to ask. Of course I didn't, because I knew how Dienstag would answer. Besides, that seemed like a pretty unlikely motive.

"What kind of person was Miles outside the courtroom?"

"Actually he was all right. A little rough around the edges, but he had a sense of humor."

"Was he friends with any of the other judges?"

"I don't know about that. I don't watch over my judges' social lives."

"You ever see him outside the courthouse?"

"I'd see him around Northbrook sometimes. We both live there, and our kids went to the same school. But I wouldn't say we were friends."

"You ever hear about him being involved in anything which could get him in trouble?"

"No."

"He have a good reputation for integrity?"

"I never heard anything to the contrary."

"You ever hear of anyone threatening him?"

"No."

"He have a good marriage?"

"Damned if I know."

I wasn't getting anything out of this, and I didn't see the interview going anywhere. Bronk the Subtle giving way to Bronk the Clueless.

I told Dienstag I had an appointment to catch, a ready excuse and one of the reasons it's better to interview someone at their place instead of yours. "I'll call you tomorrow," he said, which was too soon for my liking, but there wasn't much I could do about it. Except leave the answering machine on.

•

The next ABC meeting was Tuesday, five-thirty at Jim's office. As I got off the elevator I ran into Josh Pindler, a briefcase in his right hand, a Marshall Field's bag in the left. We said hi and talked baseball until his down elevator came. Silly kid actually thought the Cubs had a good shot at the World Series.

Again the ABC bunch gathered in the conference room. Same group as last time except for Jerry Grieg, who was out of town at a deposition.

Will was telling a story about how Judge Ramsey had stuck it to someone. The lawyer had a prepaid vacation lined up and presented a motion to continue a trial. The judge said no, there are twenty lawyers in your office, all of them capable of trying the case. The lawyer pointed out that he was the only attorney in the office who'd actually worked on the case, and that the client had specified that she only wanted him to handle it.

You should have thought of that before you booked the vacation, said the judge. But the trial date was set after the vacation was booked, replied the attorney. The judge repeated that someone else in his firm could try the case. Motion denied.

"But Ramsey never raised his voice, totally cool the whole time," said Will.

"Sometimes I think that's the worst thing of all," said Scott. "No emotion, just sticks the knife in you, deeper and deeper. Damn sadistic if you ask me."

"Anything going on with you and Billy Bob Bobb?" Jim asked me.

"Let's launch a campaign in your behalf, clear your name of that scurrilous contempt," said Will, before I could respond to Jim's question.

"You mean ABC would do that for me?"

They all laughed. "Forget ABC," said Will. "That's thinking small. We'll get the whole bar behind you."

"I think I can handle things without involving the whole bar," I said.

"Speaking of bars, how about we head down to our favorite," said Jim. "But before I forget, here's something I ran off for you, Marty." Jim handed me a membership list, with home and work addresses and phone numbers. Something I could have used the week before.

The bar talk was sports versus women, with sports getting the higher approval rating. The way Will put it, even if your favorite team is rotten or has a bad game, they can always get 'em next time. So sports is inherently optimistic. But if you're involved in a bad relationship, as were a couple of the guys, each new day is dreaded. A perpetual downer. Scott had a different take. The worse your team, the less emotional you get. You just figure the team will lose, and if they surprise you and play a good game it's an unexpected dividend. But the worse a relationship, the more emotionally draining it becomes.

"What about the opposite," I suggested. "A championship team versus a terrific relationship. Which is better?"

"If she doesn't have to be 'in the mood' to put out, and isn't always bitching about needing emotional support, I'll take the chick. Otherwise, give me a world series or Super Bowl winner anytime," said Jim.

"Championships are much rarer than a good fuck," said Dennis, "so I gotta go with the winning team."

"The Cubs won't fix you a nice dinner when you've had a rough day at the office," I said.

"Get with the program," said Scott. "These days chances are you'll be fixing the dinner because she had the rough day."

"How about women lawyers," offered Will. "Now there's a bunch of ball busters."

"Don't get us started on that," said Jim, "or we'll be here all night."

"There goes one now," said Scott, pointing to a blond in a tight suit. "A bitch on wheels. Thinks she's hot just because she has tits. Last time I had a deposition with her she kept interrupting me with a bunch of half-assed objections, like I'd roll over because I was getting a hard-on hearing her voice. Finally I had enough, so after each objection I got tougher on her client. By the time we were through he wanted to kill her."

"You handled that well," I said.

"I'd have called a break," said Jim, "and asked to talk to her outside, off the record. When we were alone I'd get real close to her, maybe grab her tit, and say 'You want to fuck me, let's do it the right way.' Guaranteed she'd quit the bullshit. Or I'd get laid." Jim delivered this deadpan, but he got the rest of us laughing.

Talk like this went on till about eight, when we called it quits. Scott declared that we'd meet again next Tuesday, usual time and place.

"How come we meet in Jim's office instead of at the bar?" I asked.

"Tradition," said Jim, "and it's central to everyone."

"And we don't always come here," said Dennis. "We'll go to O'Toole's next week."

"Oh, I almost forgot," said Jim. "Everyone be sure to get the paper tomorrow."

"I thought it'd be in today," said Will.

"I thought so too," replied Jim. "Tomorrow for sure."

"What are you talking about?" I asked.

"Just pick up the paper tomorrow. You'll see."

CHAPTER 13

I paged Amanda from the car phone, and she called back within two minutes.

"Something might be up," I said.

"What?"

"I have no idea."

"Then why are you calling?"

"I don't know, just thought you might be interested."

"You're not making sense."

I told her about Jim's comment to check out the newspaper, and his nonresponsive answer when I asked him to explain.

"Can't you find out more?"

"If they'd wanted to let me in on it they would have. Besides, I still think these guys are more into drinking and guy talk than changing the world. In the two hours I was with them we talked about law for maybe ten minutes."

"So they have other interests besides killing judges. I think these are the guys. You keep your ears open, and let me know if you hear anything more definite."

Jim's statement suggested that whatever he was referring to had already happened. But what? Nobody seemed on edge, so I doubted it was anything violent. Unless they'd become so hardened that they'd lost all feeling. Which would rank them among the worst bad-asses I'd ever encountered.

The next morning I awoke at six, then hurried through my shower and breakfast. By seven I'd bought a Sun-Times from the box outside my building and caught the 147 express bus downtown. I found a seat in the middle of the bus and started into the paper.

The two stories on the front page were about the president's new war on drugs and some high school boy who got suspended for wearing a kilt to class. I skipped the world and national news to get to the local stuff. Nothing was striking my eye. I turned some more pages; all I was seeing were the usual stories about gang shootings, drunk drivers, and suspicious fires.

And then I got to page twenty-five.

Police have no leads into the disappearance of Rebecca Ellsworth, 28, who was reported missing Monday evening by her husband Perry.

Ellsworth, of Vernon Hills and the mother of a one-year-old son, is an attorney with the Chicago firm of Markus & Stevens, where she special-izes in insurance defense law. She was last seen around 5:45 Monday evening when she left her office.

Police gave no comment regarding possible reasons for Ellsworth's dis-appearance, but say they are investigating.

I got nauseous. Rebecca seemed like the nicest person, and I couldn't imagine her being disliked, let alone hated with the passion needed to inflict harm. Maybe there was a personal or medical explanation for her disappearance, or she was the victim of a random act. But if anyone I knew was responsible, and if Rebecca was hurt, or worse, I'd beat the crap out of them.

At least that's how I felt, and even though I knew I'd settle down I was also determined to remember this emotion.

As sweet as Rebecca was, I had to remember that she was a litigation attorney, meaning that in every case she worked she faced an adversary. And litigation can create a high-charged atmosphere where a defeated lawyer may blame his opponent for his own failings. Not that I've ever heard of a lawyer killing another lawyer over a case, and Rebecca seemed like the last person someone would take offense at. Still, it was a thought, albeit one I mentally noted in pencil.

But what was it Rebecca said at the end of our meeting, that she might give me a call? I assumed it'd be about Miles, but maybe it was about something else. Damn, how I wished she'd made that call.

I phoned Amanda from my office. She'd heard something about a miss-ing lawyer but didn't have any role in the investigation. Not only wasn't it within her jurisdiction, but no connection had been established between Rebecca and the earlier cases. Even so, Amanda promised to let me know if she heard anything.

No one had hired me to investigate Rebecca's disappearance. And maybe I was taking some license here, but having met her I felt a connection. And a responsibility, because I had this sickening feeling that our meeting played a role in her disappearance. Maybe she was followed when she left the office to meet me. Or someone saw us together at the coffee house, thanks to my brilliance in picking window seats.

I liked the ABCers, and I didn't want to believe that they were involved in whatever was happening to Rebecca. But Jim's directing me to the newspaper bothered me, and the ABC talk was gratuitously disrespectful of women. Still, it's quite a leap from bad-mouthing to abduction.

But someone I'd met was directly connected to both Miles and Rebecca. Better yet, it's someone I enjoyed hassling.

No pretenses today; I just strode past Valerie and straight to Hicks Pepper's office. Once there I puffed out my chest, shut the door and said, "What have you done to Rebecca?" I expected a statement of ignorance, or maybe an order to do the anatomically impossible.

Instead I got tears.

Not a lot of them, but there they were. Pepper turned his back towards me and blew into a tissue.

"How could you accuse me of doing anything to Rebecca," he finally said, and only now did he turn to face me. "She's like a daughter to me."

"Sometimes daughters need to be disciplined. Sometimes things get out of hand."

"I'm sure you consider me a boor, but I swear on my mother's grave that I've never done anything to Rebecca." Mental note— check current status of Mrs. Hicks Pepper II.

"I know trial attorneys are known for their theatrics, but aren't you laying it on a little thick, Pepper?"

"This is no act," and he pounded his fist on the desk. "As I've already told the police, I have nothing but good to say about Rebecca, and I don't know anyone who feels differently."

"You two work pretty closely?"

"Yes, she did a lot of work for me."

"You ever get feelings for her?"

"I told you, she's like a daughter."

"Between us guys, Hicks. You ever dip your pen in the company inkwell?"

He grabbed a paperweight and threw it at my head. I ducked, and it hit his University of Michigan Alumni Association certificate, shattering the glass from its frame.

"You asshole," he screamed. "Now get the fuck out!"

People were now congregating in and near the office, and the stream didn't stop until there were about a dozen hanging around. "Excitement's over," I said and I pushed my way through the door. I could tell no one knew what to do about me, and whether they weren't willing to help because it was Pepper, or if it was simply our society's reluctance to get involved didn't matter. I kept going, and no one stopped me.

I'd provoked Pepper, and he responded with fury. But what did that prove? Could be anguish, could be guilt. Could be real, could be show.

I love investigations that raise more questions than answers.

I didn't hear from Amanda that day, and the next day the Rebecca Ellsworth story was up to page fifteen and eight paragraphs. According to her husband and co-workers she was upbeat, being particularly energized after recently winning a big case. No one could believe that she would disappear on her own. She had no problems at home (or at least none any-one knew about or would admit to knowing about), and she was too "grounded," (that was the word used by a colleague) to skip town on a whim. The consensus of those quoted was that she either had an accident or was the victim of foul play.

Looking for something to do, I walked over to the Daley Center. I hadn't seen Judge Bobb or Celia since Miles' murder, so now was a good time to see how they were holding up. And to check a few other things.

Celia was on the phone. She didn't bother to interrupt her conversation; instead she motioned her head towards the open chambers.

"Marty, can you believe what happened to Walter?" asked the judge.

"Unfortunately I can believe it all too well."

"I mean the way they found his body." Apparently word hadn't got out that it was me, not they, who discovered it. That was one reason I stopped by; to see if there'd been any leaks concerning my role.

"I admit that was odd."

"So what's the latest?"

"The trail's kind of cold."

"I don't mind telling you, Marty, I get a little nervous when judges start turning up dead. And if it's the same guy who kidnapped Celia he might have it in for me too."

"I'd be careful, but look at it this way. If he was after you he wouldn't have bothered with Judge Miles. Or Celia either for that matter."

"I suppose."

"Have you heard about that lawyer who's missing?" Yet another reason for my visit.

"Yeah, seems like a nice kid."

"You know her?"

"Vaguely. I think she's been before me a few times. At breakfast this morning a bunch of us judges were talking about her. A couple of them hear motions in law division, so they see her all the time. Said she's never been a problem. Always respectful, pleasant."

"Anything else?"

"Just that she's a good lawyer. Always comes prepared. The people at Markus & Stevens think highly of her. Even had her try some pretty big cases."

Judge Bobb gave me the names of the judges who knew Rebecca. Later I confirmed with them that Rebecca was a first rate young lawyer with a bright future and a good temperament.

Celia was hanging up the phone as I left Judge Bobb's chambers. "The asshole who got me, he killed Miles," she said.

"Looks that way."

"Can't say I'll miss him. Still..."

"Doesn't it get you thinking that it could have been you?"

"He wouldn't have killed me."

"Why not?"

"Nobody'd miss me."

"Celia, I'm sure that's not true."

"Sure it is. Anyway, way I figure, no profit in killing someone if only twenty people would go to the funeral, when you can kill someone who'd draw a couple hundred. And get big press coverage."

"Murder for publicity?"

"Yeah. I hear I never even made the papers." Which is true.

"While you were being held did you get sick to your stomach?"

"No. What kinda question is that?"

"He could have tried to poison you but botched it up."

"No, I didn't get any tummy aches. And he didn't try to drown me in the toilet neither. He kept saying he needed to teach me a lesson. You don't teach someone you're gonna kill." Good point.

Talking to Celia, and thinking about Miles, reiterated just how opposite Rebecca was from them. It didn't seem possible that the same person, or people, could be responsible for all three.

Later I'm back in the office, eating carry-out pepperoni pizza, when a fax comes in from the Northbrook Police Department.

Rebecca Ellsworth had been found. Dead. Shot four times.

CHAPTER 14

Rebecca's body had been dumped in the North Branch of the Chicago River, washing ashore in the Edgebrook community on Chicago's north-west side. She'd been shot at close range, twice in the chest, once in the abdomen and once in the thigh. The body was found fully clothed, and there were no signs of sexual assault. The preliminary estimate was that she'd been dead 24 to 48 hours when found.

I got that information from Glenn Washburn, one of the Chicago detectives on the case. Wash (a nickname which doubles as a suggestion he tends to ignore) and I go back, and if he was curious why I was asking about Rebecca he didn't say.

Most criminal offenders, even murderers, I don't hate. I may hate what they did, but apprehension and conviction, not emotion, is the best revenge. But now I felt personally violated. Someone I knew and cared for had been victimized. Worse still, I exposed her to danger. Where before I was working a job, now I was pursuing a mission.

But did my new mission involve ABC? Rebecca's murder didn't fit the ABC pattern, the most obvious difference being the lack of a note. ABC wasn't shy about taking credit for Celia's abduction and Miles' murder. An ABC riddle even suggested where Miles would be found, and the body was placed where its discovery would impart a message. Nothing like that happened with Rebecca. Another difference is the method by which the victims were killed. Poisoning shows calculation, whereas a shooting, especially one with four gunshots, is a sign of passion. And where Miles and Celia were widely disliked, perhaps even despised, Rebecca seemed like a sweetheart whose next enemy would be her first. Of course my perception of Rebecca is necessarily colored by who I am, and not everyone is like me.

But despite the differences, other things suggested an ABC connection. Jim had pointed me to the newspaper where I first learned of Rebecca's disappearance. A vague reference for sure, but after Rebecca's body turned up I went through the Sun-Times again, every page, every story, every classified ad, and nothing else even remotely pertained to ABC. And there was my connection to Rebecca, and her association with Miles' attorney. ABC had shown a lot of cunning with Miles' murder. Maybe Rebecca's was purposefully different, to throw us off the track. Or not.

The phone rang. "You get the fax?" Amanda asked.

"Unfortunately."

"You think it's one of our murders?"

"I don't know."

"Chicago doesn't think it is. And right now I don't see it either. Probably just a random act."

"Did she ever call you?"

"No. Why would she?"

"I gave her your name. She'd filed a harassment complaint against Miles with the Judicial Inquiry Board."

"No, she never called."

"Since I don't have any other leads, I guess I'll keep working the ABC angle."

"Okay. Continue to report to me."

"If the Chicago cops aren't treating this as an ABC murder, how'd you learn about it so fast?"

"After you asked about her I talked to someone I know in Vernon Hills. I got the news from him."

"I appreciate that."

"You all right, Marty? You sound different."

"I met this woman, Amanda, and I liked her. Very much. And frankly it's hard coming to grips with the evil involved in something like this."

"You need to put those feelings aside, Marty. Idealizing the victim won't help you."

"You don't have any right to tell me how to feel, Amanda."

"That's fine, Marty. But remember, she was shot four times. So she probably pissed someone off, royally. Maybe she wasn't the angel you think she was."

•

Over the next couple of days no solid leads developed. Amanda told me that Chicago assigned a detective to identify every person who had contact with Celia, Miles and Rebecca, but Wash didn't know anything about that, so I suspected someone intentionally misinformed Amanda. There's a fine line between being aggressive and being annoying, and I could see Amanda on either side. But in any event, with so many lawyers in Chicago I doubted anyone could make a complete and accurate list, and even if they could it'd have hundreds of names on it.

While I couldn't do much about ABC until the next meeting, I needed to stay active. One person I wanted to meet was Rebecca's husband, but right then he didn't need the intrusion of another investigator. Instead I visited my client.

"A real tragedy," Judge Dienstag said. "I didn't know the young woman, but the judges I've spoken to thought very well of her."

"That's certainly the consensus."

"Could it be connected to Walter Miles' murder?"

"I don't see how it could." Playing dumb. Or maybe I wasn't playing.

"It's just so odd, a judge and a litigation attorney being murdered within a week of each other."

"But I don't think the murderers are so smart."

"Why not?"

"Leaving Miles in a courthouse was dramatic, but he was found on a Sunday, and the police think he'd been dead less than 24 hours. So that limits the suspects to people who could access the building on a Saturday."

"That's not necessarily true. Walter had a key card to the building, so the murderer could have used that to get in."

"Do you know for certain that Miles had a key card?"

"Yes. About a year ago he sat temporarily in Skokie during a time when a number of judges were on vacation or out ill. So I'm sure he was issued a card then."

"He wouldn't have been required to turn it in when he was done?"

"I don't think so, but you can ask the Sheriff's office to be sure." I later confirmed with Amanda that Miles never returned the card. The Sheriff's office wouldn't talk to me; maybe they figured it was my fault Miles was found on their watch.

"And Rebecca Ellsworth left behind a clue." Not my most creative lie, but occasionally it provokes a reaction.

"Good for her. What's that?"

"I'm not at liberty to say."

"Well, you're a sharp investigator. I'm sure you'll figure things out."

Sharp investigator, am I? Is he motivating, or goading?

The next day was Friday, and over breakfast coffee I reviewed my notes of the entire case, not expecting much, but looking to identify someone, anyone, new to talk to, especially before the weekend. I surprised myself when I found him.

Michael Gelman was an associate with one of those personal injury firms you see advertised on television. Call 555-HURT 24 hours a day, seven days a week and we'll make those dirty scumbags pay up the money you rightfully deserve for your stubbed toe. These firms tend to be high volume, low class. Which didn't necessarily make Gelman a bad guy, just someone who needed a job and probably didn't have a lot of options.

I told the rather disheveled receptionist I'd been in an auto accident, and that someone recommended I see Mr. Gelman. Probably Gelman would have seen me if I played it straight, but he'd get a cut of the recovery on cases he referred into the office, so this seemed a surer bet. The new case trick might not have worked at Markus & Stevens, but at a firm like this, if you have a case, you get in the door, no appointment necessary.

Within a few minutes Michael Gelman came out and invited me back. He was average height, thin, probably late 20s even though his head showed more scalp than hair. He led me to his office, which is best described as efficient in that he could sit and be within reach of a dozen files.

After the introductions he asked "Who referred you to me?"

"Rebecca Ellsworth."

He took an extra blink before responding. "Becca's a great girl. I can't believe what happened to her. She referred you to me?"

"She said you were a good negotiator."

"Really?"

"You sound surprised."

"I guess I never thought I made much of an impression on her." Gelman needed to learn about attorney bravado if he was going to make it in the business.

"She told me about a pretrial you and she had with Judge Miles that was rather noteworthy."

This time two extra blinks. "You're not here about a new case, are you?"

"Afraid not."

"Who are you?"

I handed him my card.

"What are you investigating?" he asked.

"What do you think?"

"I guess either Judge Miles or Rebecca." Yeah, this kid was definitely green, answering questions when he could be doing the asking.

"So tell me about that pretrial."

"Shouldn't I be telling the police what I know?"

"I'm working with them."

"How do I know that?" Suspicious; there's hope for him yet.

"I can give you the name of a police detective to call, if you want to verify. But is that really necessary?"

A knock on the door, and a fiftyish man walked in without waiting for a response. "Mike, I need...oh, I didn't realize you had someone here."

"This is Mr. Bronk. He's looking into..."

"Filing suit against the jerk who rear-ended my car," I said.

"You came to the right place," the man said. "That's our specialty. We've gotten recoveries for thousands of clients. Money for people who deserve it." I think that was a line from their commercial, but I wasn't sure.

"Great. Mike comes highly recommended, so I know I'll get what I'm looking for."

"Well, I'll leave you two alone," he said, and shut the door behind him.

"He doesn't need to know our business," I said to Gelman. "Now, about that pretrial."

"Oh, sure," he said, either forgetting or changing his mind about that verification call. And he told me a story similar to Rebecca's. That she was fine when they were all in chambers together, but that she looked shaken after being alone with Miles.

"Did she say anything to you when she left his chambers?"

"That she had to be somewhere else. And then she ran out of there."

"Did Miles say anything to you about what happened?"

"He said something lame, like it must be that time of the month. Then he repeated a really bad lawyer joke I've heard dozens of time, only he made it specific to women. What do you call a female lawyer neck high in sand?"

"Not enough sand."

"That's the one."

"What'd you do?"

"I laughed. I mean, he's a judge, and even when they say stupid things you have to go along. But I wanted to punch his lights out. I've known Rebecca since law school at DePaul, and anyone who'd hurt her...Anyway, that's what happened."

"You talk to anyone about this?"

"Actually an investigator from the Judicial Inquiry Board interviewed me. And I told some of my buddies from DePaul, and maybe a couple of other guys who knew her too."

In succession I named off the ABCers, but Gelman denied having told them about the incident. Not that denials are always truthful, since even a seemingly righteous guy like Gelman could cover for a friend.

"Anybody else?"

"One other person. And I probably shouldn't have said anything to him, but it sort of slipped out."

"Who's that?"

"My Uncle Dave."

"He a reporter or something."

"No, a judge. Dave Dienstag."

•

So Dienstag knew about Miles and Rebecca. After telling me he didn't know Rebecca. Which was perhaps literally true, but he knew of her.

Despite the misinformation, for now I did nothing. No sense tipping my hand. If Dienstag was the murderer my evidence would come through investigating other sources, not interviewing him. Besides, I wanted to see how long it would take him to call me for another update.

It was now Friday afternoon, my time to deal with the little things I put off the rest of the week. Like clearing out my in box and paying bills. And sorting through the piles of papers and junk that somehow manage to accumulate on my desk.

I tossed out some stray notes and half-bent paper clips before moving to a pile of junk mail. On top was a flyer for a seminar on office finance. I already knew the secret—get paid in advance—so I frisbeed that and three other offers to relieve me of my money into the garbage can. At the bottom of the pile was the ABC membership list Jim had given me. The list he'd printed on his office computer.

Evidence was being processed in Chicago, not Northbrook, so there was no need to involve Amanda. Instead my choices were Crumpton or Washburn.

"When'd you get this list, Bronk?" asked Crumpton after I waved it before his eyes. I couldn't pass up the chance to create work for him.

"A couple days ago."

"You been withholding evidence?"

"No, I just remembered it today."

"I'll be sure the State's Attorney knows about your memory lapse."

"That's horseshit, Crumpton, and you know it. So just log in the evidence and pass it along to the guys who might actually help us solve this thing."

"I'll do my job, all right. But get this straight, Bronk, you're not part of any 'us.' Only people with guts enough to carry a badge are on this team."

"You mean you and I aren't on the same team? And I thought we were the Jordan and Pippen of law enforcement."

Crumpton's phone rang, and he shouted his name into the mouthpiece. His next sounds were "uh huh, uh huh," uttered at one-tenth the decibel level of his greeting. It was either the boss or the wife. I didn't stick around to find out which.

I had some thoughts during the ride back to the office. While I hadn't studied the ABC notes closely, and I don't have a photographic memory, my sense was that they were printed in the same font as the ABC membership list. And I was pretty sure the lab would find they came from the same printer. Even high-end laser printers have flaws or distinguishing markers like typewriters, so a definite match was possible.

But even if the lab found that the ABC notes and the membership list came from the same printer, that didn't mean Jim printed them all. ABC meetings usually began in Jim's office, so all members had access to the printer. Nevertheless I was uneasy that things might point toward Jim. He was a fun-loving guy, maybe a little misguided in his loyalty toward Michigan, but that didn't make him evil.

I was facing a moral dilemma. I considered Jim a friend, and an unlikely murderer. But if the lab came back with a positive on the list and the ABC notes, he'd become an official suspect with the police. I wanted to talk to Jim before Crumpton and his pals got their hooks into him. But if he did do it, and I somehow tipped him off, you could paint a bullseye on my ass.

What the hell, it was Friday afternoon. The perfect time to buy a buddy a beer.

CHAPTER 15

Jim and I met at the bar of the Palmer House Hotel. I figured it would be quieter than the Bar Bar, and thus more conducive to serious discussion. That was before I discovered that a franchising expo was in town, and that the Mary Kay group was headquartered at the hotel. Tables were scarce, but we managed to snare one, under the watchful eye of a blue-haired lady whose sardonic smile suggested that our proper place was the nearest sports bar.

"Good choice to meet here, Marty. You turned on by pink or something?"

"Only pink polyester."

"Then you must be in heaven, my man."

The Mary Kay ladies were running the sole waitress ragged, so I got our beers from the bar. Beck's for me, Heineken for Jim. A good sign; I'd never known a murderer to drink imported.

"You look so serious, Marty," Jim said when I got back. "Anything wrong?"

"I was just thinking about that attorney who turned up dead."

"Yeah, that was a real shame. I knew her."

"Really?"

"Yeah, we had a few cases together. I liked her."

"Never had any problems with her?"

"No, she was real easy to work with. Not like some of the ballbusters out there. Rebecca knew how the game was played. You needed a little extra time, no problem. You messed up, she wouldn't try to embarrass you."

"Any ideas why someone would kill her?"

"Who knows. I'd guess an old boyfriend. Maybe a stalker type."

"How well do you know the other ABCers?"

"Pretty well. Why?"

"Any of them ever talk about doing anything violent?"

"Yeah, a couple of us would have liked to bust up that new quarterback after he threw three interceptions against the Packers. Why, what are you talking about?"

"People connected to the judicial system keep turning up dead or missing. And I'm now a part of a group called Attorneys for the Betterment of the Courts. I know you said that's a phony name, but if there's more behind it than I've been told I'd like to know. I don't want to get involved if some of those guys are carrying reform to an extreme."

"Marty, you need to lose that cop mind set. We're not into murder, we're into having a few laughs."

"The other night, when you said that I should be sure to check the next day's paper, and then I read about Rebecca being missing. I don't know, it got me to thinking."

"You read the Tribune, didn't you?"

"No, I take the Sun-Times."

"Then you missed it. I had a trial last week against a guy I played against in college, an offensive tackle at Ohio State. The Tribune picked up on it, and it got in one of the sports columns. Shit, Marty, did you think I was pointing you to the story about Rebecca? I'm glad you have such a high opinion of us."

I took a big swallow of my Beck's, buying time. "It's not that. Like you said, it's the cop in me. Serves me right for not getting both papers."

Jim finished the last half of his beer in a single gulp. "Thanks for the brew, but I gotta get going."

"I didn't piss you off, did I?"

"No, forget it. You can't help it that you're a dick."

I stared him down, and he gave it right back at me. "Marty," he said after what was probably five seconds but seemed like five minutes, 'dick's' another word for detective, remember."

I let out a good laugh, which was just what I needed. "You got me, Jim. To show you there's no hard feelings, how about I give you a lift back to your place."

"I don't live in Lincoln Park anymore. Now I'm a suburbanite. Morton Grove. Didn't you look at that list I gave you?" Actually I never paid attention to it, except to note the font.

"What's a chick magnet like you doing away from the action?"

"I got a great deal at a foreclosure sale about six months ago. And the house gives me a chance to work with my hands. Can't do much of that in an apartment."

"That's not what you used to say."

"Different kind of hand work, pal. But not to worry, I'm still in practice. Got a hot one lined up for tomorrow night. Stewardess named Katrina."

"That's flight attendant."

"Marty, they'll always be stewardesses to me."

You've got to like an unabashed chauvinist in this day and age. Unless they live alone in a house in the suburbs. A house, no doubt, with a basement.

•

The phone rang at seven the next morning. I'm an early riser, so I was up. But I enjoy the morning quiet, and once the phone rings you never get it back.

"So clue me in on what you've been doing." It was Amanda.

"At seven a.m.?"

"I just got in from a six mile run. Didn't realize it was so early. I must have made good time."

"What do you want to know?"

"I hear you turned something over to the Chicago boys."

"Right. They've got the crime lab."

"So how come you didn't tell me about the list?"

"I'd forgotten about it."

"Who prepared it?"

"Probably Jim Lanter, my law school friend."

"How about meeting me for breakfast? We can go over what you know about this Jim."

"Breakfast, huh? You do know my weak point."

"I'm trained to pick up these things."

We met at Jack's Restaurant on Touhy Avenue in Skokie, a first-rate coffee shop. Nothing fancy, just good, stick-to-the-ribs food, and lots of it. I ordered a three egg omelette, but the eggs must have cloned between the kitchen and my table, because I'd have sworn at least five found their way onto my plate.

Amanda was wearing a red nylon jogging suit, her hair in a pony tail. The same look that turned me to mush at the health club. But I wasn't going to let my thoughts stray again. This was business, serious stuff.

"So could this Jim Lanter be the guy?" she asked.

"No way."

"But you realize there's lots of things pointing in his direction."

"True."

"Tell me about them."

"Okay. First, he's the ABC leader. Second, he knew all three of the victims. Third, I'm pretty sure that the ABC notes and the list he typed for me came from a laser printer, quite possibly the same printer. Fourth, he lives alone in a house in Morton Grove. That's close to where Judge Miles was found, and it's easily accessible to the City. And the killer figures to live alone in a house, given that Celia was held captive in a basement. Fifth, I ran into Jim in Judge Bobb's courtroom around the time the first ABC note turned up there. And sixth, last Tuesday he warned me to be on the lookout for something significant in the next day's paper. Yesterday he explained that he meant something about him in the sports pages, but it's possible he meant the news that Rebecca Ellsworth was missing."

"Marty, you have to admit that's a pretty impressive list of circumstantial evidence."

"But I know Jim, and he's a fun loving, warm-hearted guy. He's no killer."

"We've all come across people we'd never guess would commit a violent crime. Jim could be one of those."

Which reminded me that Jim was pretty mean on the football field. But I would have been too, if the coach had ever let me play.

"But the Rebecca thing doesn't fit," I offered. "Assume Jim has this dark underside, that he's this rabid psychopath trying to rid the judicial system of disrespectful, discourteous people. From everything I've seen and heard Rebecca was gentle and considerate, without an enemy in the world. I haven't heard one bad thing said about her."

"Suppose Lanter had a thing for Rebecca and she wouldn't reciprocate. Or he grabbed the wrong person by mistake, and panicked. There's lots of reasons why he could have done Rebecca even if she doesn't fit the profile."

Amanda was making sense, and if I was on her side of the table I'd have said pretty much the same thing. But still, there was no hard evidence against Jim, and no clear motive.

And there was my gut reaction, which rarely fails me.

"The next ABC meeting is Tuesday," I said. "We might as well see what happens before taking any action. In the meantime I'll see if I can dig anything up on the other members."

"Okay, good."

We turned down a fourth coffee refill. Amanda was headed to the office, and I had to make some calls if I was going to get the information on the ABCers before Tuesday. I walked her to her car, and, as usual, we promised to call if anything came up. I watched as she pulled away, admiring that damn pony tail.

•

The restaurant was less than ten minutes from my old house. In fact Randee and Gail and I used to have Sunday brunch at Jack's, when we didn't go to the Bagel on Devon. I always preferred Jack's, Randee liked the Bagel. Another irreconcilable difference.

Since I was so close I just had to stop by for a quick hello. Randee isn't thrilled when I drop in on a non-visitation day, but she knows I don't do it to cause trouble. I'm simply crazy about my kid, and Randee has resigned herself to indulging me on this point. She realizes that a lot of children face the opposite situation.

Randee answered the door. "Marty, I was just thinking about you."

"Why? You planning to take up archery?"

"Stop joking around. It's about Gail."

Randee walked away from the door and toward the living room, which I took as my cue to enter.

"Let me guess, she wants a nose job."

"Marty!"

"Okay, I'll behave. Lay it on me."

"It's about the bat mitzvah. She doesn't seem interested at all. She's not practicing, and she never even talks about it unless I bring it up first."

"She's probably just nervous, and she's coping by not overpracticing." My apologies to Colleen for not attributing this insight to her.

"Never mind overpracticing, she's not practicing, period. You know this isn't something you can cram for. It's a foreign language, and it requires a lot of work."

"Have you talked to her?"

"Of course. Her standard answers are either 'don't sweat it' or 'whatever.'"

"I'll sit her down for a chat. And if that doesn't work, I'll lay on my threat not to let her date until she's twenty-one."

"Marty, have a talk with Gail, but don't make light of it. This is a big day."

"For her or for you?" I regretted that the second it came out of my big mouth.

"For her! What do you think, this is a big Randeefest?"

"Of course not," I lied.

"It's an important day in her life, one she'll always remember. Our friends and family will be there, and yes, I'd like her to do well, show her off a little bit. If that makes me something bad, please tell me."

"No Randee, that doesn't make you bad." Frankly, I thought Randee's mention of showing Gail off confirmed that this bat mitzvah was as much about Randee as Gail. Even so I sensed the need for a strategic retreat, before Gail's Big Day became yet another round of Randee and Marty's Rumble in Rogers Park.

"What's going on down here." Gail was wearing jeans and a University of Iowa sweatshirt.

"What's with that?" Being an insufferable University of Illinois man, wearing a rival's clothes is sure to get a reaction from me.

"Katie's sister goes to school there. What are you doing here?"

"Just in the neighborhood."

"Oh."

"Want to go for a ride? I need to pick up a few things at the store."

"Okay." I usually end up getting a little something for Gail on these excursions. Today an Illinois sweatshirt topped my shopping list.

We left with Randee's blessing. "Remember that conversation we had last week about practicing for the bat mitzvah?" I asked Gail once we were in the car.

"Yeah."

"Did it do any good?"

"No."

"Well, I know your mom's a little hyper about this thing. I just want to tell you that I know you'll do great."

Gail must have expected more, but instead I turned the radio on to the classic rock station and hummed along to the Talking Heads. "Is that it?

“Of course. How long ago do you think it was?”

“I don’t know. Before TV?”

“Very funny.” Though it was around the time we got our first color set.

“What was it like?”

“I’m kind of a perfectionist, in case you didn’t know...”

“I never would have guessed.”

“No sarcasm needed. I was that way even back then. So I practiced real hard. The rabbi gave me a record with my haftorah section on it, and I’d keep playing it and repeating what was on it until I got the words just right. Some of the more difficult passages I’d keep doing over and doing over, and I’d get real upset when I messed up.”

“So how’d you do?”

“I couldn’t help but do great since I had the thing memorized. I could have done it blindfolded. Some people told me I didn’t miss a word.”

“Oh.”

“But you know what? As great as I did, I can’t say that I had fun. I mean, it’s an important day, and not just a big party. But I realized later that the roof wouldn’t have fallen if I’d goofed on a few words. And something else that didn’t dawn on me till later. Hardly any of our relatives speak Hebrew.”

“So if I don’t do it perfectly...”

“Almost no one will know. And those who will know don’t expect perfection.”

“So why’s Mom on my case to practice all the time?”

“She just wants you to do well. And don’t get me wrong, so do I. You do have to practice.”

“But I don’t have to give the best bat mitzvah of all time.”

“No you don’t. Last time I checked there was no bat mitzvah hall of fame.”

“How about talking to Mom so she’ll chill.”

“The best way to get her off your back is for you to practice. But just our little secret; she doesn’t know a word of Hebrew. So work on your haftorah a half hour a day, tell her it’s going great, and she’ll lay off. I guarantee.”

"Phat."

"Did you say fat?"

"No, phat, with a 'ph.' It means cool."

"If I was you I wouldn't use that word to your mom."

We did our shopping, but not without controversy. I told Gail that I wanted to buy her an Illinois sweatshirt, but she said the kids weren't wearing college sweatshirts, and the only reasons she was wearing the Iowa shirt was that Katie's parents got it for her, and she was going over to their house later and didn't want to hurt their feelings. A sensible approach, and a rare time when Gail suggested a way to save money.

But that didn't stop me from my mission. What did stop me was that the store was out of Illinois shirts (or maybe they just didn't stock them), though they had plenty of Michigans and Notre Dames. Gail again told me to forget about it, then in the next breath said the Michigan one was kind of cool. No way I'd buy her that. I just don't get the Michigan mystique, seeing as I'm not into ugly football helmets and underachieving basketball teams. Gail was entering the pout zone when we came up with a compromise—a Northwestern shirt. Sometimes a parent just has to take a stand.

We finished shopping, stopped at Dunkin' Donuts, then headed to the house. Gail showed off the Northwestern shirt to Randee, who is so used to me buying clothes for Gail that she doesn't bother with the spoiling-her-rotten speech anymore. Gail then ran up to her room, no doubt suffering from telephone withdrawal.

"Did you have a little talk with her?" Randee asked once our daughter was out of earshot.

"Yeah, it's taken care of. Ward Cleaver strikes again."

"What did you say?"

"That's between me and Gail. But don't worry, she'll practice."

"You blamed everything on me, right?"

"Randee, you know that's not my style."

"But are you sure she'll start practicing?"

"You worry too much. And as much as I'd love to resolve your insecurities, I have work to catch up on. Bye Gail," I shouted upstairs.

"Bye Dad, thanks," she yelled back.

"Oh, one last think Randee," I said as I neared the door. "Be sure to add Colleen Tobolski to the guest list. That's T-O-B-O-L-S-K-I."

"You're really bringing her?"

"Yeah, why not."

"You haven't been seeing her that long. And won't she feel out of place?"

"Why, because she's not Jewish?"

"No, because she won't know anyone there."

"She knows me, she knows Gail. Besides, if I go stag your cousins Roberta and Frieda will be all over me." I'm no Tom Cruise, but Randee's cousins have had the hots for me for years. Which wouldn't be bad for my ego, except they look like the offensive linemen I used to practice against.

"You're imagining things about my cousins," Randee lied. "But if you want to bring someone, go ahead."

"Thanks for your permission. I'll give you a call later in the week, to see how our Hebrew scholar is doing."

"Oh, Marty?"

"Yeah."

"Thanks for trying to set Gail straight."

"No problem. But I didn't just try, I succeeded."

"I hope so. But if she doesn't get down to it this week, I'll hold you responsible."

I was pretty sure she was serious.

CHAPTER 16

Next day I phoned Wash. Nothing new on Rebecca's case, except that her purse was found, with her wallet and money inside. That ruled out robbery as a motive.

It was a Sunday, the nicest day we'd seen all year, and work could wait. Colleen and I started on Michigan Avenue, window shopping, which was about all I could afford, assuming it was a small window. From there we strolled along the lakefront, from Oak to Fullerton. The players were out in force at the North Avenue chess pavilion, one of my favorite spots in the city. It's a three-tiered structure with inlaid chess boards, where you can spend an afternoon matching wits and appreciating either the lake's beauty or the beauties hanging out at the lake, depending on your inclination. Colleen remembered my humiliation of Fred Nickles and encouraged me to play, but this was a day for holding hands, not grabbing pawns.

Somewhere near Armitage, Colleen asked if I was seeing anyone else.

"Of course not."

"But you look at other women, right?"

What's the old saying, just because a guy's married doesn't mean he's blind. Hell, we weren't even married. "No, I only have eyes for you."

"Cut the crap," she said good naturedly. "What about this Amanda you're working with."

"What about her?"

"Is she pretty?"

"Nowhere near as pretty as you."

"Marty, I'm not fishing for compliments."

"The truth? She's not bad."

"Not bad, eh. That means she turns you on."

"We're professionals, Colleen. She's never shown any interest in me."
A reasonably accurate, albeit evasive, response.

"Why are you bringing Amanda up? Let me guess, it's a women's
thing."

"Just curious. So do you and Amanda figure to work on this case
awhile?"

"I'm really operating independently. I just coordinate with her."

"I'll bet," she smiled.

"Enough yanking my chain already."

"I'll bet Amanda does that too, but she doesn't call it a chain."

"Sexual repartee doesn't become you, Colleen."

"What does?"

I laid a big wet kiss on her. "Practically everything else."

"I hope something breaks on the case soon."

"I have a meeting on Tuesday. Hopefully something will happen then."
Something happened, all right. But on Monday, not Tuesday.

•

Bryant Weiss called at ten-thirty Monday morning and asked if I could
come right over. Jim Lanter had been arrested for the murder of Judge
Miles.

Ten minutes later Weiss led me to Jim's office. It looked as disordered
as a teenager's bedroom.

"The police were waiting for Jim when he got in this morning," said
Weiss, "then they arrested him. They had a search warrant for the office.
Really tore the place apart, as you can see."

"Did they take anything?"

"The printer, and some papers, but I don't know what they were. They
looked everywhere—his desk drawers, the filing room, his briefcase."

"Yeah, the cops mean business when they get a warrant."

"I've been calling around to some good criminal lawyers we know, but
Jim asked me to get you here right away."

"Why?"

"He said you used to be a cop, so maybe by looking around you can figure out what's going on. Maybe help him out."

"I'll take a look, but there's nothing much I can do. This isn't like a
parking ticket."

"He knows. He also thought if you knew the detectives, you could put

in the good word for him. Maybe they'd go easier on him, or even realize how ridiculous this is."

"Which detectives conducted the search?"

"I didn't catch their names. But two seemed to be in charge. A tall
woman and a loud black guy."

"I'll talk to them, see if I can get any information."

"Good. Can you imagine Jim killing anyone?"

"No." Not even with the information I knew.

Bryant left and I looked around Jim's office for a few minutes, mainly
because I was asked to, not because I thought I'd discover anything. As
expected I didn't find any ABC materials; the cops would have taken
everything related to the group. The only thing the cops missed was a
Sullivan's law directory, with the name Rebecca Ellsworth highlighted in
yellow. Judge Miles' name was not highlighted.

Josh Pindler poked his head in Jim's office as I was wrapping up my
look. "I can't believe Jim would do this," he said. "I'm like in shock."

"It is hard to believe. Do you have anything that could help Jim?"

"I don't think so, unless they want me to be a character witness. You
know...never mind."

"Go on, what were you going to say?"

"I shouldn't say this, and don't take this wrong, but if anyone in this
office was to do anything violent I'd have guessed Bryant."

"Why do you say that?"

"Jim's always even-keeled. Bryant's the one who's up and down. I
mean, he's still upset about losing a big case, and that was almost a month
ago."

"You're not suggesting that Bryant's behind this?"

"Not at all. But neither is Jim. I'm sure."

After finishing at Jim's I walked back to my office, which gave me time
to sort things through. And the more I thought the angrier I got. Amanda
and Crumpton had pulled the rug out from under me. The next ABC
meeting, just one day away, would be the one when I'd get a real handle
on things. When I'd know the guys well enough to ask the questions I
couldn't have gotten away with earlier.

Once in the office I started to dial up Crumpton, to let him know what
I thought of his tactics, but hung up before finishing the number. I'd
already fought with him too many times to get any satisfaction out of
another go-round. I needed a fresh target. I phoned Amanda, but she was-

n't available, and then didn't return my call for two hours. I don't know if that made me any angrier, but the wait sure didn't cool me off.

"What the hell are you doing, Amanda?"

"Putting away a murderer. You have a problem with that, Marty?"

"I told you to wait until after the next ABC meeting. And I also told you that Jim's not your guy."

"I didn't realize you'd been elected State's Attorney. Next time we'll be sure to clear it with you first."

"My point is, I was working to identify the real killer, and if you'd given me more time I might have done it. And what about Forrester's death? Have you looked into that?"

"I looked at it. It was a suicide, not a murder."

"I know the case was closed as a suicide, but I think there's something else there, something connected to the ABC murders."

"Lanter's your friend, so you're biased on this. I'm telling you, he's the guy."

"How can you be so sure?"

"I probably shouldn't tell you this, but I do owe you something. We found a note in his briefcase."

"What kind of note?"

"An ABC note. Threatening another murder in the next twenty-four hours."

"Who was it directed to?"

"It wasn't addressed to anyone, it was just a note."

"Why would he have an unaddressed note in his briefcase?"

"He was probably going to leave it somewhere, maybe with a judge or at a lawyer's office."

"You're reaching. Anyone could slip a note in his briefcase."

"There's something else too. We found a University of Michigan pin in Miles' car."

"Why didn't you tell me this sooner?"

"We don't have to tell you everything, you know."

"Is the pin Lanter's?"

"He denies owning a pin. But murderers have been known to lie. Face it, Marty, everything we have points to this guy."

"I assume his house was searched too."

"Of course."

"Any poisons turn up?"

"We're still analyzing some things. But we did find a gun."

"So? Miles wasn't shot."

"The Glagovic woman was threatened with a gun, and I'm sure one was used on Miles too."

"That's a stretch, Amanda."

"And of course we'll be checking to see if it matches the gun used to kill Rebecca Ellsworth."

"Is there a bathroom in Lanter's basement?"

"No; who puts a bathroom in a basement?"

"Celia said she was kept in a basement and that she had use of a bathroom."

"So, she was wrong about where she was kept."

"How can someone be mistaken about being in a basement?"

"I don't know, she's a little nutty. Or maybe Lanter's working with someone else. That's one of the reasons we do this interrogation thing, in case you forgot. To fill in the missing pieces."

"This is bullshit, Amanda."

"No Marty, this is solid, aggressive police work."

There was no point going on with the conversation. Amanda was certain she'd caught the killer, and nothing I said would change anything. At least I'd gotten some information from her. And vented.

I knew what I was going to do next. I'd need Jim's okay, but with his freedom, if not his life, at stake, I thought he'd agree.

CHAPTER 17

Blake Cardiff was the criminal lawyer to go to if you wanted a first-rate defense without a lot of glitz. There were plenty of guys in town with bigger names and flashier images, but most of them made the news by getting convictions overturned on appeal. Blake Cardiff's clients rarely had to appeal.

I met Cardiff at his office at seven o'clock the next morning, the only time he could squeeze me in. He was about fifty, and while he still had some hair on the sides and back of his head I had the feeling his barber would soon be losing a customer. He was average height and slightly built, but the running and fitness magazines in his waiting room suggested that his was a healthful frailty. He was wearing a white shirt and a blue and red repp tie. A gray, single-breasted suit jacket hung from the inside door knob. Neither a ring nor a Rolex was anywhere to be seen.

"I was pleased to receive your call," Cardiff started, "but I must say I'm confused. I know of you as a private detective, but Jim seems to believe you're an attorney."

"I have a law license, but I don't practice."

"I see. Why does Jim think you are in practice?"

"I was doing some undercover work, for the court, and needed to assume the role of attorney."

"For the court and not the police?"

"We're getting into a delicate area here, Mr. Cardiff. Let me explain why I called." I went over my infiltration of ABC and my role in tracking down the killer. I also stated my belief that Jim was not the murderer, and that I thought I could help establish his innocence.

"I'm not sure I can use you, seeing how you worked for the police.

Besides, I have certain private detectives whom I regularly employ."

"But none of them know and have the confidence of the other ABCers."

"Aren't you a witness for the State?"

"Witness to what? So far the worst thing I can say about ABC is that they're lousy tippers. Besides, I've expressed my feelings to the cops in rather strong terms, so I'd be surprised if they want, or expect, me to be part of their case."

"How do I know you're still not working for the police?"

"To spy on the defense team? Even O.J.'s attorneys never claimed that."

"Quite so. Actually I've checked up on you, and you have an excellent reputation for integrity. So how is that you expect to clear Jim?"

"I don't want to get into anything specific. But the first thing is to call an emergency session of ABC. I assume the police have the names of the members?"

"I believe their names were on some of the confiscated papers."

"What's Jim's explanation for the note in his briefcase?"

"So you know about that. Very good. Jim says he has no idea how it got there. He says he's one of those types who keeps putting papers in and doesn't take any out until the briefcase is stuffed. So the note could have been put in there anytime within the past month."

"Does Jim have any idea what's going on?"

"None. But he can't believe any of the ABCers are capable of murder."

"So, do you object to some unofficial help?"

"Are you looking to be compensated for your services?"

"Jim and I can work that out. Once he gets off."

"I like your approach. I see no problem with your assistance. But I don't need to know everything you're doing. Just tell me when you get something."

"Good. Tell Jim to keep his chin up."

"Oh, he did ask me to tell you something."

"What's that?"

"That he never thought he'd see the day when he'd ask a third-stringer to come off the bench for help."

•

I called the ABCers as soon as I got back to my office. It wasn't yet eight o'clock and none of them were in, so I left messages on their voice mail or answering machines to call me first thing. The police would talk to them before too long, and I hoped for one last meeting before then. Of course Jim's arrest was a big story; it led off the ten o'clock news the previous night, and was page one in that morning's Sun-Times and Tribune. So it's not like I'd be breaking the news.

While waiting for the return calls I thought more about the ethical implications of what I was doing. I'd been working with the police, but not for the police, and I thought that was a significant difference. I realized this wasn't the old west and that I wasn't going to be deputized, but in a sense I was in a lesser position than an informant, since I wasn't even getting paid for my information. I was free to leave at any time, and now that time had arrived. Besides, the police didn't need my help anymore, since they believed they'd found Miles' murderer. And I wasn't going to divulge any police secrets. Still, I felt uneasy. Thanks in large part to my efforts, the police made an arrest, and now I was trying to clear that very person.

My real client had been the Circuit Court of Cook County, who hired me—again without tangible compensation—to locate Judge Miles and oversee the police investigation. Helping Jim's defense wasn't inconsistent with that mission, since I was still trying to identify the murderer. If Jim really was the killer, then my future efforts would confirm that. If he wasn't the killer, I hoped to get enough exculpatory evidence to clear an innocent man, and identify the guilty one. So again I didn't see a conflict.

And Rebecca's murder still hadn't been solved.

At eight-fifteen Will Rockland called. He'd already hooked up with the rest of the ABCers, and they were meeting for breakfast at the Marquette Inn on Adams Street in fifteen minutes. I told him I'd be there. I didn't ask why my invitation was so late in arriving.

I got to the restaurant a few minutes late, and the guys were already seated at a round table in the corner. A waitress wasted no time in taking our orders.

"How can the cops think Jim would kill anyone?" asked Scott Anders. "Just because he knew Miles and Celia? We all did." Everyone nodded.

"Not only us, probably hundreds of other lawyers knew them too," said Will.

"Jim could have done it," said Dennis. Everyone froze. "Could have bored them to death with his football stories." The guys laughed harder than the joke warranted, but it temporarily loosened the tension.

"Didn't you used to be a cop?" Jerry Grieg asked me, once things settled down.

"Yeah, a detective."

"So give us some insight. What's going on here?"

"I made a few calls, and found out something that hasn't been made public. The killer has been leaving notes, and signing them ABC." Jaws dropped, heads shook and eyes blinked. In other words, everyone acted surprised by the news. Convincingly so.

Finally Will spoke up. "The cops don't think we had anything to do with this, do they?"

"One of their jobs is to gather information," I replied. "I'm sure they'll be talking to each of us soon."

"What do we do next?" asked Jerry.

"Everyone has to do some soul searching," I said, "and think about whether you've been holding any grudges against Celia and Miles. And maybe Rebecca too. Or if you know of any other members who do. You also need to think about whether you've ever discussed using violence, whether anyone heard those discussions, or if you've heard anyone talking in those terms."

The food arrived, and the table went silent. Once everything was served I continued. "I know the police routine on cases like this. If any of you want to talk to me privately, I'll be happy to give some tips on how to act and, more importantly, the things you shouldn't say. The cops don't fool around in multiple murder cases. You say the wrong thing and, even if you're innocent, you'll be in for a hard time."

All the guys had ordered hearty breakfasts, like pancakes or three egg omelettes. But no one finished more than half their food. Except me.

During breakfast conversation eventually drifted away from Jim. Somehow talk progressed from Blake Cardiff to Blake Edwards to the Pink Panther to other childhood cartoons. You didn't have to be a practicing psychologist to understand what was happening, but I was amused that this group of normally self-assured, egotistical lawyers had turned into a blathering bunch who couldn't decide whether The Flintstones or The Jetsons was the more clever.

As we left the restaurant I repeated my offer to talk privately with anyone who wanted to go over the do's and don'ts of being interrogated. I knew I'd get some takers. I hoped I'd get some information.

I didn't know how much longer I had before Crumpton dried up my sources, so while I wanted to get back to the office and hear from the ABCers, I detoured and walked the short distance to the Daley Center and

Judge Dienstag.

"I find it incredible that a lawyer would be behind this," said the judge.

"Now Judge, I don't need to remind you about innocent until proven guilty, do I?"

"I never practiced criminal law, although I do know that much. But apart from being a judge I'm also a human, and the human part thinks the police must have a pretty good case to arrest someone." Judge Dienstag got up from his chair and looked out the window. A bunch of pigeons flew by.

"Anyway," he continued while still staring out, "I guess your work is over."

"Actually there's a loose end. Do you know anybody at Markus & Stevens who'll do you a favor?"

"I suppose so, but what for?"

"I need to do some cross checking on Rebecca Ellsworth's cases. I've already tried them, and they weren't too cooperative, although Hicks Pepper III sends his regards."

"The only thing you'll get out of Pepper is a whiff of whatever he had for lunch. From both ends. Haven't they charged this Lanter with the attorney's murder too?"

"No. Do you think they're connected?"

"I don't know. I figured, the two murders being so proximate in time, they were related. But that's just an amateur talking. Still, I don't see why you want to pursue this further. I hired you to help in the Miles investigation, and now an arrest has been made. I didn't ask you to look into the lawyer's murder."

"I'm doing this one on my own. It's important to me."

"Do you have any suspects?"

"Only in a general sense. For example, some people haven't been entirely truthful where Rebecca's concerned."

"Am I supposed to be reading something into the stare you've fixed on me?"

I hadn't consciously stared, but I don't doubt doing so. "Last time I was here you said you never heard of Rebecca. But I have it on authority that you knew she'd had a problem with Miles."

"I know Miles had apparently committed certain indiscretions, but I don't know the names of the victims. She was one?"

"Yes."

"So what is it that you're thinking?"

"Nothing more than that you are one of innumerable people connected to both Miles and Rebecca."

"I don't think that's entirely it. But go ahead, do what you need to do. I wanted a first-rate investigator, so I'll have to accept the consequence that suspicion will be wide-ranging. You wanted to talk to someone at Markus & Stevens, I'll call Whit Lamberton over there."

"Thanks."

Judge Dienstag called Lamberton, explained what I needed, then put me on the phone. Lamberton sounded leery, and I half-expected his next words to be "not interested," like I was a telemarketer trying to get him to switch long distance companies. But he agreed to help. I told him I'd be there in fifteen minutes.

So my visit with Dienstag was a success on two fronts. I got a new source at Markus & Stevens. And I let Dienstag know I was still on the case. Of course he now thought I was on his case, and that wasn't really my plan. But maybe the change in status quo would lead him to make a mistake.

Next stop was Judge Bobb. "I knew it was possible an attorney could do this," he said, shaking his head, "but I really didn't believe that's how it'd turn out."

"If you ask me," Celia jumped in, "there's a whole lot more out there to watch for. No respect, everything me, me, me."

"But Lanter never gave you a problem, did he?" asked the judge.

"Who knows," replied Celia, "I pay attention to sale prices, not lawyers' faces."

"What'd you tell the cops?" I asked. "Could Lanter have been the one who kidnapped you?"

"They haven't asked."

"Really?" Even though Celia's kidnapper wore a mask, she'd be able to identify his body type. Especially if it was Jim, who's a lot larger than average. The cops could even have taken Celia to Jim's house, to confirm the basement where she was held. Maybe they'd eventually get around to talking to her. Or maybe they'd had their fill of her and figured they'd make their case without her and her rosy observations.

From there it was on to Markus & Stevens. Valerie's hair and nails were both two shades lighter than I'd remembered.

"I like the new look," I lied.

"Oh no, you're not here for Mr. Pepper again, are you?"

"Hicks the Third? No, this time I have an appointment with Whit the First."

"Mr. Lamberton? Are you in some kind of trouble?"

"Why do you ask?"

"He's our top white collar criminal attorney." A cynic could interpret that two ways.

Valerie phoned Lamberton's secretary, who came out and led me to a large office, not quite in the corner, but close.

Lamberton stood up and gave me a frosty handshake. He was a few years older than me, and fairly well put together. Maybe six-two, 215 pounds. The outside linebacker type.

"Judge Dienstag tells me you're working with the authorities on Rebecca Ellsworth's murder." I nodded, and he continued. "Even so, if I didn't have such respect for Judge Dienstag I wouldn't be inclined to give you anything without a warrant or a court order."

I wasn't in the mood for any more of the Markus & Stevens attitude. "Cut the crap, Lamberton. If you help me it's out of fear, not respect."

Lamberton tilted back in his chair until his head practically touched the window behind him. "Just what is it that you want?"

"A list of cases that Ms. Ellsworth was working on, going back two years."

"And may I ask why you need that?"

"You may certainly ask." I stared at him, stroking my chin. I needed a shave; my early meeting with Cardiff threw my grooming schedule off.

"Well," he finally said after nearly a minute of silence.

"I said you may ask. I didn't say I would answer."

"Look, I'm too busy to play sophomoric games here..."

"I'm not playing a game, Lamberton. As part of my investigation I need a list of Rebecca's cases. That's all you need to know. Now, if you will assure me that you'll help, I'll be on my way, never again to impose my persuasive powers on you." I folded my hands in front of me, and caught myself flexing my biceps.

"We must be talking about dozens of cases, if not more."

"And your billing isn't computerized, right? Come on, all you need to bring up that information is the right keystroke. Besides, I'm only interested in case names and docket numbers. You can delete all the other stuff. Now that can't be too hard, right?"

"Sally!" he barked into his phone and told her what I needed. He listened to what Sally had to say, then hung up. "It will be ready for you in an hour. Pick it up at the reception desk."

I got up from my seat. "Thanks for the help, Whit. Don't worry, I won't spoil your image by letting on that you did a good deed."

"Bronk."

"Yeah, Lamberton."

"I know you're just doing your job, but you don't have to be such an asshole."

"Let me ask you something, Whit. When you were growing up did the other kids tease you about your name? Maybe called you witless?"

"Out!"

Bronk makes another new friend.

•

While killing an hour at Starbucks I mused whether I was wasting my time looking for an ABC angle to Rebecca's murder. But despite the differences between Rebecca and Miles, I decided to go forward. Dienstag was right that the timing of the murders raised a red flag. Rebecca's name being highlighted in Jim's directory also bothered me. A yellow flag, so to speak. And even if I failed to find an ABC connection, I could stumble across something which would lead me to someone else.

After getting the list of Rebecca's cases from Markus & Stevens it was back to the Daley Center, where I had Judge Dienstag call someone in the clerk's office to print out the records on her cases. Then lunch, coincidentally at a restaurant in the same building as the Markus & Stevens office, and back again to the Daley Center to pick up the latest information. Then to Starbucks again for two grande-sized coffees to go, to get me through the afternoon, and finally to my office. Martin Bronk, human ping pong ball.

I cross-referenced the records, looking for connections between Rebecca, Judge Miles and any of the ABCers, including Jim. The closest I found was a trial before Miles eight months earlier, Jerry Grieg on one side, Markus & Stevens on the other, although there was no indication that Rebecca had worked on the case.

Markus & Stevens listed approximately 60 cases Rebecca had worked on, five of which reached trial. One of those was before Miles, about a year earlier, but according to the court record the case was dismissed pursuant to settlement. The plaintiff's attorney was a firm I wasn't familiar with, Neill & Cobb. Since an agreement to settle is unlikely to produce enemies, and the records didn't describe Rebecca's role in the case, I moved on.

Rebecca was opposed by an ABCer in seven of her cases, and each ABCer had at least one case against her. I couldn't know the extent of Rebecca's involvement in these cases without reviewing her firm's files, but those were confidential under the attorney-client privilege, and even Judge Dienstag couldn't help me there. Markus & Stevens, like most large firms, typically assigned two or three attorneys to a case. So the fact that Rebecca's name was attached to a case didn't tell me whether her role was active enough to have earned any enemies.

Rebecca had worked with a number of the firm's partners over the past two years, but Hicks Pepper III was lead attorney in the one case she had against Jim Lanter.

So here's where I stood. From my work after Miles' death I already knew that every ABCer, except Scott Anders, had tried cases before Miles. Rebecca had worked on one case which ended up in a trial before Miles, but it settled, and an ABCer wasn't on the other side. Jerry Grieg tried a case against Markus & Stevens before Miles, but Rebecca hadn't worked on that case. I hadn't considered the motions Miles heard when he served as a motion judge, because those would be too numerous to reference and analyze. Nor was Celia figured in, though I was pretty sure every ABCer had had some dealings with her.

I hoped my word processor did flow charts.

The coffee had done its job; I'd worked through till six o'clock without so much as a yawn. After finishing with the final printout I turned on the thirteen inch TV I keep on top of the file cabinet. My plan being to watch through the sports, then head home.

A guy on the northwest side was holding his mother-in-law and his postal carrier hostage, so Jim's arrest had been bumped from the lead. But it was the number two story, with a reporter live outside area three headquarters. And videotape of an interview with Amanda.

"The suspect was identified thanks to a plan we developed," she said. "We succeeded in infiltrating a secret organization of which the accused was the apparent leader, and through that learned of his alleged involvement in the two murders."

We developed a plan! And we infiltrated! And that talk about a secret organization—Amanda made them sound like a wacko militia group.

Besides, what was she doing talking on TV; the Chicago police department has a news affairs division with communication specialists to handle the media. First the rush to arrest, and now this grab for credit. I did-
n't like the way this thing was playing out.

And Amanda created another problem for me. Now that she blew my
cover I could forget about getting anything more out of ABC. Although I
just realized that none of the guys had called me since our breakfast meeting. The police must have already gotten to them, including the fact of my
infiltration.

But maybe I could salvage the ABC situation. Playing a hunch, I found
them in a corner booth at the Bar Bar. The last time I'd seen faces like
theirs was the locker room junior year of college, after losing to
Wisconsin 23-22 on a last second field goal.

"Okay guys, it's time for me to come clean," I said.

"It's a little late for that, don't you think," said Scott Anders.

"Yeah, excuse our poor manners in not buying you a round," added
Will Rockland.

"All right, here's the deal," I said. "I started off working with the cops.
But now I'm out of there—they figure they have their guy. I've told them
I don't think Jim did it, and I have no reason to believe any of you did it
either." The last part was true, but only to a point, which is why I needed
to keep communications open. "Anyway, now I'm working to clear Jim.
Go ask Cardiff if you want—I'm part of their team."

"Go on, beat it," said Jerry Grieg. "You must take us for idiots. You've
lied to us, betrayed us. Especially Jim, who was supposed to be an old
friend."

"Wait a minute," said Will. "Cardiff wouldn't use Bronk if he had any
doubts."

"Maybe Cardiff's not as smart as everyone thinks. Maybe Bronk took
him in too." That was Jerry again, his voice still edgy.

"Just what can you do for Jim?" asked Dennis.

"I'm going to keep digging. There's got to be a connection between
someone and all the victims. I'd like to speak to each of you individual-
ly, talk to you about Jim, Rebecca and Judge Miles. The more information I have the better the chance I'll find something to help Jim."

"How do we know you're not still working for the cops?"

"Let me ask you something. When the cops interviewed you, did they
tell you that ABC had been infiltrated?" They nodded. "Why would they

tell you that if I was still working for them?"

"We need to stick together on this," said Will, looking around the table. "Let's do this. We'll talk things over, maybe take a group vote, then let Bronk know in the morning what we decide."

"Fair enough," I said.

I had remained standing during our discussion, so I got moving once the guys went back to their drinking. From the car I called Colleen, hoping to hear a friendly voice, which I did, only it was the taped version. I left a message. For some reason I just wanted to kick back and listen to the latest problems facing the law school kids.

I was halfway home when I got paged. The number wasn't familiar to me.

"Law Office," they answered.

"This is Bronk."

"Bronk, it's Cardiff. You got anything for me?"

"Not yet. You're working pretty late." It was approaching seven-thirty, definitely past my office hours.

"I've got a full plate tomorrow. Including Jim's preliminary hearing. Can you be there?"

"Sure, but why?"

"It'll give you a chance for a face-to-face with Jim."

"Good idea. I have some questions for him."

"And I know Jim wants to talk to you. The hearings's at ten." He gave me the courtroom number, then hurried me off the phone. That's the thing about a full plate, no time to linger.

CHAPTER 18

The next morning something was wrong in my office. The legal pad I always leave on the right corner of my desk was missing. Well, I thought, the cleaning woman must have misplaced it. But when I neared my desk I saw an envelope on the chair seat.

The note inside defined succinct: "Easy as 1, 2, 3. ABC."

Maybe ABC was gloating over his three victims, or saying that getting into my office was simple, a piece of cake. But whether or not the note had a literal meaning, I took it as a warning that ABC had the power to mess with me. Which fit the brevity of the message; the shortest ones can be the most mysterious, and hence the most effective.

One thing about the note; it seemed to get Jim off the hook. Not that the cops would be convinced. They'd figure anyone could have created the note, including me. Although this note was different than the others, it being formed from numbers and letters which looked as if they were cut from newspaper headlines, and then taped onto a piece of paper.

I performed a quick office inventory, and the only things missing, besides my note pad, were the two CD-ROMs I kept next to the computer. One contained an assortment of computer games, the other an encyclopedia. Retail value maybe $50, so I assumed their disappearance was symbolic.

Speaking of computers, I'd have expected the intruder to take my floppy disks. I suppose he could have brought his own and copied my computer files onto them, but he'd have been better served to steal mine. Then he'd not only know what I was working on, I'd also be without my work product. The floppies were in my desk drawer, easily found, so maybe this was yet another message. The thief didn't care what I was doing, because I'd never catch up to him.

While I was thinking this through, Will Rockland called. I was in again with ABC. The consensus was, if I was okay for Cardiff, I was okay for them. I'm always pleased when my power of persuasion works. And a little surprised, too. We'd get together at noon at ABC headquarters, meaning Jim's office. As opposed to the ABC conference center, the Bar Bar.

First I had Jim's hearing. When I was a cop I'd regularly attend hearings at the criminal courts building at 26th and California, but I hadn't been there in years. I sort of missed the old place, like you miss a crotchety uncle who seems to hate you, but who always comes through with the perfect birthday gift.

I met Cardiff in the first floor courtroom, and he led me in back to a small interview room. Jim wasn't exactly GQ in his tan-colored jail uniform, the letters "DOC" stenciled on his pant leg. Despite the circumstances he gave me a big grin and a firm, dry handshake.

"Marty, what's that saying about the enemy being amongst us?" Jim's tone was more amused than accusatory.

"I was never your enemy."

"Let me guess. That whole scene in Billy Bob's courtroom, the contempt, that was a set-up, right?"

"Pretty convincing, no?"

"Not bad. Anyway, I'm glad your scheme worked. Someone's framing me, and now you're in a position to help."

"Any idea who?"

"Unfortunately, not a clue."

"That's not a good start."

"I'll bet you're thinking it's someone in ABC. But I know those guys, Marty. The only thing they shoot is the shit."

"No shooting was involved, just poison."

"Don't get literal on me. Let me explain about us. All the guys bitch and moan about the unnecessary bullshit. The judges who bully and embarrass lawyers when they could just as easily give them a pass. The lawyers who'd rather see you squirm than cut you a break. The clerks and deputies who get a high pushing us around. Even the clients who see us only as sharks, as mouthpieces. So yeah, we'd all like to see some things changed. But not out of some social concern for our colleagues and the judicial process."

"Then why?"

"Because we all want to enjoy life, have a good laugh or two. We've been forced by the passage of time to earn a living, but there's no reason we shouldn't be able to enjoy our work. But all the goddam bullshit eats away at you."

"Do any of your colleagues feel stronger about this than you?"

"I think Will feels this the most. But I've seen him walk away from bar fights. He doesn't have a violent bone in his body."

"So in your opinion no one in ABC is capable of this?"

"No way."

"Can you think of anyone, and I mean anyone, who'd want to frame you?"

"Marty, you know me, I'm the life of the party. Even Ohio State guys like me."

"Early on you told me ABC was only a social group. But Judge Dienstag showed me a letter ABC had sent him."

"We never sent a letter to Dienstag."

"I saw it."

Jim thought for a minute. "Let me back up a bit. When we first got together and decided it'd be fun to meet every week the married guys needed a story for their wives. So we came up with Attorneys for the Betterment of the Courts. I made up some stationary on the office computer. Periodically I'd mail things to the guys, phony newsletters, or copies of letters ABC supposedly sent to the newspapers, judicial commissions and so on. I even made up a dues statement. But it was all a show for the wives. I probably did a letter to Dienstag, but I wouldn't have sent it to him. Unless I mailed it by accident, or my secretary sent it out."

"The letter to Dienstag had a return address which I tracked to a mailbox center. What's that about?"

"One of the guys already had the box. I think Grieg. He said we could use the address on our mailings."

"How do you explain the note in your briefcase?"

"I can't even tell you how many people could have slipped something in there. When I'm in court I leave the briefcase unattended while I'm up at the bench. So really anybody could have put it there."

"What about the gun in your house?"

"I don't own a gun."

"You're saying someone planted it?"

"Yeah. Maybe the cops." More likely the same guy who broke into my office.

"Who knows about ABC besides the members?"

"Bryant and Josh. The married guys' wives. I don't know who else."

"How about Hicks Pepper III?"

"Hicks? Why are you asking about him?"

"His name's come up."

"Yeah, he might know. We have a case together."

"Any link to Miles?"

"No, it hasn't gone to trial."

"How would he know about ABC?"

"We were out-of-town for a deposition, and after finishing up we went out drinking."

"Why?"

"He was on expense account. Besides, I know him through the University of Michigan. He's a big booster, and I used to be a player there you know."

"So I've heard."

"We go back to my playing days there. Anyway, after the dep we had a few beers too many, and I sort of remember talking about ABC and what a great scam it is. But I'm a little hazy on the details."

"What can you tell me about Rebecca?"

"Not much. She seemed sweet, but I hardly knew her. I remember having one case with her, but that's it."

"Anything noteworthy about the case?"

"No. It was an auto collision, settled for $15,000, I think. Nothing unusual."

"You have any problems with Pepper on that case?"

"I don't remember him being involved. It probably wasn't worth a partner's time."

"Have you ever heard of Keith Forrester?"

"No."

A sheriff's officer told Cardiff that it was time to get going. I watched the hearing from the visitor's gallery. A preliminary hearing isn't a full-blown trial, but a proceeding where the State demonstrates to the judge that it has sufficient evidence to charge and try the defendant with the crime. The burden of proof at this stage is less stringent than the beyond-a-reasonable-doubt standard needed for conviction. The preliminary hearing is useful to the defense because they get a look at the State's evidence. While it's rare for a judge to find insufficient evidence, Cardiff had some hope for a ruling in Jim's favor, since everything was circumstantial. But the judge sustained the charges, and also denied bail. Ironically the judge was soft-spoken and extremely polite, not only to Jim but to everyone. I'd describe him as courtly if it wasn't such an obvious pun.

I didn't talk to Jim again after the hearing, but I waited around for Cardiff. He realized that Jim didn't give me anything solid, so after the hearing he simply told me to do what I could. Which meant go back to the office until the noontime meeting with the ABCers.

I took Michigan Avenue back downtown. State Street would have been more direct, but I felt like driving past the Art Institute to check out the lions guarding the entrance. I was looking for inspiration, like the symbolism of Jim being thrown into the den.

I first spotted it as I passed Wabash on 26th, and it stayed with me on Michigan as I worked my way back to the Loop. A white LeBaron, two car lengths back. The driver looked like a white male, as best I could tell. I couldn't make out the plate. When I turned west on Madison he followed. South on Clark he followed again. A hard right on Adams, nearly grazing a middle-aged woman as she entered the crosswalk. My tail got hung up as other pedestrians entered the intersection. I made a few lights before heading back south on Franklin, then Jackson to Clark to my garage.

It didn't make sense that I'd be tailed midday on busy city streets. But I knew I wasn't imagining it. At least I hoped I wasn't. It meant I was on to something. Too bad I had no idea what.

•

Lawyers like to cater in lunchtime meetings. But in keeping with the spirit of the group we didn't order from any fancy sandwich shop. Instead we got a couple of pizzas. Besides the four ABCers, we were joined by Bryant Weiss and Josh Pindler.

I was given the floor, and I explained that the thing I needed most was information. Not only about Jim, but about the victims too. Everyone agreed to make themselves available for private interviews. Will and Jerry were free that afternoon, the others I'd talk to the next day. I reassured them that I didn't think Jim was guilty, nor did I suspect any of them. I also pledged that anything said to me would be strictly confidential, emphasizing that nothing would be passed on to the police.

"What kind of information would you find helpful?" asked Scott.

"At this point I want to know everything about everything. Personal information, professional information, rumors, anecdotes. Whatever you have. Right now I don't see any link between the three victims, other than their obvious connection to the courts and the ABC letters. There has to be something more."

"Any chance there isn't a connection, and that we're dealing with more than one killer?" asked Bryant. "Maybe even a conspiracy?"

"For now I'm not ruling anything out. But I work off the premise that there are no coincidences. And I'm even more skeptical of conspiracies. They're just not very common. Too much danger that the weak link will blab."

Everyone had already been interviewed by the police, and talk turned to what they'd been asked and how they answered. The questioning centered on how well they knew Jim, and on Jim's state of mind. To a man they proclaimed that Jim wouldn't have done it. They were also questioned about ABC, though not very thoroughly. It seemed like the cops were focusing on the renegade member running amok theory, rather than some grand scheme. Three of the guys were interviewed by Crumpton, the other three by Amanda.

"There's one thing the police probably didn't tell you," I said. "Rebecca Ellsworth left a clue. I'm not at liberty to say what it is, but think especially hard about everything you know about her." Nothing like a little disinformation to shake things up.

Lunch was soon over. But mention of Amanda reminded me of her grandstanding to the press. I was pissed seeing her on TV, but if she was on a high from her supposed masterminding of the investigation she also might be manic enough to tell me something she shouldn't. I used Jim's phone to call Northbrook, and found out she was working out of Chicago's Area Three headquarters that afternoon. Which was a good break; I could drive over there and get back in time for my interviews with Jerry and Will.

Amanda was working from a small circular table in the lunchroom. I was surprised the cops hadn't cleared some desk space in the main room, where she'd be more visible. Young, attractive female detectives break the monotony.

"Hi Marty. Good to see you."

"Amanda."

"I didn't mean to be bitchy with you the other day."

"That's all right. You don't need an outsider telling you who or when to arrest, right?"

"You're not exactly an outsider."

Unloading on her would have felt great, but information would do more for me. And certainly more for my client.

"So you think the case is looking good?" I asked.

"Yeah. Besides the obvious, we just got confirmation that the ABC notes and your membership list came from the same printer."

"You turn up any poison yet?"

"Not so far. But poison's pretty easy to dispose of."

"What about the hair samples found in Miles' car? Are they Lanter's?"

"What if they're not? They could belong to a valet who parked the car, or a friend. These little things you're talking about don't really bother us very much."

"Maybe they should."

"Marty, just what are you doing here?"

"Just like to follow up on my work."

"Because it wouldn't be a very good idea if you started working for Lanter."

"What makes you think I'm working for Lanter?"

"Coyness doesn't fit you. I know you and Cardiff met with Lanter before court this morning. And I doubt you were talking over old football games. Anyway, my advice is to knock it off. You've heard of conflict of interest, haven't you? I know the licensing board has."

"Well, Amanda, I don't really see a conflict here. But even if I did, I think clearing an innocent man of murder would be a pretty good reason to bend a few rules. Of course you wouldn't know about that, because you do everything by the book, right?"

"Just back off. I don't need you mucking up my case."

"Aha, so it's your case."

Amanda picked up some papers with both hands, tapped the bottom edges on the table to line them up, then placed the papers back down in front of her. "I do have one tidbit for you," she finally said. "About the connection between Lanter and the Ellsworth woman." She stopped.

"Yes? What do you want me to do, beg?" She was enjoying this power trip.

"It seems Lanter had a thing for her. Started about a month ago. A chance encounter in a bar led to something a little more intimate."

"Where'd you learn that?"

"Anonymous source phoned it in this morning. And it checks out. Lanter's also going to be charged with the Ellsworth murder. Should be announced within the hour."

"Just like that? Where's the evidence."

"Oh, we have that too."

"Come on Amanda, spill it."

"I don't know if I should be telling this to a civilian. Ah, hell, you'll find out soon enough. Ballistics test came in. The gun in Lanter's house matches the one used on Ellsworth."

"Jim says he didn't own a gun."

"What do you expect him to say."

"It's a plant, Amanda. My office was broken into too."

"Did you phone it in?"

"No. Nothing of consequence was taken. The point is we have a pattern working."

Amanda paused before responding. "Far be it for me to tell Blake Cardiff how to practice law. But good luck if Lanter's defense is that someone broke into his house and put the gun there. Corroborated by the testimony of his private investigator that his office was also broken into, where the police have no record of the break-in."

"At least consider a set-up."

"Consider it considered. Now I got to get back to my paperwork before the snack crowd repossesses my table."

The gun match didn't surprise me, but if the information about Jim and Rebecca was true that would close a big hole in the State's case. Of course the information wasn't necessarily correct, since the anonymous source was likely the person setting Jim up. But at least I had something to work with.

I'd parked on Belmont, about a block from the station. As I neared my car something didn't look right. As I got to the door something didn't feel right. Probably the .38 jammed into my rib cage. Finally my steel trap of a mind figured things out; the white LeBaron was parked behind me.

I was commanded to get into the LeBaron, while simultaneously being shoved into the back seat. The guy doing the pushing was nearly my height, but even heavier than me, around 275. Another guy, average sized, got behind the wheel.

The big guy joined me in the back seat. The car was running, heater on and radio turned to WLIT, the lite FM. Maybe they were setting the mood to romance me.

"Let's get rolling," the big guy said.

"Guys, I'd love to go for a ride, but my parking meter's about to expire. Hate to mess up my clean record."

"Shut up," said the driver. Not a particularly snappy come back. The whack to the face from my back seat companion made the point more effectively.

We drove a couple miles before pulling into the rear of a lumber yard. Must have been the storage area. Nothing around but stacks of two-by-fours.

"Out," said the big guy, waving the .38.

They led me to a narrow pathway surrounded by lumber piled at least fifteen feet high.

"What's this all about?" I asked.

"You poking your nose where it don't belong." That was the driver talking. I sensed a faint Eastern European accent.

"I do that a lot. Can you be more specific."

"You know."

"I have a hunch, but I'd like to hear it from you."

"Just keep moving."

I stopped and faced them. "You don't even know what this is all about. Who hired you?"

"A colored guy."

"You're kidding. A black guy hired you two?" The only African-American involved in the case was Crumpton. And while I was critical of his police work, he wouldn't put the word out on me. Too much risk of screwing up his pension.

"Just shut up already."

A motor, like from a forklift, started up, and the two goons turned toward the noise just enough for me to make my move. I ran. I heard a shot but kept going, taking a left onto an intersecting path. I felt pretty good about my chances once I made the turn, figuring the big guy wouldn't be able to keep up with me, and even if the little guy caught me he wasn't the one with the gun. I might not have felt so confident if I'd recognized the possibility of the big guy passing the gun to the little guy.

With all the lumber piles and the pathways created between them, we would have looked pretty silly to anyone looking down from overhead. The rat in the maze routine as practiced by middle aged men. Before long I lost all sound of my pursuers. No footsteps, no labored breathing, and, most important, no more gunshots.

When I heard a car engine start up I followed that sound. The LeBaron was hightailing out of there. But this time I got the plate number.

"Hey, what's going on here." A burly guy in a flannel shirt was closing ground, walking like he'd been riding a horse, not a forklift.

"Fire inspector."

"Fire inspector?"

"Yeah, this place is a fire hazard."

"What are you talking about? This is a lumber yard. We supposed to use nonflammable wood? And I thought I heard a gunshot."

"Must have been a car backfiring."

"Bullshit. I was in the army. I know a gunshot when I hear it."

"Who am I to argue with a vet? Anyway, the wood's piled too high, and you need to leave more open area between piles. The way it is now, one pile goes up, the whole place blows."

"Now I get it. I know how this thing works."

"What thing is that?"

He peeled two twenties from his money clip. "We okay now?"

"I don't want that."

"Take it. Show your wife a good time." He pressed the bills into my hand.

It'd been two years since I had a wife, and at least two years before that when we last had a good time. But I knew some charities who'd put the cash to good use.

As I left the yard I wondered if the man was curious why a fire inspector didn't have a car.

CHAPTER 19

Thanks to the two yahoos in the LeBaron my parking meter expired and I was ticketed. But I'd fight it. Hearing examiners love unique excuses, and being abducted and dodging bullets in a lumber yard figured to rank up there.

That afternoon I started the ABC interviews. Getting shot at didn't exactly put me in the mood, and with Will Rockland I pretty much went through the motions, getting standard answers to standard questions. Jim seemed fine, he never mentioned any grudges, ABC wasn't involved in violence, blah, blah, blah.

With Jerry Grieg I was more thorough. There were some things about him that gnawed at me. Like his owning a house in the suburbs, and his absence from the last ABC meeting during the time Rebecca was missing.

I met him at his office on Clark Street, a 1920s vintage building looking every bit its age. Grieg was on the eighth floor, a traditional office with an outside room for a secretary and a main office for the boss. Just like my place.

There was no secretary or receptionist, so I gave a yell, which Jerry returned, "Come on back." His office was about 20 x 20, but felt smaller because of the clutter. File cabinets lined the walls on each side of his desk, yet a couple dozen files were lying on the floor. His desk was also a mess. Court documents, correspondence, the Tribune sports section, a scales of justice paperweight, and an airplane ticket were just some of the things spread over the desk top.

"Business or pleasure?" I pointed to the ticket.

"I got a little vacation planned for next week. I'm trying to clear off some matters before then. Not that you could tell looking at all this junk."

"You don't seem to be hurting for work."

"Quantity I have. It's quality I need. I handle a lot of workers compensation and small personal injury cases. Keeps me busy, but there're easier ways to make a buck."

"You must have a good referral network?"

"I guess. I have my regulars, and I'm of counsel to my old firm, and to Weiss & Lanter. I get a lot of their smaller cases."

"Must be stressful handling all these cases by yourself."

"It can be hectic, but I have outlets to release my stress."

"Anything fun?"

"I yell at my wife and kick the dog." He smiled, and changed subjects by asking me what I wanted to know about Jim.

"How has he seemed lately?" I asked.

"The same nut as always."

"He ever mention having any problems with Celia, Miles or Rebecca?"

"No one gets along with Celia, and Miles was an asshole, but Jim never said he wanted to kill them or anything like that."

"And Rebecca?"

"He never mentioned her."

"Did you know her?"

"Yeah, we had some cases together."

"What'd you think of her?"

"I thought she was nice, and a pretty good lawyer. And a real looker."

"That it?"

"Yeah. I mean, we didn't screw or anything. Not that I would have been opposed to the idea."

"I thought you were married."

Jerry snorted. "I can see you're a little more old-fashioned in your thinking than I am. Although these days the wife issue isn't too relevant."

"Why's that?"

"The marriage is on hiatus. My wife's been living with her parents the last six weeks."

"Sorry to hear that. Any kids involved?"

"A boy. He's with his mother." He showed me a picture of a four-year-old with shaggy brown hair.

"Cute kid. Must get his looks from his mother."

"You tell me." He handed me another picture off his desk, an attractive, brown haired woman in her late twenties.

"Yeah, definitely his mother." I handed the pictures back. "You get to see him, right?"

"Well, they're out of town."

"You dealing with things okay?"

"Yeah. I still have the dog."

"You ever see Jim get violent?"

"Jim? He's a marshmallow. I can't even imagine him ever playing football." Grieg skipped a beat, then continued. "The one with the temper is Will."

"Will? He seems pretty mild mannered."

"He is, in social settings. But he's really into his career and making money. If he loses a case he takes it personally."

"He ever say anything about any of the three victims?"

"Nothing like he wanted to kill them. But I'm pretty sure he's lost some cases before Miles."

"Any of the ABCers have problems with any of the victims?"

"Not that I know of."

"We missed you at the last ABC meeting, the one before Jim's arrest."

"Couldn't be helped."

"Were you someplace warm at least?"

"Warm?" He looked at me like I'd started speaking in tongues.

"I thought you were at an out-of-town deposition."

"Oh, that," comprehension returning to his face. "No, Ann Arbor wasn't too warm." I didn't say anything, waiting for him to break into the truth, but instead he deflected the silence by asking if I had any more questions.

"Jim said that you rented a mailbox which ABC could use on the phony mailings it sent out. Is that right?"

"Yeah."

"You use it for anything else?"

"No," he answered a little too quickly.

"Why rent a box just to have a return address?"

"I know the owner of the place. He gives me a rate. And it's a write-off."

With that I said I was through. I didn't want to tip him off that this was anything other than a meeting for me to help Jim. I'd start sounding accusatory if I kept up the questions.

Especially since a letter was on his desk from the firm of Neill & Cobb—the plaintiff's attorney in the only case Rebecca worked on which reached trial before Miles. Jerry was listed in the letterhead.

•

Plonski grumbled, but again he came through for me. The LeBaron was registered to an Edward Smejkal on West Cornelia. His license listed him as five-ten, 165 pounds, so I fingered him as the driver. Plonski also got Smejkal's sheet, which showed only a couple of misdemeanor convictions. The latest, from six months earlier, was for criminal trespass to residence, pleaded down from felony residential burglary, for which he did thirty days in County. Kind of a wimpy background for hired muscle. But it fit with the break-ins at my office and Lanter's house.

Somehow my mind melded break-ins with bat mitzvahs until a knock roused me from my daydream. Standing at the door was a tall woman, late twenties, long dark brown hair, bangs. Sort of how I imagined Gail would look in fifteen years. Gail resembled me, and I felt a little creepy about my visitor, like we could pass for brother and sister.

"Mr. Bronk?"

"Yes."

"Sorry if I startled you. I'm Elizabeth Clark. I'm a friend—I was a friend—of Rebecca Ellsworth."

She accepted my offer of a chair, and wisely declined a cup of the sludge I charitably refer to as coffee.

"How can I help you, Ms. Clark."

"Rebecca and I were very close, and she told me about your meeting. I know something which may relate to her killing."

"Why tell me?"

"Rebecca said you seem sincere, and I don't know any private investigators."

"Have you talked to the police?"

"I spoke briefly to a Detective Moyer, but she said the investigation was closed."

"No one ever interviewed you?"

"No. And I was probably Rebecca's best friend." Incredible the cops didn't talk to her in detail.

"Before you continue, Ms. Clark, you should know that I'm working for the defense."

"I heard Jim Lanter was charged. You don't think he's guilty?"

"No."

"You might be right. I'm an attorney, and I've met him on some cases. He's always seemed like an okay guy. Except he's such a flirt, a part of me thinks maybe he did do it. That's why I'm here."

"I don't understand."

"Rebecca had been getting secret admirer notes, about one a week, for the past month."

"What do you know about them?"

"They came to her office. Stuff like; Dear Rebecca, I'm crazy for you, let's run off together to some tropical island, and on and on."

"Did you see these notes?"

"Yeah, she showed them to me."

"Were they sexually suggestive?"

"Not really. They were actually sweet, in a junior high sort of way. Except there was one strange thing about them."

"What's that?"

"They weren't handwritten. Looked like they came off a word processor."

"No identification who they were from?"

"No. But they were postmarked in Chicago."

"As far as you know, did the person ever try to contact Rebecca, either in person or by phone?"

"Not that she said."

"Did she have any idea who they were from?"

"Not really. Naturally she gave that a lot of thought. She was a friendly, outgoing person, and people liked her, especially guys. So it could have been someone from her office, another lawyer, anyone. She really had no clue."

"Obviously she never got together with the guy?"

"No way. She adored Perry. And it's not that she was a mass-every-morning kind of girl, but she took her marriage vows seriously."

"Any old boyfriends?"

"Not really. She hardly dated until she met Perry."

"How long do you go back with her?"

"Since high school at Regina Dominican. We were kind of a natural pair, both from the wrong side of the tracks."

"What do you mean?"

"Maybe that's overstated. But there's lots of wealthy and snobby north shore girls at the school. We came from more middle class backgrounds, where our dads had to work two jobs so the kids could go to Catholic school. Rebecca and I just had a lot of things in common."

"And you kept close over the years?"

"Yeah. We'd meet for lunch at least once a week, and talk on the phone a couple more times. After she died I dug up this old photo of us from high school. I carry it around in my purse. That's not too weird, is it?"

"Not at all." Until now Elizabeth had been amazingly composed; nothing more than a little water in the eye, which disappeared after a few extra blinks. But now she sniffled as she handed me the photo, two schoolgirls in white blouses and plaid skirts, arms around each other, seemingly without a care in the world.

"That's a special picture," I said. "You should keep it with you."

"That's what I think. A reminder of her and what she's meant to me." She took a tissue from my desk, but didn't put it to immediate use.

"Do you mind if I ask you a few more questions, or should we do it another time?"

"No, go ahead. I'll be fine."

"Did she ever mention Jim?"

"Not that I remember."

"She never said anything about meeting him at a bar?"

"No."

"I assume Rebecca never told Perry about the notes?"

"I'm not really sure. But knowing Rebecca, she'd keep that to herself."

"If Perry found out, what would he do?"

"Hard to say. He's usually pretty mellow, but he was head-over-heals for Rebecca."

"How about the incident with Miles. Did she tell Perry about that?"

"Yeah."

"How'd he react?"

"He was upset. He talked about confronting Miles, one-on-one. But after settling down he supported Rebecca's filing the complaint."

"Do you think she would have told him about her meeting with me?"

"Probably. As far as I know she was very open with Perry about the Miles thing."

"Getting back to the love notes. Do you know what happened to them?"

"I'm not sure. She probably tossed them."

"Did she ever talk about lawyers she wasn't getting along with?"

"No. I can't think of anyone not liking Rebecca."

"What was her opinion of Hicks Pepper?"

"That he's a good lawyer, but a real pain to work for."

"She think he might have had any interest in her?"

"You mean personal?"

I nodded.

"No," she continued, "Rebecca never said anything like that. You think he could have sent her the notes?"

"I've heard of stranger things."

"I'm sure she'd have no interest in him." Which may have been the problem.

We talked a little more before Elizabeth left. What grabbed me was the stuff about the typewritten love notes. I never considered myself a hopeless romantic, but even so I'd always handwritten my notes. My penmanship isn't easy to read, but at least it's personal.

But this is the new century, where people talk through e-mail and fall in love in cyberspace, so maybe word processing is how these things work now.

But in this case the recipient might recognize the author's handwriting.

Or maybe word processing is difficult to trace, and therefore better for a frame up.

•

Perry Ellsworth worked in the residential mortgage department of the First Loop Bank on Monroe Street. I wasn't looking forward to meeting the grieving widower, but the police will tell you that the husband is always a suspect, so that was reason enough to seek him out. His cubicle was on the fifth floor, though it could just as easily have been the basement since no windows were visible from his workspace. I gave Perry my name and told him that I wanted a few minutes of his time to talk about Rebecca. We commandeered a small conference room for privacy.

"I'm very sorry for your loss, Mr. Ellsworth. From everything I hear Rebecca was a wonderful person."

"Thank you. Haven't I heard your name before?"

"I met Rebecca, once. Concerning an investigation of Judge Miles."

"That asshole. Looks like he pissed off the wrong guy."

"Who's that?"

"Lanter. The police say he killed Rebecca too. So why are you here?"

"I was hoping you could fill me in on Rebecca and Lanter."

"I've never met the guy. And anyway, what's your interest in this?"

"My investigation isn't complete."

"Rebecca is dead, Miles is dead. So what in the world are you still investigating?"

"Just wrapping things up."

"For who?"

"I've been working with the police."

"They've made their arrest. Now tell me what's going on?"

I knew I was being evasive, and actually I was relieved Ellsworth caught on. With some people you should be forthright, and surviving spouses top that list. "Truth is, I'm working for Lanter's defense now. But I really think he's innocent."

"And you have the nerve to expect me to help you! Get the fuck out of here."

"I want whoever's guilty put away too, Mr. Ellsworth. If Lanter didn't do it, that means the real killer is still out there."

Ellsworth stood up, his face a middle linebacker's scowl. "Lanter did it! He messed with my wife, and I'll be there when mister big shot football player fries."

He slammed the door on the way out.

•

It was now late afternoon. I got my car, picked up the Kennedy and headed for West Cornelia Street, near Addison and Pulaski, looking for answers from Edward Smejkal.

I'd passed Fullerton when the car phone rang. It was Jim. I'd asked Cardiff to have him call me at his next chance.

"Hi Marty. I have about five minutes till our delightful repast of chipped beef on toast. What's up?"

"Detective Moyer dropped something in my lap today. About you making it with Rebecca Ellsworth."

"Damn. I knew that was gonna bite me in the ass."

"What's the deal?"

"About a month ago, on a Friday, I went out after work with some of the guys. Rebecca was at the bar too, with the Markus & Stevens crowd. I had a few beers, and, you know how I am, I got to bragging about how I could get Rebecca in the sack. The guys laughed me off. After a few more beers I went over to talk to her. But it was a show for the guys; me and Rebecca made small talk about some of the lawyers in her firm, and that was it.

"Of course that's not what I told the guys. I told them she was hot for me. By chance she left a couple minutes later, and I followed her out. But she went one way, I went the other, and that was it."

"Anything else?"

"Well, when the guys asked me about it the next week I kinda talked about getting it on with Rebecca. Just to save face. But I swear it was only talk."

"That's the whole story?"

"Yeah."

"No follow up correspondence?"

"What are you talking about?"

"Rebecca had been getting secret admirer notes for the past month."

"Hey, I'm not the love note type. Or the secret admirer type. I dig a chick, I tell her, straight from my mouth."

"Jim, you might want to tone down that macho shit."

"Yeah, well I didn't send any notes."

"Who was with you that Friday?"

"Dennis, Jerry. And Bryant and Josh from the office."

"One last thing. You ever hear of a guy named Edward Smejkal?"

"Smejkal? I don't know. It's vaguely familiar. Uh-oh, I hear the cattle call. Got to run."

•

Cornelia was a neighborhood of three-flats. First I cruised the block without spotting the LeBaron. I doubled back using the alley, then parked and walked to Smejkal's house.

On the wall outside the front door were three mailboxes and doorbells with names affixed. None said "Smejkal."

I rang the bell marked "Rejsak," the only one with an Eastern European sounding name. A male voice came on the intercom, I told him what I wanted, and he buzzed me in.

Rejsak looked to be mid-forties, average height and weight. His distinguishing feature was his hair. It was shoe polish black, and, with the help of a generous supply of grease, he managed to direct backward every hair on his head.

"Why you wanna know about Eddie?" Rejsak asked when I was still in the hallway.

I managed to get myself invited into his apartment before answering.

"He just came into some money, and I'm trying to locate him."

"Bullshit. He's messing with you, right?"

"Something like that."

"He moved out about four months ago. I don't know where he's at now, and I don't want to know. He's nothin' but a two-bit punk."

"Anyone around here know where he'd be? Maybe a friend or relative?"

"I don't know about none of that."

"How about a big guy who hangs out with Smejkal? You know who that might be?"

"Tough guy, bigger than you?"

"Yeah."

"Sounds like Frank Ruzicka. I don't know where he lives, but he used to be a regular at the Aufderstrasse Inn on North Lincoln. Only Bohak I know who's nuts enough to hang out at a Kraut bar."

"Maybe he likes Becks."

"Over Pilsner Urquell? Then he'd really be crazy."

Rejsak let me look through his Chicago phone directory. Ruzicka wasn't listed, but I got the address for the Aufderstasse Inn.

I wouldn't say I "look Jewish," but I definitely don't look German. And while I don't have a problem with the German-Americans I deal with every day, being surrounded by dozens of children of the Fatherland in a confined setting where vast quantities of liquor are consumed was about fifteen millionth on my list of fun things do to, right after having my tongue pierced, and right before watching a Thirtysomething rerun.

A winged crest, maybe an eagle, was centered on the wooden door, below the Aufderstrasse Inn name and above some other writing which was beyond the memory of my high school German. I walked in and was greeted by an upbeat song whose words I couldn't make out, except for Gemutlichkeit. Good cheer. I hoped they meant it.

A lot of the talk was in German, but not all. The customers gave me that side-of-the-head look that any stranger gets in a neighborhood place. But no one rushed up to pin a yellow Star of David on my chest, and that was good.

In any bar the first place to get information is with the bartender. He was a big, warm-looking guy, reminding me of Sergeant Schultz from Hogan's Heroes. He asked me what I wanted, in German. At least that's what I think he asked.

"Bier, danke. Becks." I hear that in France the natives are much nicer to Americans if we at least try to speak the language, however badly we butcher it. No reason that wouldn't apply here too, I figured.

I laid a twenty on the bar. The beer, which was tapped and cold, went down smooth. I ordered another.

"Wie heisen Sie, bitte?" I asked when he brought the beer.

"Karl."

"Karl, do you mind if I ask you something."

"What happened to your German?" he asked in flawless English.

"I've pretty much exhausted it. It's not against the rules to speak English here, is it?"

"No, but some of the old-timers get ticked off. So what'd you want to ask?"

"You know a guy named Frank Ruzicka?"

"That bum? Yeah, I know him. Why you asking?"

"He came into an inheritance, and I'm trying to track him down."

"The fuck you are." That's the second time that pretense didn't work. It's what I get for not being creative.

"Why do you think I'd be looking for him?"

"You a bone breaker?"

"I can be."

"Frank don't hang out here anymore. Ran up a tab and wouldn't settle."

"Know where I can find him?"

"Ask Gunther over there." He pointed out a round guy with a flushed face and thinning blond hair. "They used to come in together sometimes."

"Thanks." I got up from my chair and headed toward Gunther.

"Your change," shouted Karl. "Keep it," I mouthed, the two words any bartender can lip read.

Gunther was seated at a round table with three other guys. A half full pitcher of beer and two empties formed the centerpiece.

"Gunther?"

"Ja, I'm Goonter."

"Karl said you might be able to help me. I'm looking for Frank Ruzicka."

"Ja, Frank. A little crazy, but nice guy. And cheap."

"Know where I can find him?"

"He live on Grace, couple blocks from Schurz hoch schule. But he usually at Joe's Tap on Irving Park. Let me guess, he owe you money."

"Something like that."

"Here, zit, haben Sie ein bier. Sprechen Sie Deutsche?"

"Ein bischen, aber nicht so gut. Thank you, I'd like to stay, but I'm working."

"I zee."

"How do you know Frank?"

"Met trough a freund. Frank say he half German, on mother's side, but he didn't fool me. He just like to come here because we good to buy him rounds. He not so good about buying back. Finally Karl kick him out. No great loss."

"Vas ist your name?" asked one of the other guys at the table.

"Bronk."

"Better than Krank," Gunther joked. Krank means sick.

"You German?" asked the guy who wanted my name.

"I'm a little of everything, as best I can figure. Anyway, I got to catch up with Frank. Thanks for the help, Gunther. Guys."

As I was walking toward the door I heard "Jude" from near Gunther's table, though I couldn't be sure exactly where it came from. I kept walking, then heard it again. This time I stopped and walked back. I looked around, but no one fessed up, so I again started to leave until it came once more. I turned back.

"If someone has something to say at least tell it to my face." The room was not very large, and my voice tends to carry. I heard some scraping of chair legs, from different directions. I'd run away from trouble at the lumber yard, and while that was the thing to do, it didn't exactly boost my ego. I didn't feel like running again.

Like magic the oompah music stopped, and the bar went silent. More chairs scraped behind me, and I got rigid as my muscles tightened. I saw Karl holding his Louisville Slugger peacemaker. I balled up my fists, anticipating he wouldn't use the bat on one of his regulars.

"Hold on there, Herr Bronk," said Gunther. This trip was quickly approaching twenty millionth on my list.

"Look," I said before Gunther could continue, "I don't want any trouble here. I got what I came for, and now I'm leaving."

"No wonder he didn't want a drink," someone at Gunther's table said, "it wasn't Mogen David."

"Hey, Rabbi," someone shouted from near the bar, "where's your beanie." That got a few laughs, which stopped as I turned and headed in the shouter's direction.

"Not so fast," said Gunther, who blocked my path.

"I don't have a problem with you, Gunther, so stay out of this."

"Just listen a minute," he shouted. "Everyone!" I stopped. "Mein Herren. Herr Bronk came in here to do a job. He didn't hassle us, he wasn't rude, he just needed information. Probably thought he wouldn't be welcome. How many of you would go into a kosher deli? He show a lot of guts. So how about everyone go back to their beer und have a good time. That's why we're here, nein?"

Slowly the barroom racket resumed. I shook Gunther's hand, and gave him my card. "You're a mensch, Gunther. You ever need anything, call. I owe you."

"You don't owe me, Herr Bronk. I'm trying to get by, you're trying to get by, that's all. Hope you find Frank and do worse to him than what he do to you."

"How'd you know..."

"Never mind. Vielen gluck."

"Danke."

•

I cruised Grace Street looking for the LeBaron or my two buddies. Coming up empty, I headed over to Joe's Tap, a hole in the wall flanked by a dry cleaners and a travel agency. The neon sign in the window read "Budwe..er."

Inside was dark, both from too much smoke and too little wattage. Alan Jackson was playing on the juke box. Beer flowed on the floor as well as on tap.

I ordered an Old Style. My protest against defective signs.

"You Joe?"

He nodded.

"You seen Frank Ruzicka?" He pointed me to a pool table in the rear of the bar.

I approached just close enough to see that Ruzicka and Smejkal were shooting a game. They were looking down at the table and didn't see me. I walked back to the bar, where I could keep on eye on them while figuring my next move.

My opening came before my plan. Ruzicka headed to the men's room, and Smejkal's back was toward me as he was racking up a new game. I hustled over and grabbed his left wrist as he was putting in the last ball, the nine.

"What the fuck..."

"Hi Eddie, remember me." I forced his hand flat on the table and took the nearest ball in my free hand. "Now before I play the fourteen into the index finger tell me who sent you after me." I raised the ball like I was going to smash it down.

"I'm thinking..."

"Stop stalling. Tell me, now!"

"My lawyer."

"His name!"

I spotted the whir of the pool cue just in time, and I blocked the blow with my upper arm. Ruzicka raised the stick again. I released Smejkal, drove my shoulder into Ruzicka's exposed midsection, wrapped my arms around his back, and took him down in a textbook tackle. He lost his grip on the pool cue. I glanced around to see if Smejkal was coming after me, but he was gone.

Ruzicka's head hit the wall with my tackle, and he was out cold. By now the other dozen or so patrons had gathered around. I didn't know if they liked Ruzicka or they didn't, but he was a regular and I wasn't, and regulars stick together.

"What'd you do to Frank?" asked a guy in a blue workshirt with "Mack" stitched above the left pocket.

"Nothing. He slipped."

"Slipped my ass."

"No, he slipped on his ass."

"You a wise guy or something?"

"Or something."

"We don't like wise guys here."

"I told you, I'm not a wise guy, I'm a something." This seemed to befuddle Mack.

"Look guys," I continued. "Frank and I had a beef, but now we're square. He'll be fine; he's already coming to." Which was true, and which spurred me to wrap things up before he'd say something to cause more problems for me.

I took the emergency fifty out of my wallet and slapped it on the bar. "Joe, keep the beer coming till this runs out. And be sure my buddy Frank gets his share. Sorry for the trouble, guys."

I'd had enough of bars for the day.

•

I had more work ahead of me that evening, but the type involving no human contact, which at that point suited me fine. Second-story work, I think they used to call it. Now it's just plain breaking and entering.

Jerry Grieg was rubbing me wrong, enough to justify a private tour of his office. After Joe's I'd gone home to change clothes. I really wanted to get in character by wearing a sharp, all black get-up, like the professional burglars you see on TV, but my left brain (or is it the right brain that controls common sense) took over, and instead I changed into a sport coat and tie, an unobtrusive look for a downtown job. Now it was six forty-five, and I was signing the after-hours register in the lobby of Grieg's building as D. Butkus.

Grieg's lock was easy to pick, especially since the dead-bolt wasn't locked. The door was solid wood, so I could work in light without fear of being seen from the hallway. My first stop was the desk, with its Oscar Madison quality. Piles of correspondence, legal briefs, deposition transcripts and other documents. Some bills were marked past due. An airplane ticket for next week, to Wichita. And a letter on ABC stationery from two months earlier, advising of an upcoming meeting.

Inside the center drawer I found Grieg's calendar, where he penciled in court appearances, due dates for papers to be filed, appointments and deposition dates. The day of the ABC meeting he missed, as well as the two days after that, had no entries. Blank days were rare; Grieg kept a busy schedule, and most days had at least three or four matters filled in. As for the upcoming week, Monday and Friday were busy, but Tuesday through Thursday were blank, although there were some stray pencil marks on those pages. It looked like things had been written, then erased.

Nothing too interesting in the other drawers, except for some raunchy magazines I'd never heard of. Not child pornography, and maybe not illegally obscene, but close to the edge.

Next I moved on to the file cabinets, where the only file of interest was for the case involving Grieg's old firm, Miles and Rebecca.

Grieg's client was involved in an automobile collision. She'd been stopped at a stop sign when she was struck in the rear by the defendant's vehicle. The plaintiff, a forty-five year old housewife, suffered a cervical strain with neck and shoulder pain, and headaches. Her medical treatment, mainly chiropractic, totalled a little less than $5000. The case settled for $8000, with Judge Miles entering the dismissal order.

That didn't strike me as a great result for the plaintiff, considering that the case was a rear-ender, meaning the defendant was most likely the only one at fault. Her medical bills were covered by the settlement, but after subtracting the attorney's fees and court costs she didn't recover anything in compensation for her pain and suffering. But cases often settle on the cheap; plaintiffs get cold feet about going to trial, judges arm-twist settlements out of the lawyers (and sometimes the clients), lawyers make mistakes which prevent all their evidence from being admitted. Maybe I'd have been able to figure out what happened if a nearby door hadn't slammed shut, followed by a clatter heading my way.

I knew what was coming, but not whether the person knew Grieg. I couldn't take a chance.

As I opened the door to the hallway I looked back into the office. "Sounds good, Jerry," I said loudly. "We'll get together next week to confirm." I shut the door with the cleaning woman still ten feet away.

"Mr. Grieg asked if you could come back in fifteen minutes," I told the woman. She didn't seem to understand, so I repeated the fifteen minutes part, slowly, then fisted and unfisted my hand three times. "Mister Grieg, five," she said in a heavy European accent, and she pushed her cart to the next office. "No, fifteen," I said, but she didn't look back.

Five minutes wouldn't give me the time I needed. I caught the elevator down.

CHAPTER 20

You'd think it'd be easy to find Edward Smejkal's attorney by checking out the criminal court's records, but you'd be wrong, and by noon the next day I'd given up trying. Attorneys are assigned identification numbers in Cook County, which are coded into the court's computer record in those cases where the lawyer files an appearance. But clerks entering the information may encode the wrong number, so it's not uncommon for the computer record to be in error. In Smejkal's case the attorney of record, according to the computer, was a Charles Linton, an eighty-year-old, semi-retired estate planner who, needless to say, never heard of Smejkal. The court documents themselves were hand-written and sloppy. For the defendant's attorney there was an initial, followed by an indecipherable name of undeterminable length.

An attorney code was written on one of the documents, but it was nearly as illegible as the handwriting. I couldn't make out the threes from the fives, or the fours from the nines. One of the numbers looked like something out of the Hebrew alphabet. I played around with various combinations and got the names of the corresponding attorneys, but none of them were familiar to me. I'd call them when I had some free time.

I also checked on Smejkal's running mate, but Frank Ruzicka didn't have a criminal record.

So it was back to the interviewing, starting today with Bryant Weiss and Josh Pindler.

I met Weiss in his office. He had a meeting in twenty minutes, so we got right down to business.

"How has Jim seemed the past month or so?" I asked.

"About the same as always."

"And how was that?"

"Good spirited. Upbeat."

"How were things going at work for him?"

"Pretty good. No problems that I knew about."

"How was Jim's social life?"

"We didn't talk about that much. Except..."

"Go on."

"This is going to sound bad for him, but he might have got lucky with Rebecca Ellsworth."

"Why do you say that?"

"He hit on her in a bar, and next day back in the office he said he scored. I didn't really believe him because he's been known to stretch the truth in that department. But now, who knows?"

"Jim says nothing happened, he was just talking macho."

"Now that sounds like Jim. But honestly, it also wouldn't surprise me if something did happen between them."

"Did Jim talk about Rebecca after that?"

"Not that I remember."

"What do you think about the ABC guys? Could any of them have done this?"

"I don't get mixed up with them. They seem like a good bunch, but that bettering the courts stuff just isn't me. I'm trying to make a buck is all. If some judge or lawyer gives me a hard time, I just shrug it off and go on to the next thing."

"Was Jim pretty involved in this activist stuff?"

"He seemed to be. I mean, a lot of the meetings were here, so I assumed he was the leader."

"What's Jerry Grieg's role with your firm?"

"Jerry? We refer some of our workers compensation cases to him. That's about it."

"Any personal injury cases?"

"Not that I know of, unless Jim does without telling me. Why, is Jerry involved in this?"

"Just curious. I noticed his name's on your letterhead."

I asked a few follow ups before Weiss had to leave for his meeting. On his way out he walked me over to Josh Pindler's office.

Pindler had that rarest of phenomena—a clean desk top. Just one stack of papers, in a basket yet. And the only two files in the office rested on the vents behind his chair, within easy reach.

"Did I catch you between assignments?" I asked, pointing to the desk.

"I'm busy all right. Just organized."

"You work here long?"

"A little over a year. I was at Jamison, Wrobel and Troon for three years before this." A large, well-paying firm. Associates don't usually leave places like that voluntarily, at least not to work for a small firm like Weiss & Lanter.

"How's working for Bryant and Jim?"

"They're good guys. Especially Jim. Bryant's a little more short-tempered, but he's not too bad either. I have to tell you, I'm shocked by this whole thing. I know Jim had a thing for Rebecca Ellsworth, and I'll bet at some time Judge Miles and that clerk Celia gave him a hard time, but still I can't believe he'd kill anyone."

"Tell me about Jim and Rebecca."

"Jim picked her up in a bar. I know, I was there. Later he told me how good she was. Said he wished things could be different."

"What kinds of things?"

"That she wasn't married, that she didn't have a kid."

"So you think he wanted a relationship with her?"

"Yeah. Not that I blame him. Rebecca was amazing; smart, attractive, funny. I hope I'm not getting Jim in any deeper trouble, but you need to know everything, right?"

"Right. How'd he seem otherwise?"

"Okay. Bryant's the one who's been down, because we lost a big case. But that didn't seem to bother Jim much."

"Tell me more about the case." I remembered Jim mentioning it, so I was interested in comparing versions. Pindler went on to describe a slip and fall on an icy sidewalk, a bad head injury, but their inability to establish an unnatural accumulation. Same description as Jim.

"Sounds like a tough case."

"It was. But get a load of this. Our client's name is Shawn O'Loughlin. Get it. SOL. Shit Outta Luck."

"I got it. Who was the judge?"

He started to say something, then hesitated. "That I don't know. Ask Bryant."

"He's gone. Besides, I don't really want to talk about this case with him, do I?"

"I suppose not, he's still touchy about it."

"You sure you don't know the judge? Weren't you working on the appeal my first time here?"

"I'm just doing research. Actually I know very little about the case, other than the basic facts. And that the defense lawyer must have been a woman, because Bryant was complaining about 'that bitch' after he came back from court that day. If you want I can check the file; it's probably in Bryant's office."

"That's all right." I'd get the information next time I was at the Daley Center. Though I had trouble believing Pindler didn't know the judge. "So you don't think losing the case stressed Jim out?"

"If it did he sure didn't show it."

"Did it affect you?"

"Not at the time. But now it's getting crazy, what with working on the appeal, plus all the other stuff going on with Jim's arrest and me taking over some of his work. So far I've avoided his divorce work; never done it and never want to. But I don't think I'll be able to fight it much longer."

"You ever go to any of the ABC meetings?"

"No."

"How come?"

"They never asked me. Not that I'd go anyway. When my work day's done I like to go home to my apartment, not attend meetings."

"Anything else I should know?"

"I just want to say something. I guess things look bad for Jim, but he couldn't have murdered anyone or kidnapped an old woman. He's not a cold blooded criminal."

"Agreed. On both counts."

•

That afternoon I interviewed the remaining ABCers, Scott Anders and Dennis Abbott. Scott seemed kind of tight lipped about everything, giving me the impression that he wasn't convinced I was on Jim's side. Naturally he doubted that Jim or any of the other ABCers was involved in the murders. He'd never heard Jim speak of Rebecca, and he didn't know of any feuds his colleagues might have had with Miles.

Every minute or two Anders would check his watch, and he never gave more than a clipped answer. He didn't know anything, and I didn't want to waste my time. So after about the fifth watch glance I called it quits.

I got to Dennis Abbott's office at four o'clock, where a very apologetic secretary explained that Dennis had our appointment in his book, but must have forgotten about it because he'd left for the day. And she couldn't reschedule for tomorrow because Dennis had the whole day blocked out. She didn't know for sure where he was, but he'd taken his gym bag, which meant he was probably playing basketball at the River North Athletic Club on Wabash.

Fortunately Abbott's office was near mine, so it only took me a couple minutes to get the workout clothes I keep in my car, then catch a cab to the club.

A young lady straight out of an aerobics video was checking ID's at the door.

"Howdy, miss," I said. Trying to affect a southern accent, but sounding like a comedian's skit. Brooklyn Sal does Texas. "I understand from my club back home that ya'll have a reciprocal agreement so's I can use your fine facilities."

"I don't think so, sir. We don't have agreements like that with any other clubs."

"Well, shoot and damn, if I don't get in my workout I'm about as much good as an infertile hen."

"Where are you from, anyway? I've never heard anyone talk like you before."

"Eastern New Mexico. Albuquerque. We talk kinda northern, kinda southern, kinda western. Takes gettin' used to."

"I'm sorry sir, but someone gave you some bad information."

"You can be my guest," came a high pitched voice from my right. I looked down and saw a brunette who couldn't have been more than five feet tall.

"Well thank ya, miss." I paid the guest fee and we went in. "I really 'preciate this..."

"Caroline. But don't get the wrong idea. I just liked your story, as ridiculous as it was."

"What do you mean?"

"I lived in New Mexico for ten years, and I never heard anyone talk like that."

"Oh."

"And Albuquerque's in the middle of the state, not the east. But you gave me a good laugh when I needed one, and that's worth something."

"Ma'am, you're as kind as a preacher's wife on Easter Sunday."

"Don't press it, you're not that funny."

After changing into my gym clothes I found Dennis at the basketball courts, playing a spirited game of three-on-three with guys who looked ten years younger than him. Despite the age difference Dennis was clearly the best player out there. He had a deadly outside shot, excellent passing skills, and quick foot movement on defense. He also held his own in the trash-talking department, as the two teams were hurling insults at each other, some good natured, some a little too personal.

The ball rolled out of bounds towards me. I picked it up and tossed it to Dennis, who, until then, had been so intent on the game he hadn't noticed me.

"Marty, I didn't know you were a member here."

"Dennis, does four o'clock ring any bells?"

"Shit! Our meeting. Tell you what, I'll catch up to you after the game. It won't be long before we kick these assholes on their butts."

Dennis was true to his word. He hit a long jumpshot, stole a pass, then made a driving layup to win the game. The teams skipped the customary postgame handshake.

Dennis was dribbling the ball as he walked over. He had that look in his eyes that good players get when they're on their game, that 'bring on the best player and I'll show him who's boss' look.

"This is what I live for," said Dennis. "Shutting up big mouths like those guys."

"You looked smooth out there."

"Thanks. Nothing like some hoops to get me going."

"Speaking of going, how about going someplace where we can talk."

"Oh yeah, you want to talk about Jim. Here's the deal. I'll tell you who the real murderer is. On one condition?"

"What's that?"

"You beat me in a game of H-O-R-S-E."

"You're kidding, right? You attended college on a basketball scholarship. I was a scrub football player."

"That's my offer."

What could I do?

In H-O-R-S-E once a player makes a shot, the other player must make the identical shot, or he gets a letter, beginning with H and working up the word "horse" to the E. If you get all five letters you lose. So the key is making difficult shots, with trick shots being especially useful.

I got the ball first. I started with a free throw, which I made, but so did Dennis. Then I tried a ten foot shot off the backboard, which clanked off the rim. Dennis then proceeded to make four long shots, one from each corner, one from the top of the free throw circle, and one from just in front of center court. I missed all four, so I was H-O-R-S before he broke a sweat.

For the coup de gras Dennis set up behind the midcourt line and let fly. The ball just grazed the rim, but that was enough to keep it from going in the basket.

This was my last chance, and I reached into my old trick bag, a remnant of a misspent summer twenty-five years earlier. Backward shots, shots while kneeling on the floor, shots while sitting on the floor, they all came back to me. Dennis wasn't happy about this "candy-assed" display, but he gamely played along. With the score tied I brought out my old specialty. I set up five feet in front of the basket, threw the ball straight upward, then, when the ball came down, hit it with my head. Nothing but net. Dennis rolled on the floor laughing, then tried it, but ended up knocking the ball backwards.

"I might be the horse, but you're the jackass," Dennis kidded as we shook hands after the game.

"Maybe, but I believe this jackass is owed some information."

"Oh yeah, that. Here's how I see it. Who gains the most if Jim's convicted?"

"I give up, who?"

"His partner."

"You think Weiss did this?"

"It makes sense. Weiss & Lanter becomes Weiss & Associates."

"If that was the motive why wouldn't Weiss just kill Lanter?"

Dennis thought about that before responding. "Then how about Jim's associate?"

"Same thing. I appreciate loyalty to your friends, Dennis, but if you know anything that could possibly be relevant, tell me."

Dennis hesitated before continuing. "All I know is, Jerry pulled me aside after our breakfast the other day and said he might have something important to announce at the next meeting. He wouldn't tell me what it's about, other than it's not something he wants to say, but that he might have to."

•

Jim called that night. I filled him in on my encounter with Smejkal and Ruzicka. I also told him what Bryant and Josh said about his post-Rebecca bragging.

"Yeah, stupid shit that I am, I probably said those things."

"What'd you mean about how you wished things could have been different?"

"It was talk. I was trying to say that if she wasn't married I could see dating her. But I was just trying to give myself an out. I'm not a wife stealer."

"So if any of the guys asked how things were going with you and Rebecca you'd say nothing was happening because she's married, and seeing a married woman wasn't your thing."

"Exactly. Seemed clever at the time."

"What more can you tell me about the O'Loughlin case?"

"It was Bryant's case. Big injury, but shitty liability, like I told you before. If we could have gotten past the summary judgment motion the defendant would have offered at least 500 grand to settle. I know Bryant gave it a good shot, but we had to prove that the defendant's shoveling made conditions worse. Bryant said we just didn't have the evidence to back it up."

"You didn't do any work on this case?"

"No."

"So you don't know who the judge or defense lawyer was?"

"No."

"Weiss never complained about them?"

"Not that I remember."

"Did Pindler work on the case?"

"A little, I think. But I'm not sure. Bryant might have hogged it to himself since it was so big."

"Did the ruling bum you out?"

"Yes and no. Objectively I thought we'd lose, so I wasn't surprised. Still, sometimes you get judges who'll help you out a little, especially where the injury is so severe. I hoped that would happen. Bryant was more upset than me. But he was also less objective about it; he was sure he'd beat the motion."

"So losing didn't cause you to go into a funk, which unleashed the killer impulse in you?"

"Fuck no. Or is it funk no."

"Pindler wants you out of the slammer. He's not anxious to take over your divorce practice."

"He really hates that shit. I'll bet his parents had an acrimonious untying of the knot. What about Bryant? Does he want me out?"

"He didn't say."

"Asshole. Probably gonna take my cases, and my fees too."

"It is hard to keep up your law practice from the hoosegow, you know."

"No shit. Hey, do me a favor Marty."

"What's that?"

"Keep an eye on things at the firm."

"You don't trust Weiss?"

"I didn't say that. Just keep an eye on things, that's all."

"Could Jerry be involved in this somehow?"

"Grieg? Are you serious?"

"Some things about him don't sit right."

"Jerry's a good guy. Maybe a little out of sorts since separating from his wife, but that's it."

"How out of sorts?"

"You've been that route, right? Sometimes you're edgy, sometimes you're mopey. Like that." I had traveled that road, and at the time I was more than a little out of sorts. Fortunately I'd had an outlet, although the scumbag offenders I pushed around probably didn't appreciate the therapeutic role they were playing.

"He ever mention having problems with any of the victims?"

"I'm sure he wasn't president of the Miles fan club. But he hasn't talked about any recent cases with him. And what could he have against Rebecca?"

"That's the thing. What did anybody have against Rebecca?" Jim couldn't answer that.

After we hung up I gave Colleen a call. "Got any ideas for Saturday night?" I asked.

"I don't recall you asking me out?"

"That's what I'm doing now."

"Oh. I didn't recognize that as a question."

"Sure it was, I asked if you have any ideas."

"What if my idea is staying home."

"Tell me what time to be over."

"Alone."

"Tell me what time to shoot myself."

"My, so dramatic. Well I'll give you a break. Professor Malkunian can't use his tickets to the symphony, so they're ours for the asking. Sound good?"

"Actually, I've got tickets to the Blackhawks game."

"So why'd you ask me if I had any ideas?"

"I figured you'd say 'No, how about you,' and I'd tell you about the tickets."

"Sorry I crossed you up. But that's what you get for playing games."

"But you don't actually have the symphony tickets, right? They're just available if we want them?"

"Right."

"Since I already have the hockey tickets, it makes more sense to use them."

"Is that how you see it?"

"Yeah."

"Why don't you just sell them to a ticket broker."

"Come on, Colleen."

"Why not? The money you get back can buy us a nice dinner."

"I don't know..."

"This case of yours must be bothering you."

"What do you mean?"

"You can't tell when I'm stringing you along."

"So the hockey game is okay?"

"Sure. You have Gail this weekend, right?"

"Yeah."

"How about I come by at six and visit with her awhile before we go."

"Sounds good."

"So what's happening on your case?"

I ran down most of the highlights, leaving out the part about being abducted and shot at.

"I'm frustrated, Colleen. I think I'm close to figuring this out, but I just can't make sense out of everything."

"Who do you least suspect?"

"You."

"Seriously."

"Jim."

"That can't be true. There're a lot of things pointing his way."

"I suppose you're right."

"Start with Jim. Until you can absolutely convince yourself that he didn't do it, you'll always have doubts."

"Anything else?"

"Figure out who'd gain the most by his being framed."

"You're a natural at this. If legal education doesn't work out for you, we may have found your new career."

My call waiting clicked in. It was Gail, and she sounded upset, so I told Colleen I'd see her Saturday.

"What's wrong, Pumpkin?"

"I got in a fight with some of my friends."

"And."

"So I told Mom, and now she doesn't want them at the bat mitzvah."

"But you do?"

"Yeah, they're my friends."

"Am I missing something here?"

"They're also my most popular friends. The party will be a disaster without them."

"Was it a big fight?"

"Kind of. Jennifer and Brittany told Jason Goldberg that I like him. Which I don't. Okay, maybe a little, but I didn't want him to know. So I got mad at them, and I told some of our other friends that they like these two dorky guys. So now they won't talk to me, and a lot of our friends are taking their side."

"Sounds like something that'll blow over."

"Yeah. But dum dum me has to tell Mom. Now she thinks we'll have problems at the party, so she's gonna call their moms and uninvite them. How uncool is that!"

"So you want me to talk to your Mom, right?"

"Yeah."

"All right. But Gail, you know that revenge stuff is pretty childish."

"I know. But they deserved it. Here's Mom."

Gail's version was pretty accurate, at least for a twelve-year-old, but according to Randee she'd left out a few things. Like coming home in tears and getting prank phone calls. And Randee's concern that we'd be stuck with the cost of the meals if these kids didn't show up.

"But the bat mitzvah's still three weeks away," I said. "Do you know how many turns a twelve-year-old's life takes in three weeks?"

"I know, Marty, I deal with Gail and her nonsense all the time. We just don't need this anxiety. Or uncertainty."

"I'm not crazy about paying for the meals if the kids don't show, but I'm willing to take that chance. Kids don't pass up parties. Besides, I'm sure their parents will make them come."

"I wouldn't be so sure about the parents. Maybe in our day they would have stepped in, but now the kids rule. They don't want to do something, they don't do it."

"Give it some time. If this is still going on the week of the bat mitzvah we'll take action. Okay?"

"That's what I like about you, Marty. You're an optimist. You haven't learned that friends aren't always what they seem. But if you want to wait, we'll wait."

"I want to wait."

Two minutes after hanging up with Randee the phone rang again. It was Cardiff, and I briefed him on my day.

"Any chance you can come up with something by the weekend?" he asked. "I hate to see Jim in longer than he has to be."

"I doubt it. Nothing's breaking."

"Keep plugging away." And he was gone.

Next, Scott Anders called. A meeting was planned for Sunday evening at Jerry Grieg's house in Glenview. Jerry thought if everyone got together in one place and put their heads together we might be able to come up with something. I was skeptical, but I told Scott I'd be there.

Before bed I made one final call. To my ticket broker. For Blackhawk tickets.

CHAPTER 21

I spent the next morning calling lawyers, and not because I was in a masochistic mood. True, the case was beating me down, but I wasn't enjoying it. Instead I was trying to track down Smejkal's attorney from the various attorney code combinations I'd come up with. I had about twenty names on my list, and between lawyers taking the day off (it was a Friday, and skipping work is hardly an unknown phenomenon among lawyers) and those out of the office for other reasons, I'd be lucky to talk to half of them.

Those I spoke with ran the gamut from sole practitioners to senior partners at major law firms. Only a couple practiced criminal law, and none of them heard of Edward Smejkal.

Until I reached number sixteen on my list. Craig Lewitt had been an assistant public defender working out of the first municipal district until a few months ago, when he became associated with a small general practice firm in Oak Lawn. He thought Smejkal's name sounded familiar, and when I described him and the charges he was pretty sure he'd represented him, although he didn't have a file and couldn't be sure. He claimed not to know Jim Lanter, except from what he'd read in the papers.

I told Lewitt what Smejkal had said, about being hired by his lawyer to put the hit on me. "It wasn't me, that I can tell you," he said.

"Why do you think he said that? Any reason he'd want to get you in trouble."

"No, I did a good job pleading him down, and he knows it. He's either lying, or he has another lawyer."

"Another lawyer? I didn't see any other criminal charges."

"Have you thought he could have been referring to his civil attorney?"

No, I hadn't thought of that at all.

•

I relate to computers as I do with people. At times we're close, other times we're strained. Since this case had started I'd frequently used the computers on the eighth floor of the Daley Center, and we'd been getting along famously. But our relationship was due for a crisis, and today it came. The system was down, and a clerk told me he didn't expect it to be up and running until Monday. Short of going through about 50,000 files there was nothing I could do.

So there I was. I had an angle, but couldn't pursue it. I could try to track Smejkal down again, but that didn't seem very promising. Even if I found him he'd probably be with Ruzicka, and Ruzicka would be with his .38.

But I couldn't stay idle, even on a Friday afternoon. After phoning Northbrook to be sure Amanda was in, I drove up there. Something was bothering me, and if I could get Amanda to talk I might get an answer.

"So, did Lanter admit his fling with Rebecca Ellsworth?" Amanda asked when she saw me.

"What do you think?"

"Probably not."

"Which reminds me, do you have any verification of this supposed fling, beyond your anonymous source?"

"I'm not at liberty to say."

"Was this anonymous source a male or female?"

"Male. What are you getting at?"

"I think someone's setting Jim up, and they're the one who tipped you off."

"You still beating that dead horse?"

"I don't think the horse is dead. In fact, I think it's coming on strong down the home stretch. If you have it, give me something that'll show I'm wrong."

An ear-piercing squeak greeted me as Amanda slowly opened her desk drawer. She took out a folder and silently handed me a piece of paper. The letter was typed:

Becca,
Now that things are different I can let my feelings out. I know we can be so happy together. What we've shared won't compare to what we can have. How does Heaven on Earth sound? Maybe you can guess who this

is from, but now's not the time to reveal myself. Just think of this until I can express myself in person.

"Where'd you get that?"

"Jim's desk."

"Assuming Jim was the killer, why would he leave a note like this in his desk, especially after killing Rebecca?"

"He must have forgotten about it."

"Come on. Our killer is sharp. He's not going to forget something as incriminating as this."

"Maybe that's part of his plan. To get us second guessing."

"What's the part about 'Now that things are different,' mean?"

"Why don't you ask your client."

"In other words, you don't know."

"I guess I should keep telling you everything, while you tell me nothing."

"Well, this note doesn't prove anything. Anyone could have put it there."

"You really think we do a half-assed job, don't you? We also got the floppy. This note was written almost a month ago. A couple days after Lanter picked Rebecca up in the bar. So now maybe you'll realize we're on to something."

"Were the other notes on the floppy too?"

"What other notes?"

"You don't know that Rebecca received a series of notes?"

"Where'd you get other notes?"

"I've heard about them, but I haven't seen them."

"Moyer, come here a minute," said someone from the hallway. "Don't move," she ordered, but I don't always listen very well, and as soon as she was out of eyesight I looked in her folder. There were at least six copies of the note. I took one of them, then rushed out of the station to my car and hurried back to the city.

I didn't say good bye. Or thank you.

•

I phoned Elizabeth Clark from the car, and she agreed to stay in her office until I got there. I made it over just before five and showed her the note.

"I don't remember this one," she said.

"Think hard. Are you positive?"

"Yeah, There's something odd about it, but I can't put my finger on it."
So I put my finger on it, literally. "Yeah, that's it," she agreed.

"Did Rebecca show you every note she got?"

"I don't know. She called me all upset right after she got the first couple, and showed me those. After that, I'm not certain. Sorry I'm not more help."

She shouldn't have underestimated herself.

CHAPTER 22

The next day was Saturday, and after picking Gail up from Hebrew school we spent the afternoon shopping. The switch being that we were looking for me. The bat mitzvah was only three weeks away, and I needed a new suit. While I'm not very particular about my clothes, I didn't want to pick out something that would mortify Gail and set her friends to giggling. I was thinking in terms of a pinstripe, but Gail said that was way too stuffy. She wanted a double breasted, but I thought they made me look like I was wearing a tent. We ended up picking out a blue suit with a subtle plaid pattern, a solid blue shirt, and a blue tie with red and green horizontal stripes. GQ might not be calling for a photo shoot, but neither would Popular Mechanics.

Gail seemed to enjoy our outing, but I think she really wanted to see Colleen. When they're together those two act like sisters. Colleen is decades older than Gail, so I don't really understand how that sort of relationship evolved. But Gail asks Colleen for advice about boys (Colleen acknowledges this fact, but refuses to reveal any details, despite my grueling interrogations), and Colleen talks clothes and make up with Gail. I enjoy seeing them together, although I'm glad Colleen doesn't copy Gail's purple nail polish, worn every other finger.

Colleen came by at six, and we all visited for about an hour. More accurately, I was present during this time, but they could have been talking about particle physics for all the good I was to their conversation. Before Colleen and I left, Gail promised she'd spend the night on her bat mitzvah studies, but I knew better, and Gail knew I knew better, but she still had to say it.

It was on to the United Center for the Blackhawks versus the Red

Wings. Colleen's good about me and sports, but calling her a fan is a stretch. This was her first time at the United Center, and I pointed out the Michael Jordan sculpture in front of the main entrance. "I'll bet Blackhawk fans feel cheated there's not a hockey statue here too," she remarked. And as godlike as Michael Jordan is in Chicago, she was probably right.

We found our seats just as the national anthem was starting. This is one of the highlights of a Blackhawks game. Shouting and applause starts early in the song, and gradually builds up until the singer is drowned out by the end. "Oh say does that" were the last words I heard. "Why are the fans so disrespectful?" Colleen asked after the crowd settled down.

"They're not disrespectful. It's just the tradition here. Helps build enthusiasm."

"For who? The team or the fans?"

"I suspect the players don't really pay much attention to it."

"So why do it?"

"It gets the fans into the game."

"But the game hasn't started yet. And once it does, won't it be exciting enough to get them enthused?"

"Let's just watch." And stop with the girly questions, I wanted to say but never would.

Colleen grew up in the Detroit area, with a dad and brothers who were Red Wings fans. So when the Wings did something good she instinctively stood up or applauded, which did not go over well with the fans around us. "Go back to murder city," someone shouted. "Stuff an octopus in it," said another. Colleen thought that was a new vulgarity she hadn't encountered living the college life, but I explained the Detroit tradition where fans throw an octopus on the ice after big goals or victories. Which, I added, was much more disrespectful than raising a ruckus during the national anthem, especially from the octopus's perspective.

The Red Wings were scoring more goals, but the Blackhawks were winning more fights, so the fans weren't altogether unhappy. Purists may decry the violence, but go to an NHL game and judge the reactions. Goals may bring the fans to their feet, but fights get them screaming.

After two periods the Red Wings were ahead 3-1. Colleen offered to buy me a hot dog and beer, seeing how her team was going to win. We took a walk in the United Center concourse, which is part concessions and part suburban shopping mall.

We checked out the gift shop which, aside from the usual Blackhawks and Bulls items for sale, also displayed old Michael Jordan and Scottie Pippen shoes, and a Tony Amonte autographed jersey. Colleen seemed surprised I was taller than some of the life-sized Bulls cutouts we passed, and that I was nearly as tall as Michael Jordan. Someone offered us a free t-shirt if we signed up for a Blackhawks or Bulls MasterCard, but as much as I like a giveaway I draw the line at something which doesn't plug in, taste good or keep me healthy.

We finally got in the food line. Colleen was ordering when I heard from my left "So, you think you've earned some time off?" Billy Bob Bobb was in full Blackhawks regalia. Not just a jersey, but a cap and a jacket too.

"I'm taking it, whether I earned it or not."

I introduced Colleen and Billy Bob. "The Dean of Wilson Law School, right?" he said. "I remember reading about your elevation in the Law Bulletin."

"That's me, but since it's Interim Dean you'll certainly be reading about my demotion some day too."

"That will be Wilson's loss, I'm sure. So Marty, you still doing anything on those murders?"

"Yeah. I'm pretty sure the police have the wrong guy. Which I might have been able to confirm except the Daley Center computers were down on Friday. I have a meeting tomorrow, and I really wanted to check out something before then."

"How sure are you that the real killer is still out there?"

"At least 90 percent."

"In that case, I can give you a hand." Billy Bob took out his wallet and handed me a plastic card. "This is a key card and building pass for the Daley Center. Use it tomorrow before your meeting. The computers were probably repaired last night, or today at the latest."

"Thanks. This really helps."

"Just be sure to get it back to me Monday. Oh, and if the guard asks, use my name."

"You mean tell them you gave me the pass?"

"No, tell them you're me. I never use the damn thing on weekends, so they won't know the difference. Just don't mention it to Fearless Leader if you run into him tonight."

"Judge Dienstag's here?"

"Yeah, he's in the Markus & Stevens skybox."

"You're kidding. How can the chief judge accept something as public as a skybox invitation?"

"As opposed to accepting something more private?"

"That's not what I meant."

"Relax, I'm playing with you. But to answer your question, I don't think David's exactly announced his presence. I happened to run into a Markus lawyer here who let it slip. So you like this get-up?"

"It certainly makes a statement," I said.

"It's high fashion in this place," said Colleen.

"My wife thinks I look ridiculous. Which is fine. She wanted to go to the opera, so I had to scramble to get game tickets from a broker. I want her to think I'm totally immersed in the game. Anyway, I better be getting back. Stop by on Monday, Marty. Colleen, nice meeting you. Hope I don't read about that demotion soon." Colleen returned his good bye, and I thanked him for the pass.

"Can you imagine, pretending to have hockey tickets just to avoid going to the opera," said Colleen when we were back in our seats.

"Some people are pretty low," I said.

"I might expect something like that from a lawyer, or a p.i., but not a judge."

"Colleen, if you're insinuating..."

"Avoidance of cultural activity is part of your charm, Marty."

I was beat, and I knew it. Then again, we were at the hockey game.

But now my interest shifted from the ice upward. Dienstag in the Markus & Stevens box didn't make sense. What if Hicks Pepper III was there? Those two socializing seemed as likely as Charlton Heston at a Spike Lee premiere. This was something I had to check out.

But how, seeing that you must present a ticket to the usher just to reach the skybox level. I could always try a bribe, or a bull rush, but my invented accent got me into a health club, so a little ingenuity was the way to go.

I headed toward the skybox access area with our food. "Where are you going with my stuff?" Colleen asked.

"I'll see you back at our seats in about fifteen minutes."

"So give me my food."

"I need it."

"Don't be a pig."

I kept walking. "I'll explain later."

"I want food, not talk," she yelled, but she didn't chase after me, so she must have known I was up to something important. With two hands I was using a cardboard carrier for the drinks and food. I shrugged as I got to the skybox usher. "Hands are kinda full," I said.

"I need to see your ticket, sir." The usher was a college age kid with glasses and an I'm-an-organic-chemistry-whiz look about him.

"C'mon, you remember me, right?"

"No I don't. Your ticket please."

I put the food carrier on the floor, and made a show of working my pockets. "I can't find it."

"You're going to have to do better than that."

"What are you talking about?"

"The hands-full-of-food trick is the oldest one in the book. And not very clever, since food's catered in the suites. No need to go out for concessions."

"Maybe I wanted to stretch my legs."

"Sure, that must be it." Hands on hips, he wasn't buying it.

"You're sharp, son. And good work deserves recognition." I fished a twenty from my pocket and extended my arm towards him.

"Here comes Security. If you don't want me to bust you, you better get back to your real seat." Next time you're getting a bull rush, you snotnosed kid.

"Here's your food," I snapped at Colleen when I got back.

"Cold hot dog and warm pop. My favorites."

"Just eat. Or don't."

"Couldn't get up to the Markus & Stevens box?"

"How'd you know where I was going?"

"Don't need a Ph.D. for that one."

"Is everyone smarter than me, or does it just seem that way?"

"If it won't bruise your male ego, how about if I check out the box."

"You?"

"Yes, me. Now tell me who I'm looking for."

I described Dienstag, Pepper, and Whit Lamberton. "If a pro like me couldn't get in there, how are you going to?"

"Don't worry your pretty little head over that. I'll see you in ten."

One shot on goal and two skirmishes later Colleen returned. "Now that's the way to see a game," she said. "TV's, private restroom, telephone. Not to mention the food and drink."

"Who are you kidding. You didn't really get in."

"Whatever you say, Marty. But I guess this is also a product of my vivid imagination." She pulled a cigar out of her purse, and even from where I sat it looked natural leaf and expensive.

"Let me see that." I reached out for it.

"Hands off! I'm saving it for someone who trusts my word. Is Macanudo a good brand?"

"Come on, Colleen."

"You can look at it, up close, if you want." She held the cigar a few inches from my eyes. "Markus & Stevens" was printed on the cellophane wrapper.

"Okay, maybe you were there. But how'd you do it?"

"Why are you more interested in how I got in than what I saw?"

"Okay, what did you see?"

"Basically a lot of men making asses of themselves. Including a fat guy with whiskey spilled on his shirt, who seemed to be your Hicks Pepper, and a short man talking about what a light read Ulysses is."

"Dienstag."

"So it would appear, especially since Pepper had his arm around him and was calling him Twin D."

"I can't believe it. And everyone was getting along?"

"Everyone was snokered. But at least they were fun drunks."

"Amazing. So how did you get in?"

"We back to that again? Let's run a little test; I'll tell you how I got in, or I'll give you the cigar. But not both."

"Posing a dilemma for me, huh? Well let me figure this out logically." I could either reinforce that Colleen beat me at my own game, or I could enjoy a quality smoke. I grabbed the Macanudo.

"Hedonist," she said. I didn't argue.

We soon left. Detroit had scored two quick goals, so the game was pretty much out of reach. Maybe I was imagining things, but it also seemed that Colleen wanted to catch Gail before bedtime.

If that was the case she got her wish. The three of us talked for a good hour before Colleen decided to get going. I'd have liked her to stay awhile longer, but the combination of Gail's presence and an evening of ice hockey didn't exactly portend romance.

After saying how cool Colleen is, Gail dropped an "Oh, by the way" on me. A man called while I was out. He didn't leave a name, only the message that he wanted to meet tomorrow at one o'clock concerning Jim Lanter. He also left an address in Glencoe. Gail was pretty sure she got the message and address right, but because of background noise on the line she wasn't certain.

Glencoe's a wealthy, North Shore suburb, the town east of Northbrook. I didn't know anyone who lived there, and the service I use to check the real estate tax records for property owner information wouldn't open until Monday. So I told myself to ease up on the curiosity, that I'd find out soon enough. Besides, surprises add interest to life. They can be so..., well, so surprising.

Too bad I hate surprises.

CHAPTER 23

Downtown Chicago at nine o'clock on a Sunday morning feels like a football stadium an hour after the game ends. Being used to the commotion of the place, the quiet and inactivity is eerie.

The Daley Center was even more unnatural. There was the lone security guard and me; otherwise nobody. The guard showed little interest in my pass, which I flashed so quickly he couldn't possibly verify what it was. Even so he nodded, had me sign a register, then wished me a good day.

I got off on Judge Bobb's floor, used his key to get into his outer office and turned on Celia's computer. It was probably only five years older than mine, but to me it seemed like a relic. It took at least two minutes to warm up, and when it finally did I wasn't greeted by any fancy graphics or music, just a blinking curser on the top left of the screen.

I moved a few papers and a Sullivan's law directory on Celia's desk to give me a clear workspace, entered the code to access civil court cases by name, then typed in the name "Smejkal." That gave me a listing of cases where a Smejkal was a plaintiff, of which there were two, neither involving an Edward or E. Smejkal. Then I accessed the defendant index. One Smejkal case there, but again it wasn't my Smejkal.

Lots of explanations for what I didn't find. Smejkal could have lied about working for his attorney. Or he was telling the truth, but the matter for which he hired the attorney isn't in suit. Or it's in suit in another county. At this point it didn't matter, because I couldn't follow up any of these possibilities before the Glencoe meeting.

Next I checked out the Shawn O'Loughlin case. I wasn't really surprised to find that Judge Walter Miles entered the dismissal, less than three weeks before his murder. What did surprise me was the defense attorney—Markus & Stevens. I double checked the information they'd supplied me; Rebecca wasn't listed as having worked on the case.

After this discovery I felt strange, like I was either farther away than ever from figuring this out, or that just one more piece would solve the puzzle, and I wasn't sure which it was.

While staring into the hallway my hand reached for the Sullivan's law directory I'd earlier moved. The book was a couple years old, but thumbing through it would give my hands something to do. When I looked down I was at the J's. J for Jim. J for Jim in jail. Damn J's.

I stared at that page a good two minutes before the adrenaline rush came. Who needs computers, this book could give me what I need! I didn't have many pages to turn before I found the missing piece.

Why is retrospect always so obvious?

As anxious as I now was for one o'clock, first was brunch with Gail. With a big day ahead I ordered the lox platter and a bowl of oatmeal. Gail thought that was a pretty gross combination. I agreed, but I was hungry.

After brunch I dropped her off at Randee's, then continued north on the Edens. During the ride I called Jerry Grieg's house. He wasn't home, but his wife answered. Which actually was a good break, because she confirmed the hunch I had about him.

I was feeling confident, but ran through my theory one final time, just to be sure I had things right. So of course that's when some excellent questions popped up.

Could someone have changed the court's computer records?

Why hadn't the cops mentioned finding my card in Rebecca's purse?

Why hadn't I thought of these earlier?

Could my missing piece of the puzzle really be just a coincidence?

No time to answer these now. It was twelve fifty-five and I was parked in front of the house, a nice-sized split-level with attached two-car garage. A Thunderbird parked on the driveway was the only car in front of the house. I approached the front door. It was open.

CHAPTER 24

The living room was to the right of the front hallway. To the left was the stairway leading to the second floor, and past that another stairway leading down to the den. The house was quiet, but when I shouted "Anyone here" someone replied "Downstairs."

I walked down the five steps to the lower level. To the right was the bathroom, a half opened door (probably leading to the laundry room) lay straight ahead, and the den was to the left.

Bryant Weiss was waiting for me, sitting on the sofa, feet propped on a marble coffee table. He was thumbing through The Complete Sherlock Holmes.

"Interesting stuff. Amazing how Holmes always solved the puzzle." He put the book down on the coffee table. "Is that how it is with you, Marty?"

"Sometimes, but not always. Nice house, Bryant."

"Thanks. Too bad it's not mine."

"Whose is it?"

"Blake Cardiff's."

"Where's he?"

"I don't know. When I got here there was a note on the door to come in, and the door was unlocked. So have you come up with anything?"

"I know who the murderer is."

"Really? Who?"

"The murderer is clever, the way Jim was set up. But not too clever. The trail leads directly to you."

"Me?"

"Yeah. You have motive. You felt cheated by the O'Loughlin case.

Dismissal order entered by Judge Miles, defense attorney Markus & Stevens. And no doubt Celia gave you a hard time at some point, but, since she was the first abduction, you could have chickened out about killing her."

"That's crazy. I could never kill anyone."

"Then there's all those little things pointing to Jim, the ABC note in his briefcase, the love note to Rebecca in his desk. That suggests an inside job."

Weiss looked calm, taking in what I was saying. "You think I killed these people and set Jim up?"

I walked over to the half opened door. "I think the murderer has been listening to everything we've said." I took two steps and opened the door to the laundry room. Josh Pindler faced me. So did a .38.

"Well done, Bronk," he said. "Good thing I cover all the angles."

"What's this all about, Josh," said Weiss.

"Shut up." Josh gestured for me to join Weiss in the den. Then he had us sit down on the couch facing him.

"What tipped you off, Bronk?" Pindler asked.

"For one, things were pointing too easily at Bryant. And another, you were too free with information in our interview. Mentioning the O'Loughlin case. Making a point that you never do divorce work, implying that you didn't know Celia. And saying that you lived in an apartment, which would be impossible if you kept Celia in a basement."

"I do live in an apartment. But my parents have a nice house with a quiet basement. And they don't return from Florida until May."

"I guessed it was something like that."

"What else have you figured out?"

"That all that ABC stuff was a smokescreen. You abducted Celia to throw everyone off the track. All along your real targets were Judge Miles and Rebecca. You worked on the O'Loughlin case and figured it would hit big for you and the firm. At the least it would get you a bonus, maybe even a promotion. But then Judge Miles ruled against you and in favor of Rebecca's firm. So your motivation was one of the oldest known to mankind—revenge." I knew this wasn't Pindler's true motivation, but I wanted him relaxed. And one way to do that was to make him believe he was the one mastering this situation.

"Is that how you figure it?"

"That's not the whole story?"

"Bronk, if this is an example of your deductive reasoning, you ought to give up your p.i. license. That is, if you were to be around after today, which you won't."

"So what is the story?"

"You got the Celia part right. I was especially proud of that, and the Michigan pin I put in Miles' car. And you're right that Miles screwed me, but not on the O'Loughlin case. About eighteen months ago, before I joined Weiss & Lanter, I worked for a defense firm. I think I even told you about that. I'd won my first three trials, which put me on the part-nership track. Then the firm gave me a dental malpractice case to try. A lady claimed a couple teeth had to be pulled and that she suffered pain because of bad periodontal care. It was bullshit, but maybe a sympathet-ic jury would throw her a little money. Judge Miles hears the case. He has a hard on for me from the beginning. Sustains objections to my opening statement, ridicules me in front of the jury. Overrules every objection I make. And the worst thing was how he reacted to the testimony. Rolling his eyes and sighing when my people are on the stand, looking all con-cerned when the plaintiff's people are on.

"So I figured I'd lose the case, but still how bad could it be. Guess what the jury came back with. Four hundred thousand dollars. For a couple of lousy teeth. It was totally absurd. We filed motions for a new trial or to reduce the judgment, and Miles denies them. So we appealed, and maybe the appellate court would have lowered the award, but the firm's bigwigs thought we couldn't take a chance, that if we lost the appeal we'd lose more than the case, we'd also lose the client. The plaintiff's attorney knew the verdict was bullshit and that the appellate court would reverse the award, so they settled for $125,000 before the appellate court could rule. That's still a ridiculous amount, and our client wasn't happy, and my bosses were furious at me. After that I was history at the firm. I had to leave and take a job as low man at a two-bit operation."

"Thanks for the high opinion of us," said Bryant.

"I'd thought about killing Miles for what he'd done to me, but never acted on it. But then he went too far."

"The O'Laughlin case," said Weiss.

"Is that all you think about," Pindler boomed. "I already said that's not it. You're so dense, no wonder you were so easy to set up."

"Why the set up?" I asked.

Pindler settled down. "Assume you're the murderer. Three things can happen. The authorities find you, the crime remains unsolved, or they convict the wrong person. Option two's not bad, except as long as the case is open they could still investigate. You're never clear."

"So you never felt secure after killing Keith Forrester."

Pindler only missed one beat. "Maybe there's hope for you yet. How'd you figure that out?"

"I came across an old law directory, where I found that you and Forrester worked at the same firm."

"He was the asshole who fired me at my other job. I waited for the right time, and once he got canned I knew the suicide angle would work. But with Miles, another suicide might look suspicious. The cops could reopen Forrester's death, and, as someone he'd fired, I'd be a suspect. I changed poisons and went with option three, the frame-up. Once there's a conviction, it's case closed.

"I needed to set someone up so I'd be off the hook. And it didn't really matter if it was Jim or Bryant, although Bryant's a bigger asshole so I hoped he'd be the one to get nailed. All while justice is served."

"And you move up the corporate ladder. So it's not only revenge, it's also greed that's behind this. You kill Miles and set up your boss so you can take over for him."

"I'm telling you, it's not about greed or revenge, it's about justice."

Pindler's voice was getting louder and shakier. Continuing the debate wasn't worth the risk of agitating him further, so I shifted gears. "Where'd you call from last night? My daughter had a hard time hearing you."

"Pay phone at a bar. Couldn't risk a tap."

"Good thinking." In a paranoid sort of way. "So how'd you get Miles' body into the Skokie courthouse?" Letting him show off.

"I picked the lock. It was a Saturday, and the guard was probably on one of his two-hour coffee breaks. We got in to the courtroom, and I gave him the poison while he was on the bench. It didn't take long to work." Maybe that story had some truth to it. Too bad there was no lock to pick. My guess is that Pindler left the getting in part to Smejkal, who'd simply lifted Miles' key card. If Pindler wanted to make himself out a master criminal, that was fine, as long as he stayed calm.

"Something I can't figure out. Why didn't you leave Miles' car in Skokie or Northbrook?"

"That's simple—I needed a ride back to my apartment."

"And why'd Smejkal steal my CD-ROMs?"

"Because he's a moron. I told him to take your computer disks, and that's what he brings me." Pindler must have found my card in Rebecca's purse.

"So tell me about justice and killing Miles."

"It's personal."

"You did it for Rebecca, right?"

"What do you know about me and her?"

"I know you loved her."

"Pardon me?"

"Don't play dumb, Josh. That note you left in Jim's drawer for the police to find, that was a mistake. Must have been a draft which never got sent, right?" He didn't respond, so I continued. "The mistake being, it was addressed to 'Becca.' Her best friend didn't call her that, or her husband, or her boss. The only person I heard call her that was a law school classmate named Michael Gelman. Which leads me to believe that law school's the only place where that nickname stuck. Where'd you go to law school, Josh?"

"None of your fucking business, man."

"My guess is you've had a crush on Rebecca for quite awhile now. Should I go on?"

Two swallows this time. "Ever since I first saw her she was my perfect woman. Gelman told me what that asshole Miles did to her. I couldn't let him go on ruining people's lives." Pindler spoke deliberately, and he seemed to sincerely believe that by killing Miles he defended Rebecca's honor. I wasn't so sure. Rebecca wasn't in the picture when he killed Forrester, Rebecca's incident with Miles occurred months earlier, and the whole plot of kidnapping Celia and setting up Jim or Bryant seemed too calculated for an emotional, love-induced revenge. Not that resolving Pindler's motivation for killing Miles was top priority. Not with a gun pointed at me.

But Rebecca was different. With her I needed to know what went wrong, gun be damned. So I asked.

Pindler sighed before responding. "For years I'd been waiting for a sign that she was available. Because whatever she saw in her husband, I knew I didn't have a chance while they were happily married. I know what you're thinking; Why didn't I kill Perry?" Actually I wasn't thinking that, but I let him continue. "Because I do have some morals, and loving Becca isn't a crime.

"Anyway, my sign came. I was with Jim when he picked her up in a bar. I figured her marriage was on the rocks. I sent her the notes, then made a point of bumping into her after work one day and asked her out for a drink. I told her I was the one who'd been writing her. She looked at me like I was nuts. She told me to get lost, and that if I ever wrote her again she'd report me to the ARDC and the police. I couldn't believe it. I loved her so much, and she treated my like that." He sobbed lightly, and his hands trembled.

"That's when you killed her," I said.

"Yeah. I didn't plan to. I just snapped. I couldn't understand why she'd have nothing to do with me, especially compared to a slob like Jim."

"But Jim didn't really pick her up."

"What are you talking about?"

"Jim exaggerated," said Weiss. "Hell, he lied. At the bar that night, he never even tried picking Rebecca up. When he talked to her, that was all show."

Pindler dropped his head, then quickly raised it back up. "So she thought I was trying to ruin her marriage. Now it makes sense why she treated me like such an asshole."

"You see, Josh, it wasn't personal," I lied.

"Damn! Then it's all that fucking Jim's fault." The tremble now progressed to an all-out shake.

"Give me the gun, Josh, and we'll get everything straightened out."

"No! Now I've got to finish my plan. Bronk, you figure out it's Weiss who set up Lanter and did the killings. You arrange this meeting to confront Weiss, with Cardiff as your witness. You accuse Weiss, he shoots you, then he kills himself. Case closed."

"That doesn't make sense. Why would Bryant kill himself?"

"What difference does it make? The cops won't worry about why."

"I was a cop, Josh. They will absolutely wonder why. And where's Cardiff?"

"He's temporarily tied up."

"What're you going to do with him?"

"Unfortunately a stray bullet kills him."

"I'm telling you, the cops won't buy any of this."

"That's my concern. Now get up and move to the center of the room."

"No problem, Josh. But you're not as clever as you think." I opened up my shirt to reveal a wire attached to a miniature microphone. "The cops have been listening the whole time. You've just made the most eloquent closing statement of your career."

"Shit!"

I pushed Weiss to the floor and raised up the coffee table as a shield. I heard a shot but it was way off target, shattering the patio door behind me. Pindler fired again, this time nicking the edge of the table. He turned around and ran up the stairs.

I dropped the table and followed. Pindler was in the middle of the living room looking out the window. All was quiet on the street outside, but he must have heard me because he turned. I ducked behind a wall just as I heard another gun shot.

There were two ways into the living room—the main hallway or the kitchen. I'd taken the hallway approach, so I creeped around into the kitchen. I could see Pindler still checking out the street, waiting for the cops. He'd have a long wait. My wire wasn't connected to anything; I wore it to throw Pindler off in case things got sticky.

I'm too big to sneak up on people, especially someone alert to unusual noises. I needed a subterfuge, and there are few better places to find noisemakers than a kitchen.

Pots and pans hung from an overhead rack. The same dark gray cookware Randee had to have one Hanukkah. Either Circulon or Calphalon, I always got them mixed up, and heard about it for years after I bought the wrong one. I grabbed a frying pan and a large pot. I took them with me as I hugged the wall in the hallway just outside the kitchen. Then I tossed them towards the middle of the kitchen.

I made my move as soon as I heard the crash. As expected Pindler responded to the noise by looking toward the kitchen. Coming from the opposite direction I was able to catch him before he realized what was happening. I put my arms around his stomach, drove my shoulder into the small of his back, and laid a perfect blindside tackle on him. His knees buckled and he fell face forward, the gun flying out of his hand into the kitchen, where it landed with a clank.

Once I had hold of him that should have been the end of the story. But Pindler thought quickly, and I didn't. I hadn't pinned his arms, so he managed to snatch a crystal candy bowl off an end table, and smashed it on the top of my head. I tried to hold on to him, but my brain shifted focus away from my muscles and toward the pain. I was conscious but woozy, and he slipped out of my grasp. He raised the bowl to hit me once again, but I rolled over just as it was coming down, and it only glanced the back of my head.

I sensed he was heading toward the kitchen, and instinctively I followed. Still unsteady, I crabbed along, hoping to spot the gun before he did. But the only things I saw were the pot and the frying pan on the floor.

Now Pindler was coming towards me, something metallic in his hand. As he got closer I saw it wasn't the gun, but a carving knife.

I retreated to the living room. I felt myself extending to my full height and puffing out my chest. I know some animals do this when threatened, to give themselves the illusion of greater strength, but I don't remember which ones. Maybe the gecko. Anyway, it may have worked, because Pindler stopped at the threshold between the kitchen and living room.

"Give it up, Pindler," I said. "Your fingerprints are all over this house."

"So? They're not on file anywhere."

"Want to bet? When the police interviewed you did you have a glass of water or a cup of coffee? Or maybe you just put your hands on the table. They took your prints off that. Standard operating procedure."

"Bullshit."

"If you say so."

"Don't try to battle wits with me, Bronk. You'll lose every time. Though I give you credit, that bit about the wire had me going."

"Can't blame a girl for trying."

"Well, you're trying's about to come to a permanent end."

"Aren't you forgetting something, Pindler?"

"What's that?"

"Where's the gun?"

"Fuck the gun."

"Well, just in case you're curious, Bryant has it, and it looks to me like it's aimed straight at your head."

"You don't give up with your asinine tricks, do you?"

"Suit yourself."

I stood still while Bryant snuck up on Pindler. Not with the gun, but with the frying pan. He handled it like a tennis racket, giving new meaning to the phrase "overhead smash." Good form, and an excellent follow through. Pindler staggered. With both hands I grabbed Pindler's right arm, the one that was holding the knife. I held on tight and squeezed hard, immobilizing the arm. Pindler cried out in pain, but he didn't release the knife. Bryant came back with a second whack of the frying pan, and I put my knee to the back of Pindler's knee and applied downward pressure. Pindler's knee buckled and he tumbled down. The knife slipped out of his hand.

This time I held on to his arms. I'd brought a pair of handcuffs, which Weiss got out of my jacket pocket. I snapped the bracelets on Pindler's wrists, and finally relaxed once I heard the locks engage.

"Where are the cops?" asked Bryant.

"That's a good question. Why didn't you call 911?"

"Why would I do that? I thought you were wired and the cops were listening."

"I was lying. Couldn't you have figured that out when no one showed?"

"I just figured they were slow."

"Well, try to find the gun. But don't touch it."

It turned out the gun had landed in the pot which I'd tossed to create noise. The black of the gun blended in with the dark gray of the pot, making it hard to spot. Bryant made a pot-kettle-black joke that was so lame I couldn't help laughing.

"You have anything you want to say now, Pindler?" I asked.

"Yeah. Tell Rebecca's husband I'm really sorry. And that she'd still be alive if Jim hadn't lied."

"What should I tell Mrs. Miles?"

"That her husband was an asshole."

CHAPTER 25

Gail looked beautiful, so, dare I say, adult, in her pale yellow dress, her hair styled something other than her usual straight down. I was the proud papa, watching from the front row of the synagogue as my little girl passed into womanhood. Well, maybe not womanhood, since she was still in the seventh grade, more interested in clothes than career, friends than family. Still, I think every parent who sees their child through a symbolic passage like a bat mitzvah feels a sense that things will now be different, less innocent, more worrisome. Even if I didn't exactly want to turn back the clock, I wished I could tinker with the inner workings, stretching out things as they were just a little longer.

I thought Gail did a great job. At least she sounded great to me, and I never saw the Rabbi wince. Not that I understood the Hebrew part when she read from the Torah, but her speech, in English, about the need to stick by your friends and believe in the good of people, rang especially true.

Following the ceremony we held a luncheon in the banquet area of the synagogue. I'd managed to finagle a last-minute invitation out of Randee, and Jim Lanter had a great time, telling everyone who would listen about his time in the slammer. While I had my doubts that he really knocked around a half dozen gangbangers, he definitely knew how to work a crowd. Even some of Gail's friends, who I figured would want nothing to do with anyone who'd graduated junior high, listened with interest. Now I understood why Gail was disappointed when my contempt citation turned out to be phony.

Colleen looked terrific in a pink dress with a matching hat, one of those flat, wide brimmed types. I love hats on women, and if some of our crotchety guests thought Colleen took a wrong turn at the Easter parade, I didn't care.

Colleen's meeting my parents proved interesting, in wildly different ways. My mom was first to seek us out.

"So you're the girl Marty's seeing," Mom said. "Nice to finally meet you."

"Same here, Mrs. Bronk."

"Please, honey, call me Gloria. I understand you work at the law school where Marty went."

"That's right. I'm an administrator there."

"Very nice. You know, I really admire the Pope, even though I'm not Polish, or Catholic for that matter."

"Good one, Mom," I said.

"What'd I say?"

"He's a very pious man," said Colleen.

"Pious. That's a good word for him. And Colleen, that's an Irish name. I like the Irish too. Who's that Irish dancer I enjoy so much?"

"Bo Jangles Robinson?"

"Very funny, Marty. No, what's his name? Kelly, Pete Kelly."

"I think you mean Gene Kelly," said Colleen.

"Yeah, that's it. You are smart, Colleen, just like Marty says. Maybe you could talk some sense into this son of mine and get him to use his law degree for something more than wall paper."

"Mom seems to think there's something disreputable about investigating wrongdoing," I said.

"No, Marty, but I think you spent a lot of time and money to get a law degree, and you could make your life easier by being a lawyer."

"To make more money, right?"

"And have a higher standing in the community. What's wrong with that?"

"Mom, just tell your friends that your son's a lawyer. They'll never know the difference."

"I do, but it's still not the same."

"I think Marty does important work," added Colleen. "He just cleared an innocent man from a murder charge, you know."

"Psssh. He can do that as a lawyer too. So Colleen, tell me, what is it about Jewish boys that Catholic girls find so attractive?"

Uncle Leonard passed by and waved hello. I hadn't spoken to him in ten years even though he only lives three blocks from me. Suddenly I felt terribly guilty about that, and I just had to renew acquaintances and introduce Colleen to him. Immediately.

Dad was an entirely different story. He'd once told me, after drinking one too many Dewars', that his biggest regret in life was never having made it with a shiksa. So he took an immediate liking to Colleen, telling her old stories I wished he'd forgotten, like the time in high school I opened up a Coke bottle with my teeth and ended up swallowing the bottle cap. Fortunately Uncle Mort came by to argue with Dad about whatever it is they always argue about. Another uncle to the rescue.

Randee was cordial to Colleen, if somewhat insincere, saying she wanted to get to know her better, but couldn't right then because of all the other things she had to do. Which to my observation was basically hanging around her side of the family, boyfriend Thad in tow.

Speaking of Thad, I learned something interesting about him. I always figured he was a Gentile; not too many Jews are named Thaddeus. But "Thad" was a nickname; his real name was Abraham Thadberg. He thought "Abe" was an old man's name, which wouldn't fit a man barely forty. I thought he looked at least fifty, and that Abe fit him fine.

Colleen was quite the party animal. She joined in on almost all the dances, including the hokey pokey and the hora. She also revealed how she infiltrated the Markus & Stevens box. Something about telling the usher the truth, how I was a private investigator and needed to check something out for a case I was working. Turns out the kid's a crime buff, so he let her in. Imagine, the truth as an investigatory tool. It'd never work twice.

All Gail's friends showed up. Apparently her little feud blew over weeks earlier. I always thought Gail hung around with a pretty good bunch of kids. Which might still be the case. But they seemed to do a lot of running around the banquet area. I even saw some of them throwing cashews at each other. My friends who'd given bar and bat mitzvahs told me to hire a security person to keep an eye on the kids, and I was glad I took their advice.

Which leads me to the biggest surprise of the afternoon. A guy in the Sheriff's Department runs a security business on the side, and he hires off-duty cops to do the actual work. So who should show up on one of the proudest days of my life—Crumpton.

He claimed to have doubted Lanter's guilt all along, but Amanda had pushed for the arrest. He also said that Amanda had been demoted, and was back to driving a patrol car on the night shift. However, he hadn't suffered any repercussions, seeing how the only thing assigned solely to him—Celia's disappearance—had turned out all right. I was going to get on his case about that when a couple of the boys walked by, heading towards the men's room, one of them holding something which looked suspiciously like a pack of cigarettes. Crumpton took off in pursuit of the suspects, something I wouldn't have believed possible. I hoped he was up to the challenge.

On the Monday following the bat mitzvah Jerry Grieg called, congratulating me on my work. I told him he'd been a suspect after that obvious lie about where he'd been the night he missed the ABC meeting. Why didn't he admit that he'd been in Kansas trying to get his wife back, I asked. Because he thought it'd sound wimpy, he said. I assured him there was nothing embarrassing about going after the woman you love, which, I realized later, is advice I should keep in mind for myself. In any event, Jerry told me he and his wife were together again, and that he was going to make things work this time. Meaning, among other things, that he was quitting ABC. Which cleared up the mystery announcement he'd hinted at with Dennis. As for his secret mailbox, I figured that was where he received his x-rated magazines. Maybe I was right, maybe I was wrong. For sure it wasn't my business.

The lead story in that afternoon's Law Bulletin was Judge Dienstag's resignation to accept a partnership at Markus & Stevens. He was quoted as expressing frustration that his efforts at reforming the circuit court had largely failed due to resistance from the legal community. Dienstag declined comment as to what role, if any, financial considerations played in his decision.

The next day I received a check drawn on Blake Cardiff's account, in an amount considerably more than I expected. Probably included a bonus for saving him. If I'd had the money before the bat mitzvah I might have done some things differently. As it was, the expenses were all accounted for. I thought about putting the check towards a vacation, me and Colleen, someplace warm, exotic, remote. But instead I called my stockbroker, and told him to put it into some growth stocks that'd show a nice appreciation over the next five to ten years. Bat mitzvah behind, college and wedding ahead. I hung up, never before having been so depressed to receive so much money.